Wild Child

KATIE CROSS

KCW

Contents

To JaiHo and Christy.
Who first read and loved Ellie so many years ago.

ELLIE

The smell of alcohol stained the air.

Grimacing, I hovered around the edges of a crowd of sweaty high school bodies clad in elaborate strappy gowns and dark tuxedos. Hairspray and perfume thickened the air. A simple dress of deep blue rustled around my legs with no design except a layer of sheer, shimmery fabric over the top. The bodice was a little tight, but my chest felt tight anyway.

Anyone would, wearing a *dress*.

Not to mention the fact that I hadn't been asked to this prom. My best friend was here with the sweetest, most popular girl in the school, and I hated crowds with an introvert's fiery passion.

Still, I pressed on.

The high school gym hadn't truly transformed despite the sparkle lights, food table, and crepe banners clogging the air. You can't hide a run-down school with cheap decorations, no matter how hard you tried. Certainly not for the last dance of the year.

The sudden absence of pulsing music left shuffles and whispers in the air. The principal, Mrs. Comstock, tapped across a stage on the far side of the gym. She wore a pair of bright pink high heels and a skirt of sheer black. Teenage couples pulled apart, turning their attention to a spotlight that illuminated her salt-and-pepper hair pulled back into a bun. She stopped at a microphone in the middle of the stage, an envelope in her left hand.

"Boys and girls," she said, voice fuzzy from the speakers. "Hope you're having a good time and thank you for behaving yourselves. The time has come to announce the King and Queen of this year's prom."

A round of applause and whoops rippled through the room, followed by a drumroll from the DJ, who worked in the corner. My stomach clenched. As if any of them needed Mrs. Comstock to tell them who would be King and Queen. We all knew who would get the crown. I crossed my arm in front of me, tucking my icy fingers away. At least I wasn't late.

Where was the perfect couple anyway?

My heart thumped as a familiar set of broad shoulders came into view on the other side of the room, near a punch bowl guarded by the towering football coach Mr. Bell. Coach Bell glowered behind the bowl in a challenge to anyone who tried to get past him with alcohol. Not far away stood my best friend Devin Blaine. His sandy, dark hair had been combed into submission for the night. I preferred it unruly. He had his arm around a girl named Cassidy, who wore a brilliant, strawberry-pink dress that fluffed around her legs.

Devin tugged her closer to the middle of the room, where a few of his football buddies had congregated. When Devin leaned down to whisper in her ear and she grinned broadly, I clenched my fingers together and resisted the urge to dart away.

This was a mistake. I shouldn't have come. It didn't matter that it was Devin's senior prom, that he'd surely take the crown with Cassidy. Both of them ruled the school with their unsought-for-popularity. I, on the other hand, kept to the shadows. Occasionally, Devin's spotlight put me in the public eye, but he largely protected me from it. His friends were his friends at school and football practice. I got the rest of him. They knew to leave me alone, and I lived happily at his side where I belonged.

This was our only opportunity to have a dance together before he exited the teenage world and stepped into the adult one.

I shouldn't have come.

But something—maybe innate loyalty or deep desperation—kept me glued to the spot as Mrs. Comstock ruffled through the envelope to pull out a piece of paper. Everybody already knew the two names there, but the formality lent a sense of routine to the whole event. Soft music started in the background, a royal accouterment with dramatic violins. Two of Devin's friends nudged him from behind. He rolled his eyes at them good-naturedly.

I wanted to vomit.

Mrs. Comstock leaned closer to the microphone, gazed out on the crowd, and grinned. The spotlight washed out her tanned face as she purposefully delayed the suspense. Given the chance, I'd willingly slash at her like a cat. Somewhere in the crowd, a girl tittered. Another called out, "Just say it already!"

My heart hiccupped as she paused for another seemingly endless minute before crying, "Devin Blaine and Cassidy Tanner!"

Music crashed through the speakers, drowning out the shouts and cries of almost everyone in the room. Applause thundered. Balloons, strapped to a net on the ceiling, rained all over the floor. Glitter cluttered the air in a metal shimmer. Devin, with his heart-stopping smile, held a bent elbow out for Cassidy. A hand covered her mouth. Her eyes—so perfectly warm and kind and compassionate I wanted to hate her but couldn't—sparkled with shock.

Really? I wanted to say. *You're surprised? No one else is.*

The perfect couple ascended the stairs on the side of the stage together, toward the awaiting student body president and vice president who held their crowns. Cassidy's tiara glittered obnoxiously as they set it on top of her head. She looked beautiful, with her dark skin offset by the white gems inlaid in her dress. She waved at her adoring public that had gone wild the moment the crown hit her head.

But it was Devin that took my breath away.

The tuxedo cut angular lines across his shoulders, and his hair now had the adorably tousled look I loved so much. Star quarterback had served him well. He *looked* like a king up there with his bowtie, wide smile, and a genuine affability for people that boggled me.

I leaned back against the wall, crushing my skirt in my hands. My heart banged so loud in my ears I couldn't hear the congratulatory screams anymore. Just the race of my blood through my body. There was only half an hour left of the dance, plenty of time to find him in the crowd and fulfill the promise of our dance. Cassidy would let me—she was good and kind that way. She wouldn't think Devin's tag-along best friend that was only a junior would be in her way.

Although I felt she was in *my* way.

An ugly truth had occurred to me earlier that night as I'd watched him get dressed for the dance. It happened the moment I comprehended that I was jealous of him being with a girl as perfect as Cassidy. Seeing him on the stage, as far from me as he'd ever been, slammed the truth into me all at once.

I freaking loved my best friend.

Now, watching them dance and whirl together, the truth was confirmed. Devin had always been more than a friend to me. He was soul. He was *all*. Tears prickled my eyes with heat and I forced them back with one last shot at my crumbling denial. No. I didn't love Devin. Not like *that*, anyway.

Devin was my best friend, not my lover. He was the other part of me. The second side of my heart that beat in tandem with mine. The last seven years living in Pineville, away from the stepfather that wanted to kill me, had been bearable because of Devin. Amazing because of Devin.

Safe because of Devin.

"Dammit," I muttered as the weak strands of my denial began to fade. Why did I even try? There was no denying the truth.

I *did* love him.

And how could that ever work? It couldn't. Because love was fickle and men left. Even the ones you loved. Mama had made that lesson very clear.

You fall in love, she told me, *and men leave. It's the way of things for girls like us. Besides, baby, you're the kind of girl that will always take care of yourself. You deserve the truth. Stay away from them.*

Never mind that Mama had had some weird views on life and had led my older sisters down terrible paths with her advice. While Mama whispered sweet tales of romantic passion to Lizbeth, she told me the cold hard facts of life and love. Men leave. Love fades. Take care of yourself first.

Jim, my abusive stepfather, made it very clear that I wasn't good enough for him. And my real father had left me to die with Jim. While I had glowing examples of worthy men in my life now that Mama was out of it—my adopted father Maverick, my brother-in-law JJ, and of course Devin—the truth always rang in my ears like a high-pitched reminder.

Men leave.

Love dies.

You take care of yourself.

So, no. If I loved Devin and lost him too, I'd lose myself. Was it worth the risk? Well . . . maybe. Because wasn't Devin already inextricably tied up in me? *Besides,* I thought as I watched him and Cassidy twirl around the stage to an especially pungent romance song, *Devin deserves the princess, and I am the sword maiden.*

Dev and I were too alike.

It would never work.

That felt easier. Brutal, cold, hard reality. Not the dreams of me being the girl in his arms. Me in the tiara. Me in the dress and actually enjoying it, which would never happen. No, this was reality, and reality was far safer than dreams.

With all my strength, I swallowed back my emotion. Pushed back the truth that had dangled at the edge of my mind for years now and tipped it into a safe, metal box that it could never escape. The lid slammed shut. Even though I'd only just acknowledged my feelings for him today, I happily shoved that box into the corner of my mind to ignore. There it would pulse like a little heart, reminding me that it knew the truth, even as I strove to live a lie.

The crowd surged into the dance as Dev escorted Cassidy off the stage. Suddenly, my tendency to keep to myself and ignore almost everyone but Devin swamped me. There was no one else here I knew well aside from a few acquaintances who waved while we passed in the halls. Most of them were friends with Devin, and they accepted that being friends with him meant tolerating me taking up his time outside of school. No reason to stay.

Stay and dance and tell Devin how I really felt?

No thanks.

Locked away now.

A tap on my shoulder distracted me. My shoulders bunched as I glanced to my left, then relaxed. My only other friend in the junior class, Jax, stood there with a wry smile. His long, wiry arms and legs were hidden in a tuxedo tonight. He had the gangly look of someone that still hadn't grown into his body yet, even though his blue eyes had always been kind.

"Ellie?"

"Hey." He tilted his head to Devin. "How you doing?"

My tension faded. No punch in Jax's hand. No alcohol on his breath. Instead, I swallowed and said, "Great. Just wanted to see it happen."

"You knew they'd get it?"

"Who didn't?"

He grinned. "They look great together, don't they? The two

nicest people in the school deserve the crowns." His eyebrows rose with an intentionally interested gaze. "Don't you think?"

"Yep."

"You all right?"

I tilted my head to crack my neck. The room felt like a warm swamp filled with cheap perfume. Mr. Bell abandoned the punch bowl to escort a kid out of the room by his shoulders. Two other kids slipped up, emptying a new bottle of what appeared to be rum inside the punch with a snicker. Idiots.

"I'm good."

He nodded knowingly as if I'd said something wise, but I caught the hint of sarcasm in his face. "Sure. You're good. You just got here?"

"Yep. I'm on my way out now."

Wrinkles appeared in his brow. "Why? Don't you want to dance with D–"

"Nope."

"Ellie—"

"You look handsome tonight, Jax." I patted his lapel, where a red rose graced the pocket. "I need to go."

His gaze darted behind me, then his lips twitched. I sensed someone approaching as Jax stepped to the side a little.

"Good luck with that," he sang. A second later, a hand grabbed mine. I whirled around, coming face-to-face with a grinning Devin.

"Hey E. I *knew* you'd come, even though you threatened not to."

My heart stalled like a dying star at the excitement in his tone. I sucked in a breath to get it going again, arrested by the overwhelming presence of Devin, my best friend. The guy who was usually sweaty, smelly, and fell asleep with his body half on top of mine most Friday nights while we watched zombie movies. The guy that made a mean grilled cheese sandwich and never had a sip of alcohol just for my sake.

The little box in the corner of my brain, built from metal and reinforced with sheer grit, exploded.

Somehow, I managed a smile. "Hey."

As easily as breathing, he tugged me closer, put his hand on my waist, and whisked me onto the dance floor. I caught a quick glimpse of Jax over Devin's shoulder as I whirled away. Concern waited in his furrowed brows. Before I could figure it out, Devin spoke.

"So . . . you came."

An undercurrent of joy infused his words, not to mention surprise. Annoyance washed through me. Of *course* I came. But I let it go. Parties were not my thing and he knew that. His words were a comment on my loyalty to him, in a roundabout way. Still, the sparkle of the gaudy, fake crown, tipped a little sideways on his head, made everything more real.

"Of course," I said quietly.

I couldn't look him in the eye. For the first time in my life, I didn't see the muddy little boy that caught fish with me. I saw Devin the almost-man. The graduating senior. The guy that planned to work a filthy construction job for the next nine months until I graduated high school early, and we moved to the state university together.

If he looked in my eyes, he'd see it all.

The utter vulnerability of my feelings took my breath away. Still, with his smell banishing the trace amount of alcohol in the air, I couldn't help but relax. This was Devin. Devin was home. Even in a crowd of people that thought me reclusive and strange, Devin was safety.

"You looked great up there," I managed to say. "Cassidy is beautiful. So . . . congratulations?"

He made a noise in his throat. I risked a quick glance up and couldn't help a laugh when I saw his crown. Up close, it appeared cheap. A pliable metal with laurels and berries on it, sprinkled with green glass gems that mimicked the school colors of gold and emerald.

Devin smirked. "Laugh it up," he muttered. "I can't wait to take this thing off. Will you have food for me when this finishes? I'm taking Cassidy home as soon as it's over, and then I'll head your way. I'm freaking *starving*."

"You ate like three cheeseburgers three hours ago."

"I know! And I've been dancing and talking all night. That makes a man hungry."

Suddenly, I relaxed. The irony in his voice. The ease of his escape to me. Even if I wasn't Cassidy, I still had Devin.

"Of course, Your Highness. All the bananas, fudge, and ice cream a high school quarterback could dream of."

He pinned me with a glare. I laughed.

"Calm down. Bethany just went shopping and also bought your favorite pizza rolls, bread, milk, and fruit."

He pulled me a little closer. I closed my eyes as we moved together, breathing in his scent. I'd hate myself for it later, even as the gentle hint of pine lifted from his skin. We'd gone on a hike before he left to pick up Cassidy. I could still smell traces of the outdoors on him.

"Thank you," he said quietly, and I knew he meant for coming. For braving a crowd with hidden alcohol that made me extremely uncomfortable. For venturing out in a dress, with my hair freshly washed and straightened. For being here with him in this transitory moment, even though I didn't have to be. I should have been flattered, but instead, I felt scared. His breath was hot on my neck and sent a shiver down my spine.

"Always," I whispered.

His hold on me tightened. My temple pressed to his jaw. Could he feel my heartbeat? Did he sense how breathless this made me?

"There's something I wanted to tell you tonight," he said.

His voice turned down slightly. With the music still blaring around us, it was almost imperceptible. I thought I imagined it, but then his palm turned clammy against mine.

"What's that?" I asked. My voice was a rasp, but he didn't seem to notice. The slow song shuffled into another one.

"I, uh, received some news earlier today. Good news, but it will surprise you. Maybe not really news. More of a confirmed decision?"

He became a rigid board around me as he rambled around a blind topic. He paused for a beat, then plowed forward before I could tell him to just spit it out already. "I enlisted, Ellie. I've joined the Marines. I leave for San Diego in two weeks. Two days after I graduate."

I blinked, fuzzy with the sense of impending doom. Of everything about to change. Of the world sliding away from me like a mudflow. I didn't even have to speak.

We were too close together for me to see him, but I didn't need to. The steadiness of his voice, slightly hushed around the edges, let me know he was scared. Scared of what I'd say. How I'd react. We stopped dancing somewhere near the edge of the gymnasium, not far from a bright green EXIT sign.

I've joined the Marines.

It echoed through my mind with undulations. For half a breath, I almost laughed. Told him that it was a funny joke and the timing was poor, but the rigid way he held me in his arms—almost like he didn't *want* to see my face—told me this wasn't a joke.

He had joined the Marines.

"What?"

"Ellie, let me explain before you run off, okay? It's . . . it's the money. I can't afford to go to college, even if I stay home for nine months and work and save it all. The scholarship I was hoping for didn't come through."

While he continued to explain, the words filtered through my mind. *GI Bill* and *no stress about finances now* and *we'll be okay* vaguely occurred to me. My mind narrowed into a fuzzy tunnel of thoughts that all revolved around one tiny phrase that whispered through my thoughts in Mama's voice.

They always leave.

Heart thumping, I pulled away. A panicked expression filled his face, but I didn't look right at him.

"I-I need to go."

Before he could protest, I headed toward the glowing sign and pushed through the heavy doors. It spilled me into the parking lot, and the cool air from late spring shocked me out of the tunnel. Out of the questions.

My movement felt clumsy as I stumbled toward the truck. The sound of the wind outside too loud. The sense of shock at the cooler air too dramatic on my skin. Behind me, the door slammed open against the wall, then wheezed closed again. Footsteps ran to me.

"Ellie!"

He reached for me, but I moved my arm too fast. Livid, I whirled around to face him. This time, I looked him right in the eyes.

"How long have you had this planned?"

He faltered for only a moment. "Since last summer."

"Last summer?" I cried. "That's over a year."

Uneasy now, he nodded.

"Last summer is when we started talking about going to the state university together. When we *toured* it together. Do you remember that? Do you remember us discussing plans and talking this out and you agreeing?"

He shifted. "Ellie—"

But I plowed over his plea, too hot to stop now. "Did you know then that you wanted to go into the Marines?"

"I don't *want* to, Ellie. I just don't have a choice."

"Did you know?" I asked again, my voice expanding.

His jaw became rigid as he stared at me, so gorgeous in the low light that it made my heart ache. Finally, he looked at the ground and nodded. His voice was low when he whispered, "Yes."

"Yes, you've been lying to me for a year?"

His nostrils flared. "Yes, but—"

He stopped on his own this time. When he finally set his eyes back on mine, I had to look away. There was pain and fear and disappointment and maybe, just maybe, a hint of resentment. It was that chance of resentment that sent a shockwave through me.

I stepped back, shaking. Another tremor of pain crashed through me. *Resentment.* Was I holding him back? Did he feel trapped with my friendship? He must, or he wouldn't have done something to run away. That meant there was nothing else to do. I had to escape. Had to leave. Had to get out of here before I . . .

Exploded.

"Okay," I whispered.

"Okay?"

"Okay."

What else could I say? For the last year, Devin had been sneaking behind my back, letting me believe we had a future together. All that time, he knew he would betray me to go to the Marines. He allowed me to believe in a dream where we moved forward together. That we'd leave this small mountain town and conquer the world.

It was all a lie.

The heat in my eyes returned, this time with ferocity. I blinked the tears back with the maddening thought that Mama had been right.

Men leave.

Love dies.

You take care of yourself.

Although I'd talked myself out of believing her for the last couple of years because Devin was different, Mama had been absolutely right all this time. Maybe it was just a matter of time for *all* of us. For Maverick to leave Bethany. For JJ to escape from

Lizbeth and Serafina to lose Benjamin. Maybe we all ended up alone.

"Ellie." He put a hand on my shoulder and I realized I'd stopped moving away from him to stare at the ground. "Please tell me what you're thinking. I know you feel betrayed and this is frightening and . . . "

He trailed away again. My heart fought my head, which hurt from all the confusion. Everything felt like a big, ugly trap that rolled around me. And, pulsing in the corner of my mind, was the remnants of the shredded box where I'd tucked the truth. It screamed at me now in maniacal revenge for having ever tried to ignore it.

You love him. You love him.

And now?

He's leaving, Mama whispered. *Because they always do.*

I stepped back. "I have to go," I said. "I . . . I have to go."

With that, I picked up the dress that I'd carefully chosen, grateful that I'd worn my tennis shoes, and I disappeared into the night with a carefully masked sob.

* * *

10 days later

Laughter and the clicking sound of pop cans opening filled the air.

I climbed up the back of a favorite tree behind the Frolicking Moose and carefully settled onto a branch in the middle. The rough bark scraped against the back of my legs, but the black material of my yoga pants and my oversized camouflage hunting shirt would hide me. My black hair skirted my shoulders and a matching camouflage hat pulled low over my eyes hid as much skin as possible.

Through twigs and leaves, I made out the small gathering on

the parking lot below. Twenty people lingered around a grill and several red-and-white checkered picnic tables. The early summer air smelled like charred beef and hotdogs. Three children scuttled around, chasing each other with water balloons. They belonged to Kendra, Devin's older sister. She was twenty-seven years old and stood near the shop, laughing at something a neighbor said. Over it all flapped an American flag, crisp in the wind.

Devin stood out amongst the crowd right away. He stood next to his mother, Millie. At the grill was Mac, his father. Mac sat on a chair when he wasn't flipping burgers or rolling hot dogs because he couldn't stand for long periods of time. A debilitating back injury had nearly paralyzed him years ago, and they'd almost lost their small home.

Other members of the Pineville community littered the lot. A banner across the Frolicking Moose said *Good Luck Devin* in red, white, and blue font with a camouflage background. The whole thing made the back of my throat tighten.

This farewell party shouldn't have to happen at all.

A week and a half had passed since I'd last spoken to him at the prom. I felt like a coward for ignoring his calls, his text messages, and avoiding him at school. I had changed my usual routes and acted as if he didn't exist. The limelight of prom King and his announcement of his commitment to the Marines kept him busy in the halls. Everyone wanted to talk with the new hero.

Which is right when I'd turned into a coward.

Maverick turned Devin away when he came over on prom night because I demanded it. I didn't want to see Devin, even though he'd chased after me. Devin had lied to me. He'd taken the dreams that we'd made together. Unsafe dreams I probably shouldn't have invested in in the first place.

Most of all, he *chose* to leave.

No amount of Maverick staying up with me and trying to explain why Devin did it dulled the pain. *It will be good for both of you,* he said. *You need to find yourself without him,* he said. The words ran in and right back out of my mind.

Yes, the Marines cleared up his financial issues.

It eased the burden on his parents.

It gave him a chance to see the world.

It created opportunities for him later.

But none of that helped my broken heart, so I'd turned to the only thing that would: reality. Dirty, crusty, say-it-like-it-is reality. Devin had chosen a different life. I couldn't change that. So, if he was going to leave, he needed to stay gone.

If he didn't bounce in and out of my life, I'd be able to move on. Because, for the last seven years, I had pictured my life happening one way. That way always had Devin in it. Maybe Devin dated other girls, the way he did in high school, but he was there. That stable, permanent figure.

For the last ten days, I'd grappled with who I'd be and what my life would look like without him, and it robbed me of my courage.

That's why I sat in the tree with camouflage hiding my body and watched most of Pineville come and go. Watched them shake his hand, clap his shoulder, give him advice, thank him for his service. I watched his eyes go to the road, and his shoulders fall in disappointment every time someone new came that wasn't me. I watched while Maverick and Bethany bustled in and out of the Frolicking Moose. Both had been angry with Devin, but worked through it faster than me.

Not for what he did, but the *way* he did it.

My sister-mama had a territorial streak in her that frightened even me.

Near the end of the picnic, Maverick glanced up and met my eyes. I scowled. He winked. Then he turned his back and acted as if I weren't there. A few minutes later, he gave Devin an envelope that would have a lot of money in it. Devin smiled with gratitude, but the tone of the smile remained empty. Several times he tried to speak, but couldn't. Eventually, Maverick saved him with a clap on the shoulder and something I couldn't hear.

The bark pressed into my stomach and I felt sick. Thor whined on the ground beneath me, but still, I watched. Watched Cassidy when she gave him a hug and a warm smile and another hug that lingered seconds longer than I liked.

Watched Devin wait, and wait, and wait.

Despite dusk falling and the gradual clearing of the party, I watched. Despite knowing he'd leave early the next morning to take a flight to San Diego and I didn't know when I'd talk to him again, I stayed in the tree. I didn't climb down, throw myself into his arms, and sob the way I wanted.

Devin was moving into his new life, and he'd chosen to do it without me. He'd chosen to lie for a year, and now he put us on separate paths. We weren't tied together. He wouldn't know my daily life and I wouldn't know his. That was his choice, and I'd honor it the only way I knew how.

It was better if people just stayed gone.

And so, I stayed in the tree like a coward while darkness fell and I let Devin go. After everyone left, I trekked back to my truck hidden in the trees with Thor at my side. Those were the last tears I'd let fall for Devin Blaine.

Now, it was time to watch out for myself.

Chapter One

ELLIE

Three years later

My birthday candle burned bright in the middle of a frosting-free vanilla cupcake.

The single flame in the coffee shop made Maverick's cheek twitch. His eyes flickered from the flame to the wall to the ceiling. Bethany smirked. He had good reason. This coffee shop had almost burned to the ground three-and-a-half years ago. Just to prolong his torture, I let it burn a second more. Then I snuffed it out with a sharp exhale.

He loosed a breath of relief.

"Happy twentieth birthday Ellie!" Bethany cried, clapping. My three-and-a-half-year-old nephew Shane clapped his already grubby hands. Blue frosting lined his upper lip as he clung to me, laughing when I bounced him. His own cupcake lay in his hands, a crumbly disaster already.

"Happy Birfday, Lee," he chimed, giggling when I dug a finger into his ribs. He had black hair like his Mama and wide golden eyes that earned whatever he wanted. Freckles smattered his cheeks, folding into adorable wrinkles when he smiled. I pressed a quick kiss to his temple.

"Thank you very much."

"I fed your chickens with the breakfast leftovers," Bethany said as she gathered her purse. "I have a few clients that are meeting me here tomorrow morning, by the way, so keep the back room reserved."

"Always."

Behind us lay the renovated Frolicking Moose Coffee Shop. Bad wiring, an old building, and dry walls led to a fire years ago that almost burned the entire thing to the ground. Maverick and Bethany had thrown money into renovations, and the new Frolicking Moose sparkled, a gem on the landscape of the small mountain town of Pineville.

Part of the changes had expanded the dining and prep areas, increasing our capacity. Renovations also created a back room that allowed Bethany to meet with real estate clients and ply them with free coffee and baked goods. Some people held birthday parties back there, and Lizbeth always hosted her monthly book club.

Everything glimmered brightly and smelled like espresso.

"Also, Lizbeth and JJ will be in for your birthday dinner tonight." Bethany slung her purse strap over her shoulder. "Don't worry. JJ is bringing dessert. I will not have any part of that."

I quelled a silent exclamation of relief. Despite being my sister-mama for the last seven years, Bethany had no culinary skills whatsoever. JJ, on the other hand, bought out a bakery in nearby Jackson City and ran it with the help of his wife, my sister, Lizbeth. Lizbeth's redesign of their website and her online savvy led to a booming business. They supplied the shop's baked goods and used the money for their own eco-friendly house.

"No other plans today?" Bethany eyed me with mama-like concern. "No . . . lunch with a friend?"

The words almost died on her lips. Maverick coughed a bad

cover for a laugh. My smile tightened imperceptibly. Regret followed her question.

"Sorry." She grimaced. "I just . . ."

"I know. You think I need friends, but I'm fine. Jax took me to dinner last night, and Lizbeth had breakfast with me this morning."

Maverick sent Bethany a not-so-subtle shake of the head.

She sighed.

"Fine. I'll stop being a mother hen. I just . . . I just love you. Like, a lot. And I want you to be happy."

"Then put me on a trail."

She grinned. "I'm sure you already have an extensive hike planned out for this afternoon?"

My own grin responded.

Bethany fussed over Shane for a moment before Maverick shooed her away. She wore a cream-colored pants suit with a pair of crimson heels that disappeared into the flowing material. Her lipstick was more purple than red, which had a striking effect against her dark black hair. She pressed a quick kiss to Maverick's lips, then Shane's cheek. She gave me a wink.

"Love you, Ellie."

"Love you too, Bethie."

"Gotta run to a showing." She waved over her shoulder. "See you at our place for dinner. Love you all!"

Shane lunged for his father, so I passed him over and peeled the cupcake liner off my own dessert.

"Happy birthday, Ellie," Maverick said, his deep rolling voice a reassuring part of this place. There was something about Maverick in the Frolicking Moose that felt safe.

"Thanks."

He lifted an inquiring eyebrow. "Taking the horse out with you on the trail, I presume?"

"Yep. Alone outside? Best birthday ever."

He glanced at the clock.

2:25.

"Stay until three, and you can have the rest of the day off. Deal?"

I hesitated. What did it matter? These were the slowest hours of the day, and we closed at 4:00 on Wednesdays anyway. No one had come in for over an hour. Still, Maverick and Bethany owned this place, not me.

"Sure."

He nodded but made no move to go. Instead, he hesitated. His gaze lingered on mine and I had the distinct feeling he was stalling with his question.

"What's the news from Pineville Outfitters?"

My heart skipped another beat. Pineville Outfitters was a store owned by our neighbor and family friend, Daniel. Two years ago, he opened up a position for a new employee to help run the rental and retail portion of the Outfitters shop, and I had applied. It would be my best shot to my ultimate dream: an outdoor guide.

"I'll take you, Ellie," Daniel said at the end of my interview, "because I know you want to be a guide. Prove yourself first. Work in the store for a while, then learn. We'll get you in the mountains on paid hikes once I know you're not going to kill anyone."

College had been a dramatic fail that I had not yet recovered any interest in, so I poured my focus into every outdoor educational opportunity I could find. Professional mountain climbing with JJ. Memorizing the best trails for horseback riding. Avalanche training. CPR. First aid. My life focused around sculpting my resume to one single goal: overnight outdoor guiding. I wanted to be paid to live in the mountains all year round.

And it was just about to happen.

Any day now, Daniel would confirm my first overnight guide with paying clients. Then Mav could hire more help for the Frolicking Moose, and I'd spend my time outside, where I belonged. The money would open up travel opportunities so I could get out of Pineville and see the world.

Which had been my plan all along, although this path was a different route.

"Daniel has booked three overnight guides for the summer so far," I said to Maverick. "Two in August, one in July. I should get all three. There could be one sooner. He wasn't sure when. Said the client hadn't decided yet."

Maverick nodded, but I could see his thoughts whirl. He didn't like the thought of me alone in the mountains with people he didn't know. The very nature of me taking someone else into the forest meant they had no idea what they were doing. I could outlast and outlive any of them. Besides, I was better with a knife than most men. Three years of self-defense lessons with Benjamin Mercedey gave me a leg up. I'd saved my own life twice at college.

Shane squirmed in Mav's arms, but Mav didn't seem to notice. His thoughts brewed deep today, which meant something was definitely up.

"Why?" I drawled.

Maverick shrugged. "No reason, just wondering."

"Liar."

He rolled his eyes. "We'll need to onboard someone else to pick up the hours, or we might give them to the new girl Dahlia if she wants them. Dagny dropped her hours to weekends only while doing an internship with a construction company after graduating in the winter. I'm just thinking ahead."

Fair enough excuse, but I wasn't buying it. Mav shook it off and gave me his usual roguish smile, even if something belied it.

"Have fun on your ride and be safe."

"Always."

Shane blew me a sloppy kiss as they headed out the door. The Frolicking Moose fell into quiet again. The scent of vanilla and coffee combined when I bit into the first piece of cupcake. Sweet things weren't my preference, and neither were cupcakes, but I appreciated the subdued party.

Attention *also* wasn't my thing, not even on the first birthday of my twenties. A milestone, for sure.

One I should be celebrating with Devin.

The traitorous thought passed through my mind so sneakily I almost didn't hear it. As soon as I realized he'd snuck back in, I turned him away again.

Three years ago, Devin made his choice. The first year, he stayed away. Hadn't returned once. After finishing recruit training in San Diego, he'd flown his parents out to see him at his assigned duty station in North Carolina twice. He ghosted this town. Almost two years passed before he returned. I made myself scarce for the two weeks he'd been here, thanks to Millie's inside knowledge on his schedule. A backpacking trip by myself through the mountains. It had been redeeming. I returned the morning he left and didn't once see him.

Shortly after, he deployed to Afghanistan for a year. According to his mother, he'd recently returned.

Despite the errant thought of Devin that I tried to dismiss, my stubborn mind held on. Thoughts of my fifteenth birthday came next, when he'd helped me pick out Thor, my Rhodesian Ridgeback dog. Then my sixteenth birthday, when he sat in the passenger seat of my junker car with a helmet on after my license became official. Pain followed the memories like a river, so I turned my thoughts away again.

This is why birthdays sucked. Too many memories stacked behind them.

I eyed the clock. In fact, it was almost time to *really* celebrate. I had a few canyons to refresh myself on. There were back trails I'd taken before that avoided the highway, which saved time. I could ride for a few hours and be back for family dinner.

No one headed in from the parking lot outside, so I dashed out the back door, over to the outside loft entrance, and upstairs to the attic apartment where I lived. Hiking boots and maps littered my bed and floor as I shucked off my black pants and yanked on my jeans.

The distant sound of the door jingled below.

"Coming!" I called.

After I stuffed my feet into my boots, I grabbed a hair tie and slipped back down the winding stairs. Millie came to see me almost every day in between hair appointments for a caffeine boost. No doubt, she'd sneak in today. Boots untied, I carefully descended the stairs and hurried back through the door into the main area.

"Sorry about that. I—"

I jerked to a stop before I knew why. Tall figure. Broad shoulders with stacked muscles and thick arms. Sandy blond hair with slivers of brown, cropped too short to tell.

Devin.

For five seconds, I stared at him without comprehending fully. He pulled off a pair of reflective aviators, and those chocolate brown eyes met mine.

"Ellie."

The word was tentative, maybe yearning. I couldn't tell because my throat had closed off. Instead of responding, I stared at him.

Devin.

Devin.

Devin.

"Dev," I heard myself say.

We stared at each other for a small eternity, nothing in the room but charged air and unspoken emotions. Dark emotions. Relieved emotions. Something that lived on the edge of hysteria and joy.

He looked so good. So . . . tan. So . . . torn. Was the edge in his eyes because of me? Millie kept me updated on him. Secretly, I sucked up every single word. He had supposedly returned from a twelve-month deployment at some point a few weeks ago, but the details were vague and uncertain, and I'd been busy at the outfitters. No one had mentioned him visiting.

I must have been staring at him too long because his gaze dropped. My heart pounded in my chest as I tried to slow my breathing.

"I . . ." He clacked his teeth together. "I just got into town."

"Oh."

By sheer instinct, I stepped behind the counter and reached for my apron. My brain hardly comprehended what I did, but I felt purpose and stabilization in the movement.

"Can I get you something to drink?"

My voice was a breathy sound. A choked sob, maybe? I didn't dare look at him to read his face. This entire sequence felt unreal. Like I moved through water. Like this was one of the thousands of dreams I'd had over the last three years where he'd walk back into my life, and I'd wake up to realize it was the last three years that had been the dream.

"No, thanks."

I started making something anyway because I couldn't just stand there. Nor could I look at him. The memories came too fast. Like whips, they burned.

"Glad you're home safe," I managed to say, and I meant it. I snuck a quick glance at him. Something dark clouded his features when he nodded, but he looked outside now, jaw tight.

"I didn't tell my parents that I was coming. Wanted to surprise them."

"Your Mom will cry."

He chuckled again, and the darkness had passed. My heart cracked with a Devin-deep fissure. He was the same. Three years, two deployments, and countless hours of unknown life separated us, but he was still Devin.

How could he just show up?

Another burdened silence weighed heavy in the air as I grabbed a cup and filled it with coffee. Then I added cream, sugar, and a hint of cinnamon on top. Once I finished, I set the lid on, then stared at it.

My brain whirled in two capacities:

1. Do something so he'd go away.
2. Figure out why Devin had returned.

Neither was feasible at this moment. He cleared his throat.

"I, uh . . . I didn't tell anyone because I was afraid you'd disappear again, like you did a year or so ago." His shoulders lifted as he drew in a deep breath. "I was afraid you'd leave, and I wouldn't get a chance to see you. Or talk to you."

Shock dropped all pretenses. "I would have."

He winced. "I know."

My hands shook as I reached for another empty cup, set it back down in a different spot, then grabbed a rag from the sink.

I'm not the only one that's been running away, I wanted to say.

Tables. I could wipe those down. Because there was a dusty, forgotten box in the corner of my mind trembling with the urge to break. To remind me of the past, of what I'd locked away. But I clamped back down on it because that box had been destroyed the night of prom. Somehow, it had built itself back up. Now, it sat there with thick armor and a low growl that dared anything that might poke it. Inside the ravaged box waited affection, adoration, hope, dreams, and lo— . . . the box would be gone now. Empty, demolished by time. But wasn't that the scariest part of all?

Maybe, inside that box, there was nothing left.

"I'm glad you stopped by." I avoided his gaze as I shoved a chair under a table, then wiped the already clean surface. I could feel his eyes on my back. "But I need to be going soon. Just getting ready to clear out of here."

"It's your birthday."

I bit back my instant retort. *You don't get to know everything about me now, Dev. You gave that up.*

So I said nothing.

"I brought you something."

The sound of a box settling on the counter followed. Whatever it was, it must be pocket-sized, because he hadn't been holding anything when he'd walked in. With ferocious intent, I wiped down the next table. My throat had nearly swollen closed.

He hesitated, somewhere behind me out of arms reach. I stopped, straightened, and for one moment gave into the thoughts that streamed through my head.

How dare you?

Don't ever come back again.

Please don't die out there.

You left.

Tell me everything.

I'd dreamed—consciously and unconsciously—of this moment so many times. Most of them revolved around him coming home while I dated someone else, or just finished a guide, returned from South America, or some other big, awesome life event. Then I'd smile, act delighted to see him, and prove that I didn't need him to be happy. Then *I* would leave *him,* so he'd know that he made the right mistake by lying and abandoning me and my dreams.

Instead, I leaned both palms against the table and tried to catch my breath. Tried to convince myself that I could shove my happiness in his face and that I wanted to. But I could barely organize my thoughts.

"Ellie—"

"Don't."

The word came out sharp as a knife and with more feeling than I meant. Lost in the pain now, I whirled around.

"Tell me you didn't come back with some sort of hope for us. Tell me that your life has been exactly what you wanted it to be, and it was worth it and you want to go back to it after you spend some time here."

He opened his mouth, then closed it again. But I didn't save him. I sat in that waiting space until he finally said, "I came because I wanted to see you. I wanted to clear the air between us after what happened."

My shoulders snapped back. "Oh, well, that's easy enough. You are absolved of any guilt that you feel. I forgive you for lying and altering the course of my life. For avoiding me for three years and then for showing up without warning." My chin lifted, and righteous indignation gave me the strength to power through. "Do you want me to say that you made the right choice? Because I will. I'll say that you did the right thing, and now you can go back to it without residual guilt. Does that feel better?"

The pain in my own voice bothered me. Hadn't I dealt with this? Hadn't I tucked it all away or thought it out of my brain yet? Apparently not, because the fire of a thousand suns burned in my chest now.

"No."

He said it so quietly I almost didn't hear it at first.

"Then what do you want?"

His eyes met mine, more burnt sienna than brown now. The pain there cut through my own, and an instinct buried deep in my chest wanted to reach out and console him. But I held it back because Devin didn't need me anymore.

"I want a chance."

"To what?"

"To explain."

My breath still came too fast, my thoughts too slow. Just seeing him there, as familiar and yet as unknown as a stranger, made it almost impossible to think.

"I want to explain why I did it." He pressed on because I hadn't spoken. "I want a chance to at least explain why . . ."

He sighed. I waited for him to finish the thought, but he didn't. Something broke inside me, and I didn't know what it was, but I couldn't take another moment of this. Although subtle and layered with the overwhelming scent of coffee, there was a hint of pine in the air. *His* smell. The smell that had carried me through each day as a young girl.

Give him a chance, I thought, *and he'll just leave again.*

Because men leave.

Love dies.

You take care of yourself.

With a quick spin, I headed behind the counter. Ditched the cloth in the sink, locked the drive-thru window, and grabbed my backpack. My keys jangled in the outside pocket as I riffled around it and blatantly ignored his birthday present.

"Maybe some other time," I said. "I need to go."

He said nothing at first, but nodded, looking uncertain. There were harder edges to him now, hiding the softer, kinder Devin I once knew. This was an older version of Devin. The version of Devin that had seen the world. What had happened to him to cause the emotional callous over once-gentle eyes?

I slung the backpack over one shoulder and motioned to the door.

"Goodbye, Dev."

With one last look, he headed to the door and stepped outside. The moment it closed, I flipped the lock and fled out the back door, relieved to get some space between us.

I darted away before I begged him to take me into his arms and never let me go.

Chapter Two

DEVIN

Early summer sunshine glowed hot on my back as I stepped outside the Frolicking Moose and headed for my rental car. The lock flipped behind me with a final *thud* as Ellie shut me out.

Yet again.

Less than two minutes later, a beater truck appeared from behind the shop. Without a glance my way, Ellie pulled onto Main Street and headed out. No doubt she was headed home. Or maybe to my parents' house to saddle the horse and run to the mountains. That sounded more like her.

But how would I know anyway? Three years separated us. All I had now was supposition.

Now that she'd left, I could close my eyes and let out the longest exhale ever. Could calm the roiling panic, fear, and terror that had been wreaking havoc on my body for the last four days. All the questions I'd been secretly obsessing over had died away. *What is she like now? Does she utterly hate me?*

Is there any chance?

Harsh reception aside, her response had been better than I'd expected. My brow furrowed on the thought. What *had* I expected? I didn't know, but cold indifference seemed most likely.

Rage, perhaps. Ellie never made a scene, she just left. Disappeared. Like a cat, she had a way of slipping away to never be found again if she wanted. Kind of like now.

So, at least she'd spoken to me.

Maybe I'd expected silence, too, because that's certainly what I'd experienced the last three years.

I tilted my head back to look at the clouds and let the quiet settle my thoughts. The worst of it was over. At least I'd broken the ice. Clapped my eyes on her after three years of dreaming what she'd look like. Her dark hair was still long, brushing past her shoulders. Her eyes like evergreens, skin tanned and rough, body slim. Her expression had matured. She'd lost the gentle roundness of youth but certainly hadn't gained any laugh lines. She was stronger now, a wiriness built under the flannel shirt that hid a tank top. Glimpses of her shoulder had peeked out as she'd frantically scrubbed the tables to avoid me.

My left shoulder ached, so I reached over to rub it just as my phone chimed with a text message. I shook my head to pull myself back to the present. Texting took some getting used to after returning back to civilization, just like everything else. The chatter on the radio felt like too much noise. The people in the grocery store stood too close.

Pineville seemed surreal, with its calm temperatures and people walking everywhere without fear. While my world had constantly changed into new landscapes for the last three years, Pineville hadn't changed much at all. Except for the new Frolicking Moose, everything else was just like home.

Whether that was comfort or frustration, I couldn't tell.

Maverick: You survive?

Devin: Barely.

Maverick: How'd she take it?

Devin: As expected. Shock. A bit of rage. Then she ran.

Maverick: Did she say she'd give you a chance to explain?

My finger tapped against the back of my phone as I thought about the answer. She hadn't said no. At least, not directly. Hadn't outright refused me. *Maybe some other time* was infinitely better than *go to hell*.

Or was it the same thing?

Devin: She said maybe later.

Maverick: That's something.

Devin: Let's hope. I have three weeks to clear this up with her before I have to head back.

Maverick: Have faith. Ellie needs you. She's not the same girl. She'll see it if you keep after it. I'll enlist Lizbeth's help tonight. She always talks sense into her.

Devin: Thanks, Mav.

Maverick: I'm here. Reintegration after a deployment like yours is scary as hell. Sometimes, it takes another soldier to understand. I've got you, brother.

I closed my phone. Didn't want to think about that yet, or name it, but I silently appreciated it all the same. Being in love with my best friend, who effectively hated me now, was traumatic enough.

Almost losing the chance to tell her how I felt, however, was far more frightening. Being two shades away from death several times had a way of bringing clarity to the greatest darkness. I wouldn't lose this chance again.

Before I returned back to North Carolina, Ellie would know that I loved her then and I love her now. Ellie was worth fighting for, even if she could be compared to the ice queen. She was worth doing now what I didn't do then.

Even if she hated me.

The crack of a car door closing outside brought me out of my spiraling thoughts. *Can't control this,* I thought as I loosened my tense fists. *Can't let this send me into another spiral. Everything is fine. I'm fine. I'm here. I'm not there.*

With great effort, I mentally set Ellie aside and shoved my phone into my back pocket. She wasn't the only one I came to see. With a quick smile, I shut the door, and headed to Mom's hair salon.

Time to scare the highlights out of her.

Chapter Three

ELLIE

"Those chickens won't water themselves, you know."

My head jerked up at the familiar, lyrical sound of Lizbeth's voice. She tossed a bowl of food on the ground, and a flurry of feathers flocked to it. In the distance, the guinea hen screeched. I sighed and set the canister for the water trough down. Water glugged into a metal bowl.

"I know."

Lizbeth leaned against the fence next to me. She wore a pair of jeans and a t-shirt that said, *Get your buns frosted.* It covered an adorable, rounded belly. Even at seven months pregnant, she looked lovely as ever. Shimmering locks of bright red hair spilled onto her shoulders. A tattered romance book lingered under one of her arms. She'd probably read it in the car on the way down the canyon from where she lived in Jackson City.

"It's your birthday, so why do you look like someone just kicked Thor?"

My dog prowled around outside, attempting to stuff his face between the slats of the fence to get to my hens. I shooed him away with a little tap of my shoe near his face, and he snorted.

"Devin's home."

Her expression turned so pale I thought she'd faint, but she waved me off with a hand before I could reach for her. Her shock comforted me, and I didn't know why.

"What?"

I nodded, barely able to believe it myself. "He stopped by the coffee shop earlier today."

I recounted what I could remember in odd snippets that didn't string together well. Lizbeth asked for more details to clarify the confusing five minutes in which I'd seen him. All the while, my mind seemed to unwind. Talking it out helped it not feel so stuffed and heavy in my head.

"Sweet baby pineapple."

Lizbeth shook her head as chickens cluttered our feet. Something about the flurry of feathers and constant cooing eased me. I reached down, grabbed my favorite hen, and held her against me. The soft, downy feathers were silk on my fingertips and soothed the prickles inside.

"How are you?" she asked.

"Fine."

She tilted her head with a fierce glare. For being so lithe and thin, she was a powerful little thing.

"Stop it. How are you?"

Fractured. Stunned. Startled. Relieved. Uncertain.

"I'm not really sure," I said, which was true enough. She seemed to take that in stride. How should I feel? Devin had returned from the dead after three years. Part of my heart couldn't stop caring that he'd made it back from deployment. We had seven years of inseparable friendship before those three of absence. Not even his awful departure could take those years back.

But did they mean anything now?

"Fair," she murmured. "I'm pretty shocked, and I didn't love him like you did."

I scowled.

She grinned brightly.

"It wasn't what I thought it would be," I admitted quietly. "Seeing him again, I mean. It was . . . weird. He seems the same, but he's also so different. That's probably what he thought of me, too."

Although surely I hadn't changed like he had. Or had I? Did I have the same sharp edges? Did I seem more mature?

Piecing my life back together after the shock of his enlistment and into something totally new had been intentional and painstaking. My senior year of high school had been the loneliest I'd ever known. Devin's departure had thrust me into a world without him I hadn't been ready for.

"How did he look?" She cast a sly glance my way. "I mean, how did he *really* look? All buffed up from those push-ups, I bet?"

My teeth clenched. "He looked like Devin."

She held up two hands. "Sweet baby pineapple! Be fair, Ellie. He's probably a stunner. He was already good-looking as a senior, but now he's a freaking Marine. I know, I know you're still hurt and bitter and—"

"I'm not hurt. And I'm not bitter."

The words came out a bit too forcefully. She smirked.

I frowned.

"Right," she drawled. "I'll remove bitter, but not hurt. You didn't wallow out loud and you moved on. But you're definitely still hurt, and you have reason to be. He left you without closure. You need to find it now. This is a massive chance from the universe! You gotta take it."

"Maybe."

She rolled her eyes. "If not that, then what *do* you want right now, Ellie?"

I want him to leave, was my first thought, but it didn't sit well. Did I really want him to leave without us finally smoothing this down?

No, I didn't.

Part of me had thirsted for Devin since he left. Had craved him like an addict. Time hadn't entirely dulled the ache, even if the need had slowly throbbed away in that long year after he first left.

"Have you considered that one of the reasons you still feel hurt is because of the way he left?" Lizbeth turned and leaned her shoulder against the fence to face me fully. "Until today, you haven't spoken about him since that awful night at prom. I think it made you jaded about other men, so you haven't really dated."

"I've dated."

"First dates."

"And that's all they ever amounted to."

"Because you ignored them."

That was the truth. Plenty of those first dates would have come back for second, third, and more dates. But I'd stopped there, because . . . why bother? Men left. I didn't want them back. It felt coldhearted, but it was an attempt to be kind.

"I don't want to find someone else." The chicken squawked as I set her back down to scavenge with the others. In the distance, Thor's snorts as he prowled the property filled the evening air. My goats bleated from their pen not far away.

"Why not?" she asked. "Dating sucks, but marriage is the best."

"Because love sucks."

"Sometimes it totally does." She poked a finger into my rib. "But the moments that it rocks are worth it. You and I have been over this countless times. Mama was wrong about *parts* of romance and love, but not all of it. It's worth fighting for, Ellie."

My heart reviewed the surface of all the good times with Devin. The light. The joy. The connection. The feel of his body next to mine, my stalwart best friend. My safety. Then the emptiness when he was gone. The scattered life that remained in his wake.

Was it worth it?

"I don't want a boyfriend, Lizbeth. I don't want a husband. That's not my life."

She shrugged. "That's fine. If you clear things up with Devin, then at least you'd be ready then if someone else *did* come along. The right one makes you want it. You can't force it."

That didn't sit great either. Marriage. Love. Babies. That wasn't my thing. Mama and Devin had left big enough holes in my heart. No reason to do that again. JJ and Lizbeth were genuinely imperfect and adorable. Maverick and Bethany were so well matched they suited each other's intensity. But me?

No.

I'd rather have my chickens, goats, and dogs. Drooling babies and staying in the same place for decades on decades behind a white picket fence wasn't my jam. Yet . . . I didn't leave Pineville much on my own, either.

"Maybe you're right," I said as I shoved those thoughts aside. "I can take the chance to clear the air and be done. At least hear his side."

She exhaled dramatically as if relieved. "Good. Let him explain." She met my gaze with bright, clear eyes. "What do you have to lose? A burden of grief? If moving on without Devin is what you really want, Ellie, then you've just been given your chance. Hear him out, then move forward again. It's a process you've perfected the last three years, and I couldn't be more proud of you."

Reluctantly, I nodded. Devin needed to stay gone, but I wasn't sure I wanted to know what he'd say. What if he had great reasons for what he did? Although, I couldn't think of any good reason to harbor a lie.

No, I just wanted to tuck this back into the box and shove it off a cliff. Once we spoke, that stalwart box wouldn't have a place in my mind any longer, with its gentle pulse and quiet reminders as it collected age and dust.

This time, Devin would go away, and there he'd stay.

"C'mon." Lizbeth hooked her arm through mine. "JJ made this scrumptious naked Black Forest cake that is to die for. The cherry glaze?" She shivered. "Let's just say it makes baby Lizbeth so very, very happy."

Chapter Four

DEVIN

When the dull *thud* of a fist hitting a bag rang in my ears, I knew I'd found the right place.

Dawn hinted on the horizon as I stepped inside the MMA Center. Sweat from my 4:00 a.m. run drenched my shirt, making it cling to my back. The run had worked out the kinks of crappy sleep. Returning from the other side of the globe was never going to be easy, but this time transition really sucked. At least I could remove the dreams and residual darkness that lingered.

But now, I needed to hit something.

Something *hard.*

"Devin Blaine."

A familiar face approached me from behind a counter. Short, stocky body. Muscles on muscles. Quick grin and short blonde hair buzzed low on the sides and spiked on top. I almost didn't recognize him.

"Jax?"

He grinned and held out a hand that I clasped and pulled into a quick man-hug with a thunderous back pounding. When he stepped back, I could hardly believe my eyes.

"Gentle Jax." I shook my head. "My, my, how you've grown."

He laughed and slapped me on the shoulder. "It's been a few years, my friend." His arms spread to encompass the gym. "Welcome."

"This is yours?"

"Nah, I just help Ben run it. He wanted it all MMA-focused, but I've convinced him to make it a real gym where people come to work out. He lets me run classes and the gym side. He does all the rest."

"Benjamin Mercedy?"

"The one."

I whistled low. The guys would die if they knew where I stood. Retired MMA fighter Benjamin Mercedy still had everyone's attention with the training gym he opened after his career-making final fight.

I glanced around the gleaming space with floor-to-ceiling windows and alternating black-and-red mats on the ground. Groups of workout equipment cluttered the back of the room. Several joggers kept treadmills busy or stacked bumper plates on bars near the squat racks. More than I would have expected little Pineville to produce at 5:00 am.

"Sweet place, man."

"Thanks. How are you? Didn't know you were back."

"Surprised everyone," I said with a quick smile.

Jax's eyebrows rose. "Everyone?"

The drawl in his voice immediately clued me in. He meant Ellie, which likely meant that Ellie and Jax were still friends. Of course, they were. Who else lived in Pineville, population 300?

Before I could change the subject, he chuckled. "Actually, you showing up this morning explains a lot."

"What do you mean?"

He tilted his head toward the back of the room. I had to side-step to peer around a TRX system before I saw a black ponytail swishing through the air. A pair of fists flew against a bag, interspersed with an occasional roundhouse kick and grunt. Sweat gleamed down Ellie's face as she danced back and forth, focused on the punching bag.

"Yeah," I drawled. "She's picturing me right there."

Jax laughed outright. "Then she wants to destroy you. I haven't seen her this worked up in months. It's an impressive sight when Ellie gets in her rage."

My gut clenched at the thought. I watched her for a minute more, then turned away. The deep grooves in her expression, and intense concentration, made it feel like I intruded on something. She had skill, that was for sure. The bag wasn't something new, clearly, which hurt even more.

Did I know this Ellie?

The door opened behind me, admitting a cool brush of morning air against the back of my neck. Jax lifted his head in a short nod to someone back there.

"Hey, Kimball. Class will start in ten."

A tall guy nodded to him and kept going. He had an uncertain gait as he strode past, bag slung over his shoulder. He slowed, canvassing the room until he saw Ellie in the back corner. A quick twitch of his lips gave him away. A second later, he headed for a changing room at the back. His eyes didn't stray from her much before he slipped inside.

I didn't like that guy at all.

"Who's he?" I asked with a jerk of my head.

"Summer visitor, I think. Came in a few days ago and only signed up through the end of the month. His family owned a cabin in the mountains they'd never visited before or something? Can't remember his story." Jax shrugged. "Nice enough. Bit . . . chatty."

"Huh."

"So, how long are you back?"

While Jax and I devolved into the usual questions that I'd braced myself to answer—how long are you here for? Where are you stationed? How was deployment?— I stayed where I could see

Ellie. She pounded the bag for a few more minutes before she ripped the gloves off and grabbed some water.

Thankfully, Jax kept the conversation on the surface. He didn't ask any questions I'd already decided I wouldn't answer. Ellie sat on the floor to stretch just as Kimball came back out. The people running on the treadmill had started to gather on the mats, where another tall, slender guy fiddled with some music.

Kimball headed right for Ellie. My shoulders tensed.

"She's not yours anymore."

Jax said the words so easily I thought I'd misunderstood him. Startled, I looked at him in wordless question. There was no animosity in his tone, but something lurked underneath.

"What?"

"Ellie isn't yours, so you can act as possessive as you want, but I'm not going to let it fly in here."

A flash of amusement crossed his expression. Maybe I looked pissed. I *felt* pissed. Defensive.

But he was absolutely right.

Jax folded his arms across his chest. "Ellie moved on. She had to. You left her, and she rebuilt her life slowly. One piece at a time. So, yes. Kimball is flirting with her. He has been for the past couple of days. He comes in early, looks for her, changes, and they talk until his class starts. She leaves. He hasn't come any other day except the ones when she shows up. And that's his right."

His words felt like glass under the skin, but I couldn't deny their truth. Coming back, I knew that Ellie would be different. That our friendship wouldn't be the same. That we'd be new people and the likelihood of things ever reconciling were slim to none. Ellie's sense of survival had always been greater than her sense of happiness. She no longer saw me as safe, so she wouldn't invest time or trust in me.

At least not yet.

The only hope that I had was that those years of friendship and connection *had* happened. Maybe there was a foundation that she couldn't deny. If there wasn't, I came home to tell her how I felt then and now. That mission wouldn't change, Kimball notwithstanding.

"Roger," I said.

Jax had the gall to look amused again, and I almost tackled him right there. I needed to hit something, and he'd suffice.

"Listen, Dev, I don't have any more claim on Ellie than you do. We're friends in a held-at-arms-length kind of way, and I'm fine with that. No one has any claim on a woman like her. She goes on first dates, and they never hear back. I've warned Kimball, but he doesn't care. She seems to have silently committed herself to the single life. If you're hoping to reconcile, be fair. I won't let you break her heart again."

"You won't?"

He shrugged, but he didn't take it back. "I am the only friend she has in this town, and I take that very seriously."

"You're the nice guy around here?"

"I guess so."

I scowled. "I won't break her heart."

Jax's brow had grown heavy. "You will. Even if you don't mean to. She still cares for you, Dev. You have to see that. Why else do you think she's so pissed off today? Ellie tells off the people she doesn't care about. The ones she avoids are the ones she loves."

My gaze drifted back to her. She warily smiled at Kimball from a runner's lunge, her legs long and strong in a pair of tight black pants. A towel had mopped away her sweat, but she still had that devastating smile. Her natural uncertainty around people only added to her sense of appeal. It would be so easy to believe that she had once had feelings for me. That I hadn't been the only one madly in love.

That was a dangerous road to go down without proof. For the millionth time, I forced myself away from it.

"I was stupid," I admitted. "I shouldn't have lied to her."

"Duh."

"But I had to leave."

"Why?"

My nostrils flared. That wasn't my story to tell.

Ellie had stood up and started to walk our way, stopping my thought process. Halfway across the mats, her gaze met mine. She stumbled slightly, and I couldn't tell what the flash in her eyes meant. She'd been hard to read on a good day when we were inseparable.

Practically impossible now.

"I'm on her side, my brother." Jax slammed a palm into my shoulder as he moved away. "Don't mess her up and then leave again, or I'll take it personally. You won't ever want to come back then."

A litany of curse words streamed through my head because he'd already voiced my greatest fear. I quieted them, but the questions invaded anyway. Was it wrong to sweep in, tell her how I felt, and then leave again? Was this about me, or her? It should be about her, but I couldn't deny my own selfish interests.

Ellie had recovered her wits and kept walking, her gaze on the floor now. Kimball reluctantly ambled over to the class, but his eyes hadn't left Ellie's back. They darted to mine next, and I met them. My expression hardened. He kept my gaze. Something in his face didn't sit right with me. He was harmless enough, probably, but I still didn't like him.

Kimball turned away as Ellie slowed to a stop a few feet away from me. I turned to give her my full attention.

"Hey."

"Hi."

With a jerk of my head, I motioned to the bag. "Great form."

"Thanks."

All right. The awkward conversation had returned.

"Listen, can I—"

"About yesterday—"

We both spoke at the same time, but she quieted first. A hint of amusement lingered in her half-raised lips before it faded into a frown. The fact that she hadn't swept by with her middle finger in the air encouraged me.

"I'm sorry about surprising you yesterday." I let out a breath, infusing as much honesty into it that I could. "Maybe it wasn't fair, but I just wanted to explain myself. And now that I'm here, I want to know what it's been like for you since I left. I want to . . . take responsibility for what I did."

The words hurt to say, and they seemed to startle her. Was it the first time I'd taken responsibility for the fact that I massively broke her heart? Probably. I'd avoided her for years, unable to reconcile my true feelings over what I'd done. I'd been a coward then, but life had a way of changing.

No more cowards now.

She hesitated, then nodded. "That's fine."

"That's fine, I can explain, or it's fine that I surprised you?"

Lines formed between her eyebrows. "Both, I guess. If you want a chance to explain, I'll give it. I have to work until four, but you can come to the shop then. We'll go out on the lake. I still have the boat. We can talk there."

Relief tripled through me. "Thank you."

She lifted one eyebrow. Behind her, Kimball's eyes bored into her back. I ignored him. *Yeah,* I wanted to say, *you definitely have competition.*

"All right." I nodded. The air conditioning made goosebumps prickle on my arms. "I'll see you at the back of the Frolicking Moose at four."

Ellie nodded, then brushed past without another word. Kimball stared at me from across the room before I nodded to Jax and left with a mental middle finger in the air, pointed right at Kimball.

Chapter Five

ELLIE

Cool water lapped against my ankles as I shoved the old canoe halfway into the lake. A short rope would keep it from going anywhere while I watched for leaks. It was the first time I'd brought the canoe out this year.

In three years, actually.

The sound of tires on gravel followed shortly after I'd satisfied my curiosity that we wouldn't sink and drown. My lips twitched. Sinking had happened once, actually, when I was fourteen and Devin was fifteen. We took an old canoe out, it sank halfway out of the peninsula, and we had to swim back together. He tried to convince me he was manly enough to give me a piggyback ride *and* swim back to shore, but almost ended up killing both of us instead.

A car door shut and drew me from the memory. Feet approached with the crunch of gravel under shoes. My heart fluttered a little knowing Devin would be there. I straightened as a tackle box and fishing pole landed in the canoe. When I looked up, he had a lopsided smile.

"Figured I might as well."

I couldn't help but half-heartedly return it. He looked so goofy. So boyish. He stopped to roll up an old pair of jeans that fit his narrow hips well. An old t-shirt stretched across his shoulders, a bit too tight. Likely one he'd found at home and tried it on because his laundry wasn't done, I'd bet. He'd put on at least twenty pounds since I'd last seen him, but it had all been mass. Devin had seemed strong and indomitable in high school, but he was puny then compared to now.

"Ready?" I asked as I put the paddles inside.

He rubbed his hands together. "Been waiting all day."

After I pushed the canoe out the rest of the way, I climbed in. He gave us another little jolt, then leaped in behind me with smoother agility than I'd expected. We assumed our childhood positions with me at the front, him at the back. The canoe rode lower in the water than last time with his bulkier weight, but felt more stable. We faced out to the reservoir and began to paddle.

For almost twenty minutes, nothing but the glide of smooth water beneath us could be heard. The sounds of Pineville disappeared as we rowed out in silence to the empty, still heart of the reservoir. My heart lay heavy in my throat. I both dreaded and anticipated what he would say. For years I had tried to understand what led him to the decision, but it had all been questions.

Until he could explain it, I'd never truly know. Now, it seemed surreal that I'd soon understand the machinations behind the hard years at my back.

"Can we try here?"

The sound of his voice in the silence was like a gunshot. Drops of water splatted my back as he pulled his paddle in. I nodded and did the same. While he flipped open his tackle box and started to rummage through, I grabbed the bag I'd stowed. After I removed my flip-flops and set them aside, I turned around to face him. I'd been a coward in the tree before, but not this time.

The sun felt hot on my skin, countering the still, cool water, chilled from snow run-off in the highest mountains. Sunglasses hid my eyes, which made it easier to study him while he worked. He seemed at ease. His face was smooth and movements intent. He didn't stammer or try to make small talk. He never had.

Out here, like this, without the clutter of Pineville around us, he seemed to be the old Devin. So much so that I half grinned when he muttered under his breath about a missing lure. I reached behind me, grabbed my own tackle box that I'd hidden under my bag, and passed it over.

"I raided yours."

His head lifted. He looked at me, then the tackle box, and back to me.

"After you left." I motioned to his box with a hand. "I raided it. All your best lures are in here, I would bet."

A quick grin took me by surprise. "Took all the good stuff, I see."

"You deserved it."

He laughed, then dove into my tackle box. The tension eased while he prepped his line with the lure and fresh bait. The smell of earth and worms and slime filled the air like a reassuring memory. Minutes later, he cast the line. It flopped a few feet away.

"Embarrassing," he muttered as he reeled it back in.

I laughed.

"Worst time of day to fish anyway," he said. "Except, it's—"

"It's not about the fish," I replied, echoing his usual line so quickly it startled both of us. For a brief tangle, our eyes met, then skated away. I reached for my water bottle just to have something to do and took a sip.

"Yeah," he agreed quietly. "It never was."

Silence fell between us. Seconds stretched into minutes. My lips were tied. I had no idea what to say or where to start.

His voice broke the stillness like a firework again.

"I meant it when I said I didn't want to go."

He leaned back a little, looking perfectly at ease. As if we weren't about to hash into our dark history. As if the secrets that had been smoldering in the background for years weren't about to be thrown wide open. Like me, sunglasses hid his eyes. It seemed to make everything less intense.

"But you went."

"Yeah." He nodded. "And damn, if I haven't regretted it every day."

There was nothing to say, so I waited. A few moments later, he continued. "Dad's back surgery set my parents back financially quite a bit. Do you remember that?"

I nodded, awash with vague memories of hospitals. Millie's exhausted, fearful expression. Devin's father had been in the hospital and then rehab for what felt like months. He'd regained his ability to walk, but the pain still plagued him for years. Even now, after recent physical therapy, he still had to take it easy.

"That sort of hospital stay, the rehab?" He tsked under his breath. "Just about wiped them out. We didn't have health insurance at the time and had to take out a second mortgage to cover the bills. Mom applied for charities, tried to find ways to fundraise, you name it. Credit cards maxed out, that kind of thing."

He let out a soft breath, a half-chuckle, as he shook his head. He tugged on his line as he admitted, "Maverick paid for my senior football season."

I reared back. "What?"

He nodded and looked right at me. "Yeah. I was too embarrassed to tell anyone that we couldn't afford all the gear, new cleats, that kind of stuff. Maverick offered after I told the coach I couldn't play. Mav found out somehow." He shrugged. "Don't know how. He paid for everything."

"I didn't know that."

Devin lifted his shoulders. "He promised he wouldn't say. All the times I ate at your house? I did it because we didn't have the money for a lot of food. Maverick and Bethany were always so generous. I was a teenager and a football player. Mom couldn't keep up with my appetite. We were on food stamps. Bethany even paid for my tux for prom in exchange for free haircuts from Mom. She lied to my Mom and said it cost half of what it did."

"Is that why you always ate at the coffee shop while we worked?" I asked, recalling days when he'd wolf down three sandwiches, five drinks, and a few scones. He'd forfeit his pay for the day.

He nodded.

My gut clenched. Money had always been tight at the Blaine household, but I hadn't realized just how much. After his dad broke his back, they lived off what Millie could make as a hairstylist, which couldn't have been much. Now that I looked back, it seemed like an obvious problem. Only a teenager would miss something like that.

Devin kept going, jaw tight as he gazed over the lake.

"So I practically lived with and ate with your family, which relieved some of the cost of food. Most of my clothes were thrift store finds out of Jackson City. I guess Mom would stay there for hours looking for stuff that seemed new so that I wasn't embarrassed. I wouldn't have cared, but she didn't want me to be ashamed. She tried so hard, but there was no making that kind of money back."

He leaned forward. He was more lost in the story than here on the canoe, now.

"When we started making those plans the summer before I graduated, I really meant to follow through." He frowned. "Going to the state university with you? Sounded like a dream. Saving up money and then going to college with you would have been awesome. I didn't . . . I didn't want you to go alone. It didn't seem safe or . . ." He paused, shook his head, and kept going. "As time went on, however, I started to do the math. The jobs I could get as an eighteen-year-old were mostly minimum wage. Even working two jobs and saving everything I could meant that I'd barely save enough for the first semester. But I couldn't work like that *and* go to school once it started."

Devin had always been gifted with learning. While I struggled with math and hated to read because it bored me, he sailed through his classes. Quarterback. Straight A student. Well-liked everywhere. College scholarships seemed inevitable.

But they hadn't been.

"Then I lost the big scholarship I applied for, and I still don't know why," he said as if he'd just read my mind. "Jobs were hard to secure. I saw the writing on the wall."

He let out a long breath and finally looked back at me. His fishing pole lay on the side of the canoe. Nothing would nibble now, and we'd both known it. But it felt better to act like we still participated in one of the things we both loved.

"Then my parents' debts were called. They had to put a $7,000 payment down or lose the house and be forced to file for bankruptcy." He held out his hands in a helpless gesture. "We have no family to fall back on. My parents would have been homeless or a charity case."

Breath fled my chest. Without knowing the details, I saw where this slowly moved. Saw how the pieces stacked together. How the dominos were about to fall. A fluttery feeling had become my heart. If it came together the way I imagined it would, I made a grave mistake three years ago.

Dev kept going, even though I wanted to ask him to stop. It felt like we careened down a train track and couldn't stop. My stomach felt like a wrung-out old rag.

"The Marines offered a $5,000 sign-on bonus if I enlisted with the infantry for six years. So I signed the damn paper and gave the bonus to my parents. They were able to come up with the rest and keep the house. Once I got a paycheck, I tried to send money home, but they wouldn't take it. Dad's pride barely allowed him to take the $5,000. Eventually, Dad found a job he can do without standing all day, which helped. Without me there taking up gas money and food and other stuff, they were able to make ends meet."

He exhaled a long breath. "But the debt still remained, as did their pride. So, I approached Maverick with an idea to be a blind investor for my mom. He and Mark Bailey went to her with the idea to renovate her salon, then slowly offer more things, like a spa. Apparently, Mark had been trying to open a spa but, because Stella still hadn't agreed with him on it, it never happened. Anyway, the plan worked. She took the bait and made more money. Their debts went down.

"I sent Mark more money, and Mark convinced her to open another business in Jackson City. That increased her revenue more so that they could upgrade the house a bit and start Dad with physical therapy. The house desperately needs improvements, and they've been able to start into them. They're almost out of the worst debt now and back to just the mortgage."

I silently agreed that their house needed a lot of work, then almost laughed. The shining new fridge suddenly made more sense. Millie had cried when they delivered it, clutching her Bible and muttering prayers of thanks under her breath.

Despite a moment of levity, my entire body felt cold, like I'd plunged back into the lake. All of *this* lay behind his decision. All of this history suddenly brought intense clarity to the story.

And he'd never told me.

Or maybe I just hadn't listened.

The last three years lay like a graveyard between us—a useless graveyard. Could all of this have been prevented? Had I done something wrong? My breath felt thready and weak, like I couldn't catch it no matter how hard I tried.

"Dev, I didn't know they struggled so much. I—"

"I know." His gaze dropped then. "I know, and that is my

fault. I just didn't want you to know. You've always worried about things, and I think I had a little too much pride." His brow furrowed. "Like my parents. Anyway, my parents still think that Mark was the investor behind the idea, but it's me. I've fronted almost $30,000 over the last three years for them to do it, and now it's paying out. One day I'll tell them, but not now, so please—"

"I wouldn't."

"Thank you."

I swallowed hard because I didn't know what to say. Several long minutes passed while I comprehended all that he told me. Understanding it came with a surprising amount of rage. If he had just *trusted* me. If he had just *told* me. The last three years could have been avoided. I could have supported him in the Marines. Helped his family. I could have done something to keep us together and avoided all those dark nights crying myself to sleep.

You could have supported him regardless of the history, came the thought. For the first time, I didn't brush it away. There were opportunities I didn't give him to explain. The weight of the last three years also lay on me.

Our current position was as much my fault as it was his. The silence waited for my response, and I was grateful that he gave me time to think it over. To deal with the overwhelm of my own responsibility in this.

"Thank you for telling me, Dev. I . . . admire your loyalty to your parents. That's a big sacrifice to make."

He waved that off.

My whisper came out quietly. "I'm sorry."

After I said it, the gentle lap of the lake against the boat filled the air. Did he know how much my words truly encompassed? That I was sorry for not trusting him enough to get an explanation sooner? That I was sorry so much time had passed that we couldn't take back now? That he'd made such a decision without once consulting me in all that time? I felt sorry and sad for both of us.

He licked his lips, then shook his head. Before he could say another word, I forced the rest out.

"I'm sorry that I didn't give you a chance to explain. You tried."

He opened his mouth, then closed it again. Several moments later, he said, "It's my fault, Ellie. I'm the one that should be apologizing."

The sound of my name off his lips sent a physical thrill through me.

"It's my fault that these three years happened this way," he said with feeling. "That I chickened out and didn't come home. That I didn't tell you sooner and explain sooner instead of rowing you out here on this damn canoe and telling you when you couldn't escape. To tell you at prom? I . . ."

Frustration made his entire body rigid. I could feel the sincerity of his regret, and it cut deep. Didn't we both bear responsibility? If just one of us had trusted the other enough. If we had just—

I cut that thought off. We could have done a lot, but we didn't. Now we had a three-year chasm to either ignore or try to gap.

"We're both at fault, Dev."

He frowned, not seeming any better for the admission. I appreciated the sentiment because, while I was grateful to understand, I felt worse. I drew in a deep breath and rubbed my hands over my knees, cold despite the persuasive heat from the warm summer sun on my skin.

"The question is, what do we do now?" I murmured.

Several attempts to speak yielded nothing on his part. I wrapped my arms around my knees and let the silence ride. The canoe gently rocked. The smell of the lake, the occasional *blip* of the water, soothed me.

Devin seemed to be at war with himself, as if he had something he wanted to say but didn't know how to say it. I wondered what thoughts lay behind those tight lips.

"What makes you happy now, Ellie?"

The question caught me by surprise. "What?"

"There's so much I don't know about the last three years, so I want to know what makes you happy now."

Startled, I responded with my instinct. "Freedom."

He lifted an eyebrow in silent question.

"College wasn't a good fit for me." My nose wrinkled. "I tried half of a semester at the state university, but I couldn't do it."

What I didn't tell him was that ghosts chased me away. That his absence was a living entity that walked me to class. His ghost accompanied me home and sat with me in a loud apartment cluttered with girls swapping mascara and sequined shirts. Their drunk boyfriend-of-the-day laughed loudly in the other room as if they owned the place. Always unpredictable. Sometimes in my stuff. When I became angry that they entered my room without permission, they laughed it off. The scent of alcohol stained the air every weekend. Memories of Jim had come back to haunt me in big ways, making it impossible to feel safe.

I skipped over the memory of the guy that pawed at me when my roommates held a party. I'd dislocated his arm and had to file a report with the police. Or the group of guys that surrounded me on campus as if to ask me directions. They tried to back me up against a wall. I'd kicked one in the throat, slashed another in the eyes with my keys, and the third one fled before I could turn on him.

Those things didn't need to be said yet.

"What didn't you like?" he asked.

I shrugged.

"Everything. Classes. Restrictions. A single career path. Someone else telling me to pay them money to educate me on something I might not want to do in ten years."

Most people recoiled when I stated my opinions about college. They judged my job at the coffee shop and seemed to quietly ask: *and this is so much better?* Some people just smiled at my less-than-popular opinions, acting as if I was young and would rush back to college later when I learned the truth.

"I didn't need a professor to tell me how to start a fire without matches. How to survive for three days with only the clothes on my back. I already did those things, and that's all I wanted to keep doing. I wanted freedom in the mountains. So, I came home."

To my surprise, he grinned. "I always thought you'd hate college."

I chuckled. "Turns out you were right."

"What happened next?"

He leaned forward again, arms braced on his knees, as if hungry for the details. Genuine interest lay there.

"I came home," I said. "Dagny and Hernandez married in a Christmas ceremony at his abuela's house, so I moved into the loft and took over the Frolicking Moose. JJ Bailey has been taking me on climbs with him a few times a month, so I'm skilled at that. Got my boaters certification. First aid. CPR. Avalanche training. Licenses. Practiced downhill winter skiing. Anything I could do outside that would eventually get me to where I wanted to be."

"Adventure guiding."

It wasn't a question.

My grin grew. "Guiding."

Devin scoffed.

"I had to earn Daniel's trust somehow, so I dove into all the outdoor adventure things I could find. He thought I was too young and inexperienced at first, and . . . he might have been right."

I winced. Admitting that concession always stung. Devin grinned, but it was half-hearted and quiet.

"He has let me start small. Half-day hikes, full-day hikes. Some boating and fishing. Winter traffic is big, especially for back-country skiing. After working for him for two years, assisting on some guides, and learning a bit more, I'm going to do my first overnight guide this summer."

"Freaking sweet." He grinned wide, and the skin around his sunglasses wrinkled. "You've been busy."

My heart settled a little. No judgment from him, of course.

"It's perfect for you." He tugged on the fishing pole. "When is the first overnight guide?"

"Soon, I hope."

He studied me for a moment. "Being outside makes you happy, just like always."

I tilted my head back to the sun.

"Like always."

"Wild child," he murmured my most used childhood nickname with an undeniable warmth.

We fell back into thinking, but this time it felt easier. I filtered through all he'd revealed while I leaned back and surrounded myself with sunshine. Devin tugged on the worm, which had long since sunk, and recast it. We lacked only Thor, who we used to bring out with us as a puppy, and with him this would have been a perfect canoe trip.

For the next hour, occasional small talk filled the time, but not much of it. Devin seemed content to sit with his pole and not get a bite. His thoughts, like mine, were far from fishing. The quiet was a welcome reprieve after the day at the shop, and we fell into it the way we used to.

Just as my stomach started to grumble, Devin reached for the paddle. Wordless, I grabbed mine, and we started our way back.

White strings of lights from the Frolicking Moose welcomed us back. Inside, our new barista Dahlia bustled around, visible through the drive thru window as she attended to customers. Lizbeth's book club filled the back room, which looked out over the lake. They'd see us out here together, and Lizbeth would have questions.

I had questions.

We docked the boat together. He helped me pull it out of reach, and I tucked the paddles at the bottom. Full tourist season hadn't started yet, so it would be safe to rest out here for now. Then we headed toward the front of the shop.

At his car, he turned to me.

"Where do we go from here, Ellie?" he asked.

Devin tucked his sunglasses onto his shirt, where they hung around the neckline, giving me full access to his eyes. Their natural warmth had returned, but the receding wariness remained. His pant legs were still rolled around his calves and his tackle box dangled next to his thigh.

"Where we left off," I said.

"Friends?"

"Friends."

A thousand days of pain lay behind us that I couldn't forget, but he didn't ask me to forget them. We wouldn't be the same people right this moment that we were then, but we didn't have to ignore each other. The little box rumbled in my mind, but I ignored it and all the truths within. Friends came and went. That was fine. They were supposed to. I'd accepted that years ago.

As friends, Devin could come and go. He could go back to the life he had to live for at least six years—maybe he'd do more—and I could continue on the path I'd carefully sculpted for myself.

This life was what I wanted.

He fiddled with car keys. "I have two and a half weeks left before I have to return to North Carolina. Can I spend some of those days with you?"

I nodded, unable to commit to an amount of time but just as unable to turn him away. My emotions were in turmoil inside me, torn between regret for what I hadn't done but should have, relief that his decision hadn't been about me, and fear. Fear of what this meant. Fear of the expression of hope that had returned to his face. Fear of more pain. More empty years. More of the truth I already knew to the depths of my bones.

Men leave.

Love dies.

You take care of yourself.
"I'll text you?" he said.
"Sure."
"Same number?"
I nodded.
He ducked into the truck, and with one last wave, disappeared onto Main Street. I watched him go with immense relief, my heart a slow plod inside me.

Chapter Six

DEVIN

The brakes of my parents' truck screeched as I slid to a stop outside of a wooden cabin at Adventura mountain camp.

Through the open truck window, the distant cry of kids rattled through the trees. I stepped out of the truck and slammed the door behind me. A familiar head of red hair rushed out of the cabin, then skidded to a stop.

Lizbeth's mouth dropped open.

Seconds later, she'd crossed the space between us, and her pregnant little body slammed into mine with a tight hug.

"Devin!" she cried.

I wrapped my arms around her in an awkward embrace, her baby belly between us, gratified to see her again. When she pulled away, she nailed me on the shoulder with a fist.

"That's for not coming to see us last time you came home! What's the matter with you?"

"I'm sorry!"

Fury showed in those bright emerald eyes, sprinkled with hints of love. Despite being one of the sweetest people I had ever met, I definitely wouldn't mess with her. Her hair was pulled into a bun at the base of her neck, but red tendrils flew off her forehead in the summer breeze.

"Well." She frowned. "My sister is terrifying. I probably would have avoided her too. But still . . ."

Something else lingered in her gaze as she trailed off. Concern, maybe. I braced myself, ready to hear the inevitable sympathy, and wasn't disappointed.

"Your Mom told me about . . . everything. I'm sorry, Dev. Sounds like it was hell over there."

Before I could change the subject, another body stepped out of the cabin and waved, locks of hair flowing free around his face. JJ saved me as he strode over wearing a matching polo t-shirt to Lizbeth's. Both said *Adventura Summer Camp*. I met him halfway, eager to avoid the conversation Lizbeth started.

"How are you?" JJ asked and clapped me on the back. I pulled him close and returned the pounding.

"Glad to be back in the mountains," I said. "Nothing quite like the scent of pine, is there?"

He grinned. "You're here to see Mark, right?"

"Yeah."

JJ jerked his head back. "He's waiting for you inside."

"Sweet, thanks. Can't wait to come up to your bakery in Jackson City. I heard it's starting to be legendary with the tourists."

He grinned. "We're there on the weekends. Hired some people to run it during the week in the summer while we're here. Come up, and we'll give you a tour and free slice of cheesecake. Or a whole cake, whatever you want."

Lizbeth held up a thumb. "It is *the* best cheesecake."

"Soon," I promised.

"Get in there." JJ added, gesturing to the cabin again. "He's waiting for you."

With a nod of thanks, I headed for the cabin while JJ looped an arm around Lizbeth's waist, pulled her close, and then headed in the opposite direction. The gentle swish of pine needles in a summer breeze escorted me into the camp office. That scent was the final piece of returning home I needed.

JJ and Mark Bailey had been out exploring the world for most of my teen years. Our budding friendship started when Lizbeth and JJ began dating, became engaged, and then married. With JJ around Lizbeth all the time and me practically living with Ellie and her family, Mark inevitably tagged along every now and then. My business interests with Mark had brought us closer than I'd ever expected, and now I saw him as a brother.

I rapped on the cabin door, then stepped inside. Despite early summer heat rising from the carpet of pine needles outside, this cabin greeted me with a brush of cooler air. At the back of the room sat Mark, feet propped up on a desk cluttered with paperwork and pens.

Mark set his feet on the ground, pointed to his phone, and rolled his eyes. "I promise I won't do anything stupid. Swear it. Okay, gotta go. I'll tell him hi. Yeah, love you too. Bye."

He hung up.

"Stella is visiting her grandma in Florida. She thinks I'm going to try to buy an old strip mall in Nebraska and renovate it into a gym while she's gone."

"Are you?"

He laughed as he stood. "Totally."

Mark stepped around the desk, threw his arms wide, and enveloped me in a shameless, full-on hug. Then he gripped my shoulders and pulled me away.

"Dude, you look awesome."

"Thanks."

"Lifting?"

I shrugged. "When I could."

"Must be hard in the sandbox."

I chuckled as he sat back down. *You have no idea,* I thought. His chair groaned, but he ignored it. Despite the hurricane of paperwork on his desk—and was that a candle?—the rest of the cabin felt cozy and well-cared for. Coffee mugs hung from the wall over the sink. Pale drapes fluttered from an open window. Lizbeth definitely had a hand in all the changing decor when she first arrived, but Mark had a wife now. No doubt Stella kept up with it in Lizbeth's place.

"Place looks better," I said. "Bigger. Did you expand?"

"We did. Added a couple of rooms out back and on the side. Stella finally got a kitchen in here, too. It's the only project we've ever agreed on."

I laughed, "And it's way less smelly."

He grinned and ran a hand through his hair, then scrubbed his jaw. "We live upstairs most of the time. Stella won't let me be a slob."

"Stella likes it here?"

He nodded. "Loves it here." His gaze roamed the rafters. "Imperfect or not, Adventura is home. I'm not running the summer camp anymore. Sione, one of my counselors, has swapped his love for the ocean to the mountains. He runs the camp, Stella runs the basic-admin and bookkeeping, and I do big-picture stuff with the investors. We're working on getting a high-ropes course next summer. I can't leave it, so we live here."

"Seems great to me."

Mark studied me a second, then leaned forward. If it came down to a weightlifting competition, I'd have no chance against a guy like him. He'd always been bulkier than JJ, who had the wiry power of a climber. Mark could wrestle a bear and take it down. And sometimes, when he let his hair go full shag and his beard grew out, he *looked* like a bear.

But the sudden intensity in his expression told me he'd switched to business mode.

"What's up?" he asked. "I know we're friends *and* business partners now, but I have a feeling you didn't drive out to Adventura to take me on a date. If you did, you suck at it. You didn't even bring lunch."

"Came to check on my investment."

He grinned with one side of his lips. "Your Mom is a whiz, you know that? She didn't really trust me and Maverick at first, but once I told her she should take it to her pastor and pray about it," He snapped his thumb and forefinger, "—I had her."

A chuckle escaped me. "She's nothing if not devoted."

"Hey, we all got something. Honestly, Dev, things look good. She has steady contractors right now, the revenue coming in is strong. She's set aside some cash flow for hiccups in the future. I've stepped back. She mostly does this herself now. You've seen the investment dashboard Lizbeth put together for us. It's looking strong. Solid profile. Some of my other contacts have discussed requesting that she expand into some other mountain towns, but I haven't broached it yet. The time isn't right because she isn't bored yet."

I nodded, expecting to feel more relief at his report, but he wasn't saying anything that I didn't know already. Nothing that we couldn't have covered on a call.

So why was I here?

"That's not why you came," Mark said. He leaned back against the chair but stayed upright instead of lounging all the way back. "But you already knew that. So what's up?"

My gaze met his. "Honestly?"

"Always."

The cagey feeling I'd been battling since I returned home welled back up. It grew every day, more and more suffocating. More and more diabolical. Darker. Heavier. Filled with flashes of fire and light and explosions all around me.

This last deployment hadn't been my first, but it had been my longest. A damn year in Afghanistan, cut off from the world. My parents emailed, sent packages, but it had been the emptiest, most terrifying year of my life.

Without Ellie, everything felt empty.

But that deployment had been hell unleashed, which only made it all feel worse. Disaster riddled it like holes in an old boat. The attacks didn't stop. The sense of impending doom never left. The hits from the border never stopped smacking us on the back of the head, no matter how much aerial support we fed over there to prevent them from killing us first. On our "mission of peace."

There was no peace.

Even on American soil, peace had eluded me. Sometimes I woke up at night in a cold sweat. Minutes would pass before reality became clear, but sleep never returned. The lack of deep rest made me feel like a zombie, and I stumbled through the day with thoughts of Ellie and naps that only made it worse.

And I didn't know how to tell anyone.

Didn't know how to form the words that would sound something like *I'm back and I'm struggling and everything feels too close. Like it's pressing on me. Text messages come too fast. The radio is too loud. People talk too much to strangers they don't know. I don't know what to say when people ask how I'm doing. My parents' house feels too different to be mine. I don't belong here anymore.*

I don't know how to be back.

"I need to beat the shit out of something," I said in a croak.

Mark studied me with a shrewd gaze. Eternities seemed to pass before he nodded without a hint of question, pity, or compassion.

"You know I have it," he said. "If there's anything we specialize in around here, it's destruction."

With a jerk of his head, he motioned to the back door and stood. Relief filled me. He didn't ask. Wouldn't question. There were no answers I had to avoid, make up, or lie about. As I'd hoped, Mark got it.

And now I could vent the rage over my relentless deployment

and all the lives lost somewhere safe. Maybe, just *maybe,* I'd get a full night's sleep tonight.

"Come on." Mark grabbed my shoulders and shoved me down a back hallway ahead of him. "I have a woodpile and an ax with your name on it. Don't come back until the whole thing is split and ready to keep my wife warm through the winter."

Chapter Seven

ELLIE

A pile of skewed undershirts commanded my attention two days later.

The smell of coffee followed me while I walked around Pineville Outfitters setting things straight. I attempted to contact our sister company in Jackson City to coordinate canoe rentals, and haphazardly managed inventory. Thanks to the Frolicking Moose, I smelled like espresso all day. An eight-hour shift at the shop had preceded my six-hour shift at the Outfitters. Tonight, I'd drop into bed exhausted.

But not because of work.

Devin haunted my thoughts since our quiet canoe ride. The truths he'd unveiled had slowly unwound in my head. I reviewed the last three years—particularly time with his parents, Millie and Mac—with a new understanding. As if I had to relive my life now that I could see it through a new lens.

Through the *truth*.

And what he said made sense. Mac's pride. Millie's natural piousness and humility meant she rarely spoke about money, not even the seemingly sudden success of her company. In some ways, it seemed to come from nowhere. She'd never explained where the funds to expand came from, and I hadn't asked.

In other words, history really *did* stack up.

No texts had come through from Devin, and I didn't have his number. The distance was a relief. I needed space away from . . . him. I'd just wrapped my mind around the idea that we could be friends again. Maybe acquaintances was a better word. What was the difference? In my world, not much, and that didn't seem right either.

Devin would go back to his life in a few weeks, and I'd continue on mine. It had taken two days to wrap my head around the idea that I could spend time with him without regretting it later. Without yearning to feel his touch. Without falling even more in love with him. That was the old Ellie.

We had never *been* lovers, no matter how badly I had once wished it.

Now I could really set the past behind me and move forward without Devin. At some point, I'd be able to settle into that idea. Once I could comprehend that Devin was living in his own world as my friend, not occupying my world as . . . everything. Friendship with Devin had, at times, felt more like soulship.

Could it be different now?

Yes. It had to be.

I nodded once to reaffirm it.

Friends.

I got this.

"Ellie!"

A scratchy voice brought me out of my thoughts. I slipped around a corner display of new hiking boots and stopped a few feet away from Daniel. He stood behind the cash register, brow furrowed as he flipped through receipts. A fishing vest hung over his torso filled with brightly colored lures, a few old patches he'd sewn on, and a name tag that said "Old Hoss" instead of his name.

Salt-and-pepper hair topped his head in dusty strands. Wrinkles lined his neck.

These days, he was as familiar to me as the mountains and twice as cranky. My loyalty ran deep.

"Yes?"

"Just got a call from a man named Kimball."

My mind instantly slipped to Kimball, the carefree guy who had come to Pineville a week ago. Nice enough guy. Seemed to be everywhere and, according to Jax, probably had a little crush on me. I'd turned him down on a few date attempts. *Just checking this place out for a long, overnight hike,* he told me a few days ago. *You know of any?*

That was a *very* interesting conversation for a girl that longed to do overnight mountain guides but needed someone to pay for it.

I leaned against the front counter, riddled with stickers from gear companies and old bumper stickers that didn't sell. Something fuzzy took residence in my stomach when Daniel gazed at me with inquisition beneath his eyebrows. That furry thing called hope wriggled like a caterpillar.

"And?" I drawled.

"He wants an overnight guide. Five nights."

Schooling my *whoop* came with serious control. I lifted my brow and cleared my throat, the picture of serious professionalism. Daniel loved me because I didn't react to stuff. In other words, women still frightened this perpetual, middle-aged bachelor that was surprisingly attractive for his salty personality.

Instead of celebrating, I focused on the rigid frown that had overtaken his face.

"You don't seem happy about this, Daniel."

"They requested you."

"Shows they're wise."

"Or Kimball has the hots for you."

I rolled my eyes. "First, it's weird that you say *hots* in that tone.

Please never do that again. Second, I can take care of myself. Kimball is harmless, and I've already turned him down twice for a date. Third—"

He jabbed a finger at me, cutting me off. "First, you don't make the call here. I do. So don't inform me how to run my company."

Properly chastised, I backed down. Daniel might be—definitely was—rough around the edges. It's why we got along so well. But I knew when to capitulate. When that tone came out, I didn't have a chance to win.

"Second." His eyebrows lifted halfway to his hairline as if to emphasize a point. "I don't care how badly you want to be an adventure guide. I won't compromise your safety. They aren't local."

"They?"

"He has a friend, named Steve, that he wants to come along."

Fair point. Two strange men plus me in the mountains wasn't desirable arithmetic. But I wasn't about to lose this chance.

"I accept the risk along with my Glock."

"Of course you do," he muttered. "You're twenty, and all twenty-somethings are stupid, with one exception, and it's not you."

I rolled my eyes. He said that stupid line at least once a week, and, in years of working together, he had never mentioned the identity of the *not* stupid twenty-something of his acquaintance.

"Daniel—"

He held up two hands, shutting me up again. "However," he drawled, "this would be a great learning experience for you, and they specifically asked. I don't want to tell them no. But," he held up that finger again when I opened my mouth, "I'm not about to send you into the mountains for five nights with two men I don't know that well. Sorry." He slammed the cash register shut. "Not going to happen."

My lips clamped shut again, and my nostrils flared. Yes, I

resented the insinuation that I couldn't take care of myself, but I also understood it at the same time. Did I think Kimball would be an issue? Definitely not one I couldn't handle. But that didn't speak for his friend Steve or the entire situation.

If life had taught me anything, it was that most men couldn't be trusted. The rest had to be verified through years of proof, like Mav, JJ, and Daniel.

And Devin, at one point.

To that point, I also didn't trust Kimball entirely either.

"Okay," I said.

Daniel blinked twice. His head tilted to the side slightly. "What?"

"I said okay."

"So I heard you correctly?" he asked. "There has now been a moment where we've actually agreed on something?"

I rolled my eyes again, just for emphasis. "Yes. I agreed with you."

"That's why I'm questioning it. You never agree with me."

"Ha ha," I muttered. "I'm not going to fight you on it."

He leaned back a little. "Why?"

"You're not wrong."

"You want the guide so bad you're buttering me up by agreeing with me, so I'll eventually give in."

"Yes and no." I folded my arms across my chest and shrugged. "It's probably a wise move to have someone else out there with me. Besides, how hard could it be to find another person to go with me? Someone who wants to give up days of their life to go into the mountains, without reception or amenities? Especially someone I could trust?"

He scowled, eyebrows low.

"Of course, that's one more person for you to pay," I continued doggedly, "which would kill all profit from the guide. But who needs to make money? It's not like you run a company with skin-tight margins while you live on a prayer that more people book more guides or buy more t-shirts."

His eyes tapered to slashes now, but I wasn't about to stop.

"Especially considering my extensive history with self-defense," I continued, "my intimate knowledge of every inch of these mountains and my skill with a knife. We already know I'm not afraid to take almost-lethal action to save myself. But . . . that's your decision, Daniel."

His eyes had become thin lines. He was onto me, but my argument would still work into his brain to nestle some doubt. Oh, I knew the source of his bleeding heart: money. Profit. Dollar bills. He expected me to fight back, but he just didn't know my game yet.

"Nice try," he muttered. "But I'm ahead of you. Already got someone!" He grinned. "Should be a good guide. Kimball said they want to see beautiful things. Pitch their own tent, eat fish from a stream, that kind of idea."

A careful bud of hope revived in my chest. Was he giving this guide to me then? Who had he asked?

"Sounds great." I straightened up, arms falling to my side. "I'll take them up Buccaneer road and into the canyon to Nightingale Pass. It has all they requested, and the hikes aren't too challenging. Easy river valley in most spots. So many moose to see, if they want wildlife."

He grunted, which meant he approved. At least he hadn't *told* me where I'd have to take them. That morsel of trust was something, and I'd worked hard for it. The only thing that puzzled me was *who* he had found.

There was really only one option.

"Are you coming with us?" I asked.

He snorted. "No."

"Then what are you going to do?"

He grinned. "Here's the part you *will* fight me on."

The growing excitement slowly started to deflate again.

Although I didn't know what the dark premonition inside of me meant, it couldn't be good.

"Who?" I asked.

He paused for annoying, dramatic effect, then said, "The only twenty-something I know that isn't an idiot: Devin Blaine."

Dev's name rippled through me like a shockwave. Daniel watched without apology while I grappled with his revelation. The Blaine family and Daniel went back farther than me and Daniel. Daniel and Mac fished together all the time. When Devin enlisted in the Marines, Daniel had given him $500 and had tears in his eyes when he thanked him.

Daniel knew I'd balk at Devin coming, just as I knew he wouldn't back down. He'd given me what I wanted: a professional, overnight guide. I'd seen that look in Daniel before. Those wise eyes *asked* me to rebuff him because, if I did, I'd have to forfeit the guide.

"What?" was all I managed.

"He's here, available, and willing. Most importantly, he has survival skills beyond even yours and a vested interest in keeping you safe. Besides, have you seen him yet? The man could be a tank himself." He grinned. "Seemed pretty great to me."

"He's almost as much a stranger to me as Kimball!"

Daniel snorted. "You'll never convince me of that."

For a moment, I regretted my comment. Devin wasn't a stranger. Was he? I didn't know yet, but it *felt* true. The Devin that revealed his secrets was not the same boy I knew for years. He'd turned into a man without me. He'd experienced so many things we could never have together.

But underneath it all, he *was* still Devin.

Regardless, this wasn't a complication that I could afford. No, I'd just barely wrapped my mind around being an acquaintance-friend to Devin. I'd let him have a sliver of space back into my life so that I could easily nudge him back out. Just telling him that we could spend time together had been throat-closing terrifying.

Five nights in the mountains with him?

No. Way.

Daniel turned and started to walk away. I ran along the counter and followed before he hid in the back office behind a locked door. Knowing him, he'd stay there until midnight just to avoid me.

We could both be persistent.

"You've already talked to him?" I asked.

"Yep."

Fury bubbled under my skin, but I schooled it back as I jogged to keep up with his long gait. "And he said yes?"

"Yep."

"When does the guide start?"

Daniel smiled over at me as he reached for the doorknob to his office. "You leave the day after tomorrow at 5:00 am. Get ready, girl. This is your chance to prove to me that you're ready to do it, twenty years old notwithstanding."

* * *

Dawn cracked early a day and a half later. At 4:45 am, I stood in the parking lot of Pineville Outfitters under a star-studded sky, my hands shoved into a zippered fleece jacket. Ebony mountains rippled in the sky like dark ribbons, the trees a looming presence even from far away. The temperature was in the low 60's, but it felt cold.

Or maybe that was dread.

No matter what came of these five days in the mountains with Devin there—the way it always used to be—nothing will have changed in our circumstances. We would part afterward as acquaintance-friends and nothing more. Devin and I wouldn't ease back into what we used to be because that ship had sailed.

Nor would the box in my head open up with a thunderous roar.

No.

We'd hike. He'd provide further security and insight. We'd walk away from each other feeling exactly the same as this very moment. Daniel would book more guides for me. I would live my best life.

That would be absolutely true.

It would be.

Eventually, I would convince myself of that.

A pair of headlights approached and drew me from my too-desperate thoughts, then stopped in a parking spot. Seconds later, a head of not-so-natural blonde hair appeared, then warm arms wrapped me in a hug. I held Devin's mother, Millie, close to me for a full five seconds. The smell of chamomile and potpourri gave me an undeniable comfort.

"I'd ask you where you've been the past few days," she murmured quietly, "but I already know the answer, so I'm satisfied with just letting you know that you have been missed by both Mac and me and the horses."

When she pulled away, I gave her a sheepish smile. Normally, I stopped by the Blaine house three or four times a week. I rode their horses, cleaned the barn, dealt with the hay, and did odd jobs outside that Mac's back wouldn't allow him to do. With Devin home, they didn't need me to do that work.

Or that's what I told myself.

"Thanks," I said.

Behind her came the rummaging sounds of someone in the bed of a truck. I caught a glimpse of Devin's muscled arm just before he hopped in the truck bed and reached for something. Millie squeezed my hands, then let them go.

"Later," she said earnestly. "We need to talk."

I nodded. She had likely come to drop him off just to see me, and I appreciated the quick, maternal connection that she provided. Bethany had become my sister-mama, but there was something about Millie that felt more naturally maternal. My brightest memory of Millie was the moments after I'd attacked, toppled, and almost killed Jim at the Frolicking Moose. Both Devin and I had been terrified and shaking. The moment Millie had seen me, she clucked, reprimanded, and hugged me as fiercely as she did Devin, as if I was her own.

That's when I knew that I belonged to her, too.

The thud of a falling bag brought me out of my memories. Devin shut the tailgate, a stuffed backpacking bag at his feet. For being almost 5:00 am, he didn't seem like he'd just gotten up. Did he struggle with sleeping after his deployment?

His eyes were clear as glass as they met mine.

"Hey," he said quietly.

"Hey."

Millie blew us both a kiss, admonished us to be safe, promised to pray for us with her Bible study group, and the truck drove away minutes later. That left Devin and I staring at each other in the parking lot. My tongue felt glued to the roof of my mouth. Was I supposed to thank him for coming? Probably. I couldn't deny there was a sense of relief and safety that came with him being there.

But on the other hand . . .

"Thanks," I said. "I'm not sure you wanted to spend almost six days away from your parents when you were just deployed."

He grinned and ripped open a zipper in his bag to rummage inside. "No worries, Ellie. I can't tell you how much I've wanted to get back into the mountains. Daniel approached me the day after our canoe ride. Couldn't say yes fast enough." He stood, one eyebrow raised. "Are you okay with it?"

My nostrils flared, and I took too long to consider my answer.

"Yes," I finally said, "with the understanding that we're . . . I mean . . . there's no expectation for more."

His expression became a wordless question. I swallowed hard. *Idiot,* I thought to myself. What was I babbling about? Why would there be an expectation for more? All Devin had ever expected of me was friendship.

This weekend was off to a great start.

"I just mean that . . . we . . . let's leave everything behind us. The history is back there and doesn't matter for now. So . . . we can do this guide and then part as acquaintances, the way we are now."

Acquaintances made my brain trip, and I almost couldn't get the word out. He paused for the briefest breath. In that span, his gaze darkened a little. The shadow passed when he nodded.

"Of course."

His quick response should have been a relief, but it stung instead. I forced a smile.

"Great. Once they get here, we'll drive up to the trailhead in separate cars. You can ride with me."

"You got it."

I tried to find the sarcasm in his tone, but there was none. He opened his mouth as if to say something, but closed it when another pair of headlights appeared in the parking lot. I gratefully turned my attention to the approaching black SUV with bright, shiny rims. Kimball pulled to a stop next to us. Sleep lingered in his eyes as he rolled the window down and grinned widely.

"Hey, Ellie. Pretty early for our first date, don't you think?"

Kimball's gaze fluttered to Devin and his smile ebbed ever-so-slightly. I didn't turn around to see what Devin's reaction was because it didn't matter.

"Early? I've been up for hours," I quipped lightly and let the weird date comment slide.

A burly man sat in the passenger seat. He had mousey colored hair, a soft beard, and barely folded his broad body into the SUV. His hazel eyes had a quiet look about them when his gaze connected with mine, then dropped.

"This is Steve." Kimball motioned with a dismissive wave. "He's coming, too."

"Nice to meet you," I said, then pointed to Devin. "This is Devin. He's going as a guide with me. No extra charge," I added quickly when a weird look crossed his face. "So if you need anything, either of us is here for you. Are you ready to get started?"

Kimball and Steve exchanged a glance, then Kimball nodded. "Uh, yeah. Sure. Let us just gather our stuff in here, then we'll pull our gear out of the back."

There was a true sense of excitement in his eyes, and that meant a lot. These mountains were my world. I felt honored to give him a tour through the most beautiful country I'd ever seen. A bright mood settled on my shoulders. Knowing I was going to be in my mountains liberated me from the baggage with Devin I'd clung to lately. This would be my first *real* step into the life I had planned, and it sent a shot of energy through my body.

I slapped the side of the truck. "Don't worry about that. Just follow us, and we'll start at the trailhead."

This guide was going to be just fine. The hike would be lovely this time of year. The weather forecast was perfect, and Devin was here as an . . . acquaintance. Friend. Whatever. There he'd stay until we parted again when he went back to his life, and I went to mine, where I could be safe from ever going through losing him again.

I'd see to it.

Chapter Eight

DEVIN

This guide was going to be a disaster.

Ellie had an unusual sense of optimism about her as she started the outfitter's truck and drove off. Her jaw was set, evidently deep in thought. She didn't seem to notice the two creepy guys in the SUV who weren't keen to have me be a part of this guide. Kimball was fit enough, but Steve was an absolute tank. That alone had set my teeth on edge. Why would two thirty-something guys like them need a guide to go into the mountains?

This math didn't add up.

"We'll take them up the Nightingale Pass in three days," she said, more to herself than to me. "That'll give them some acclimation time with the altitude."

Maybe she didn't want to see the truth: these were two guys who probably hoped to win her over and then score big. Although in their mid-thirties, neither of them appeared overly ambitious with cardio. Steve had too much brawn for long-distance, and I doubted they would make it to the trailhead over the pass. Not in three days. And I seriously doubted whether they cared if the view was breathtaking or not.

In my mind, they had their sights on Ellie. Based on his attention at the gym, and the startled look on his face when she introduced me, the only view Kimball wanted was of her.

With a sigh, I peered at the fading darkness. Maybe I'd be wrong. I hoped so. She seemed intent on this going well, as if one guide determined the rest of her future. But that had always been Ellie. All in or all out.

My thoughts had all jumbled together over the last couple of days. Sitting next to her in the same truck she'd driven in high school didn't help. Slamming an ax into sun-hardened wood for three hours at Adventura had been the therapy I'd needed because I just wasn't ready to talk about deployment yet. Eventually, I would. I had to. I knew that.

But not yet.

The easy dinner that followed with Mark, JJ, Lizbeth, and a few of their camp counselors loosened me the rest of the way. Their counselors didn't know me, so they didn't ask deployment questions. Instead, we talked about the camp. Expectations for how things would continue to grow. Where the counselors were from. JJ served up a too-delicious cake and everything had felt normal.

For the first time.

But Daniel's call and plea for help the next morning had started my brain back up after the first full night's sleep I'd had since returning. Now, I was back with Ellie.

And she wanted nothing to do with me.

The word *acquaintance* rang back through my head. Had she even said the word *friend* once? Yes. After the canoe. But cold reality had settled in between then and now, and her walls were back up. Way up. She'd seemed calm enough in our short discussion about the guide, but panic lived in her eyes.

What was an acquaintance anyway?

We'd *never* been acquaintances, not even when we first met. The moment I saw her for the first time, she'd grabbed my hand, pulled me outside, and we'd scoured the mud in search of worms and lures for hours.

So what was there to panic about?

"I don't know if it needs to be pointed out," I said, "but I've learned my lesson after not telling you everything I should have. I appreciate clear communication more than ever, so I'm going to say what's on my mind. Hope that's okay."

My words broke the silence, which had been slightly strained. Her knuckles tightened on the steering wheel and her face illuminated with the bouncing glow of the headlights behind us. With her hair pulled back on her head in a messy bun, she reminded me of high school all over again.

When she said nothing, I continued.

"I'm not here to cause problems or be the man in charge or whatever else. You're in charge. I'll do what you ask, and I'll give my thoughts when you ask. Other than that, I'm here to keep any idiots from doing idiotic things. Is there anything else you want to add to my list of responsibilities?"

Her fingers loosened.

"No."

"Anything you want to say?"

She cast me a sidelong glance. "I've already decided on a route, itinerary, and some options for camping. Steve looks kind of . . . not ready for this . . . so I don't know how far we'll get at first, but we can work with that. Daniel already gave Kimball a tent and did his usual lecture on packing. I'm not sure about Steve."

My teeth ached from clenching so hard.

"You don't have to be silent," she continued. "You can make suggestions or help. I just . . . I need this to convince Daniel that I could take more of these guides. This is my chance to get into guiding bigger adventures with more options. This first one has to prove my skill."

"Got it."

She opened her mouth to speak again, then closed it. "Thank you."

I nodded, and we stopped talking. Darkness passed on either side of us in flashes of vague trees and creeks. Ellie drove us into a north-south canyon that would soon turn to a dirt road. An hour of winding hills that vaguely followed a river would take us to a turn-off that few people knew about. Then we'd drive on a vague two-track, let the trucks go as far as they could, and hike into a beautiful, lush meadow that afforded a striking view of the still-snowy peaks. I reached for my left shoulder. No tightness. I'd walked around with the pack for half an hour last night, and the injury hadn't flared up.

A good sign.

As easy as Ellie's plan sounded—and as simple as I knew the terrain to be because Ellie and I had been there several times before —I doubted it would go well. My natural optimism had faded dramatically over the last three years.

Deployments had a way of shoving you into reality.

Ellie would get her reality soon enough. These men weren't here to prove her as a guide. They wouldn't want to hike the way she'd probably very meticulously planned. I was here to make sure she ended this trip safely, even if the end result didn't meet her expectations. I couldn't give her much these days.

But I could give her that.

Chapter Nine

ELLIE

The scent of pine thickened the air when we rolled to a stop at the edge of a two-track road. Light warmed the far edge of the sky, washing the clouds overhead in pink, but the sun hadn't risen above the peaks yet.

A trail hidden in the trees wound through foothills and ridges for a couple of miles, then would end on a secluded mountain meadow. We'd camp there for the night. It would keep us off the road and away from other hikers.

"Want me to hide the keys under the truck when they aren't looking?" Dev asked, one hand on the doorknob. "Like we used to?"

"Oh, no." I fingered the keys against my palm, ready to jump out of the cab. "We can take them with us. That's what . . . it's what I do now. I don't leave them with the truck like we did when we were teenagers."

"Right." He nodded once, as if pretending we both didn't feel totally awkward that something he'd taught me hadn't carried through. "Got it."

Devin slipped out of the truck, and I followed suit. Kimball hurried out of his SUV with a smile, then stepped back to study his door. He rubbed a few spots off the paint with his palm, seemed relieved nothing had been permanently marred, and headed for the back. Steve followed him without saying anything.

"Devin and I will walk at the back," I said to them as they finished strapping on their packs. "That allows you to set the pace so it's not too strenuous. We'll follow a trail for four or five miles before an incline at the end, so go at whatever pace will preserve your energy. We can decide what you want to do after that."

Kimball squinted as he peered into the foliage, which still held onto shadows. Next to me, Devin adjusted his pack on his shoulders.

"Sounds good," Kimball finally said. "Steve, you take the lead."

Steve stepped onto the trail and started up the path without once looking at any of us. I glanced back in wordless question and Devin shrugged with one shoulder. He'd bring up the very end, and I felt good about that. He knew to keep an eye on our backs.

"Where are we going again?" Kimball asked. He'd stopped to tilt his head back and regard the forested mountains that rolled out on either side.

"You gave no clear itinerary when you talked to Daniel," I said, "so I thought about a place called Nightingale Peak. It's a mountain pass two days hike away. I planned on getting us there before our third night. We'll summit the pass, then head back down the same way we came up."

He made a noise in his throat. When I glanced back, Devin had an eye on Kimball, but I couldn't read his expression. Up the trail a bit, Steve had stopped to look back.

"I heard rumors in town about an old, haunted cabin up here somewhere," Kimball said without moving. "Some trapper that lived here in the 1800's. Do you know anything about that?"

Devin's brow furrowed. He'd lived here his whole life, and so had his parents. If there were rumors of anything like that, the Blaine's would know it.

"I haven't heard of that," I said. "Not at Nightingale pass."

"Could be kind of cool." Kimball paused. "They said it was somewhere around Granite Ridge?"

Despite wracking my brain, I couldn't figure out if those words were familiar. "Doesn't ring a bell," I said.

"You got a map?"

I nodded. Kimball waved an arm. "Then we can look at it tonight, not a big deal. Let's proceed as you planned. Can't wait."

With that, he trudged on. I hesitated for only a moment before I followed a few steps behind him. My thoughts whirred for a moment until I turned around and mouthed to Devin, "Granite Ridge?"

His brow furrowed when he shook his head and mouthed, "Idiots," back.

Something in the offhand comment from Kimball unsettled me. Did he even know what mountains we were in? His awareness of such a place seemed . . . odd. Particularly for an out-of-towner. If he wanted to check out a specific cabin, why didn't he tell Daniel when we started the guide? From what little I knew of Kimball while talking to him at the gym, he was only visiting for a few weeks and hadn't been here before.

I knew these mountains as well as anyone except Daniel, who tracked herds of animals through these hills as a hobby and had been hiking here for over fifty years. I'd heard of almost every interesting point and knew most ridges like the back of my hand. Mountains were tricky that way, though. Get too close and you would lose all perspective. Their indomitable heights hid behind lesser peaks that would fool you for days before you realized that what you thought was your tallest challenge was nothing but a step on the path to it.

"You good, Steve?" I called after twenty minutes had passed.

He held up a hand, his back to us, and kept going. For such a large man, he held his own pretty well. I studied him from the back. His shirt hung loose, and so did the skin around his neck, as if he'd lost weight recently. A strange silence fell on the group as we continued on, at odds with the usual, bright chatter most groups maintained.

By nature, I wasn't a talkative person. The day-trip groups that I'd guided so far most often kept up conversation amongst themselves or would ask me questions along the way. Daniel would keep a steady flow of facts about wildflowers, trees, and weather in the mountains. To this crowd, however, I felt no desire to speak, and no idea what they'd want to hear if we did.

But *should* I?

The debate over whether or not my role as guide required me to talk about useless facts or keep up information waged in my head and kept me occupied for almost an hour. If I *did* need to do that for five days, that would dramatically lessen my enjoyment of these trips.

"So," Kimball called, moments before I felt obligated to give some random facts about avalanches in the area. "How long have you two known each other?"

Thankfully, my pack hid the sudden stiffness in my shoulders from Devin, and Steve and Kimball faced away from me. Although I wasn't sure *what* I expected them to ask, questions about me and Devin weren't it.

"Our whole lives," I finally said when I realized Devin wasn't going to reply. The words *we used to be best friends* almost followed, but it sounded too trite. Almost like a punishment, particularly when Devin had expressed interest in being friends again. In the end, not knowing what to say, I left it at that.

"Cool. You hike a lot?"

"I do," I said. I couldn't speak for Devin anymore, could I?

Devin remained quiet. Kimball didn't push him, and I was grateful. Annoyance burned hot in me. *Seriously?* I wanted to say to Devin. *You can't just answer the question?* Before the lacking reply could make things awkward, Kimball picked the conversation back up.

"You look military to me, Dev," Kimball called. "You in the service?"

Kimball's casual use of my nickname for Devin curled my toes, but I let it pass. Devin wouldn't like him being that familiar either, I would imagine.

"Yeah," Dev replied.

Relief that he'd responded, even so minutely, slipped through me. I'd take it as a step in the right direction. Kimball made a sound in his throat. I stepped off the trail to peer ahead of Kimball's bulky backpack. Steve continued in the lead, but his pace had slowed a little as we faced a gentle incline. Sweat ringed his arms and neck. He panted, but didn't seem inclined to stop. The pace he set was steady, but not impressively fast. Exactly what I'd expected from a thirty-something guy unaccustomed to the altitude.

"How do the two of you know each other?" I asked as I stepped back onto the trail.

Kimball chuckled. "Steve and I met on a dare with some friends, actually, and have spent a lot of time together since then. We both wanted to see what we thought of the mountains." He spread his arms. "And here we are."

"Oh. Where are you from?"

"Lots of places."

His vague response left empty air that I struggled to know how to fill. In the end, I didn't need to.

"Doing good, Stevie boy?" Kimball asked. He reached forward, close enough now to clap Steve on the shoulder, then give him a shove that seemed just a bit too forceful. "We don't want a girl to out-hike you."

My teeth gritted at the sexist remark, and I wanted to snap back, "I'll out-hike you any day you arrogant swine." My future as a guide depended on my professionalism, so I bit it back.

Not surprisingly, the conversation fell flat for the next hour.

* * *

"You doing all right, Steve?"

That afternoon, Steve waved a vague hand from where he stood at a burbling stream, doubled over and dry heaving. Bright red splotches colored his face, and one of his water bottles lay empty on the ground next to him. He dunked a kerchief back in the water, then wiped his face off and left the soaked material across the back of his neck. We'd been hiking for six hours. He'd grown more uncomfortable and fatigued every hour, but hadn't complained.

My shoulders were ready for a break as I dropped my pack and reached for a water bottle. Devin stopped behind me with a little grunt of pain. He grimaced when he dropped his pack, then moved his left shoulder in a few circles. Did it bother him? His bag was heavier than mine by at least fifty pounds.

Kimball lay in the grass and stared up at the sky. "Quiet up here," he murmured, then frowned. "Kinda weird."

Weird wasn't my preferred description of the peaceful, gentle calm, but not everyone appreciated the mountains, so I let that go.

"How much longer until we get to the pass?" Kimball asked.

"Two days from now is the earliest," I said, "but it's harder going up, so we may need more time."

"If we keep going today, will that help?"

"Well, yes."

"Good. We'll take a short break, then keep going."

He said it so easily, as if his friend wasn't gasping on the rock next to him after retching his stomach dry.

"At the rate we've maintained today," I said, "I'd plan on arriving at the pass the day after tomorrow. We'll come down much faster than we ascend, so it'll keep us within the five-day window."

Kimball frowned. "Huh."

I shot Devin a quick glance. Ridges furrowed his brow. I

turned back to Kimball, unsure how to read Steve's tense shoulders and Kimball's contemplative stare. Did Kimball have somewhere to be, or something? Why rush through the hike?

"Will that work?" I asked.

"Should be fine for now." He waved a hand, a frown on his face. "We'll just keep track of time as we go."

"Are you concerned about it?"

"Nah. We're good."

Startled by the strange interaction—and unusual questioning —I turned back to my water bottle and focused on rehydrating. The simple beauty of rustling grass drew my gaze in a momentary distraction from the heavy air.

The trees we'd just trekked out of gave way to a mountain meadow with a few late-spring wildflowers that nodded in a breeze. Beyond those, Nightingale Pass and the two peaks we'd eventually summit loomed in the far horizon as imposing slate sentinels.

"I want to be done for the night," Steve said.

They were the first words I'd heard from him so far, and he said them to Kimball. His jaw was tense, gaze challenging. The two of them stared at each other for a long moment before Kimball finally nodded.

"The man needs a break," he said brightly. "Thirty minutes should do it."

"No. I want to camp."

Another moment of tense silence swelled. My gaze darted between them in shock. For friends, they really sucked at getting along. Which one would throw the first punch?

"We can make camp here," I said to stave off the rising agitation, "or we can take an hour off, then hike a few more miles before we camp." I eyed Steve. "First night is always the roughest if you're still acclimating."

Again to Kimball, Steve said, "Camp now. We will make up the time tomorrow." His eyebrows rose, as if questioning whether

Kimball would challenge him. Kimball smiled in a saccharine way I didn't entirely trust.

"Stevie declares it, and it is so," Kimball said with a sweep of his arms. "We camp here tonight."

Devin stood not far behind me, his pack at his feet. He had a canteen in his hands while he scoured the meadow with his gaze. Then he pointed out a little spot I'd already been eyeing. "That would be a good spot there to camp," he murmured. "Not too close to the creek."

Kimball glanced over. "Being near water is a bad thing?"

"Only because of sound," I replied. "You want to be far enough away that you can still hear."

"Like if something is approaching?"

"Yeah."

"Huh."

"Looks good to me," I said to Devin.

The campsite would be ours alone. I'd never seen another person around here, plus we'd veered off the main trail and through a game track I'd found while hiking with Thor. This meadow wasn't a well-known part of the mountain. Quaking aspen trees lined the edges of where Devin pointed, fluttering together like bright green coins. Did he remember that I loved the sound of the trees overhead? That seemed like something the old Devin would recall, then camp beneath because he knew I loved it.

Same Devin, I thought.

Yet, it wasn't entirely true.

"Let's set up camp then," I said to stop that thought. "Do you need any help with your tents?"

"I got mine." Kimball rolled to his knees, then sprang up. "Stevie-boy will be sleeping under the stars."

Steve stared into the distance now and didn't say a word. A suspicious feeling started to crawl up my back. Something here wasn't right. Sleeping under the stars wasn't entirely unusual on a backpacking trip, but it was odd for a guy like Steve. Most flatlanders feared animals, even when they slept in a tent. Rarely did they feel comfortable without a canvas covering.

"You sure?" I asked Steve.

He didn't look at me, but he nodded. Kimball grinned, his smile wide, and turned to the meadow.

"So, boss. Where do you want us?"

Chapter Ten

DEVIN

Thirty minutes after the decision to camp had been made, I called out to Ellie. "Hey, E. Let's go filter some water. I'm almost out."

Ellie glanced up at my casual statement, eyed me for a second, then nodded. She retrieved her water filter from the pack and followed. We strode side-by-side through the knee-high grasses without saying a word. Kimball wrestled the canvas of his tent while Steve lay on the ground, his hat over his face. His even breathing likely meant he'd fallen asleep, but I couldn't really tell if he'd let his guard down like that.

The trees that surrounded the burbling, snow-run-off stream embraced us as we stepped into them. This creek would die down within a few weeks and verdant green hills would crackle into brown under the baking sun. The process of life often struck me as unequivocally sad when spring faded.

Ellie dropped to one knee and unrolled the filter bag. Her furrowed expression made her seem burdened with thought.

"So," I drawled. "Something is weird."

She leaned back on her haunches. "Yeah. There's an odd dynamic going on between them."

Odd? She had to be kidding. There was an almost *feral*

dynamic between them. The fact that Ellie didn't have red flags waving over Kimball's vague story or concerns about the fact that Steve had no tent, no real hiking ability, and no words was more surprising than the weirdos on this trip.

But this was her gig, so my approach to this topic had to be careful.

Ellie glanced at me over her shoulder while water trickled from the stream and into the filter bag. "Steve put on a long-sleeve shirt over his sweaty one. Think I should wake him up and tell him to change?"

"He'll figure it out when he's cold from the sweaty shirt tonight."

Her frown deepened. "He doesn't have a tent, either."

"Weird, right?"

"A little."

"C'mon, Ellie." I crouched next to her so I could drop my voice even further. The strange acoustics up here were always unpredictable. Sounds bounced in weird ways and I didn't want them to risk hearing us. "I don't think this whole trip is a good idea. We need to go back."

"What?"

"I don't feel good about this."

And the last time I didn't feel good about something, I almost added, *people died.*

"I . . ."

The words stuck in my throat, and I wasn't sure what to really say next. Explaining my deployment ghosts, the ones she didn't know about, wasn't on the table right now. Maybe I was being too sensitive or queasy over these two weirdos, but I didn't think so. Steve might have been a quiet guy, I could accept that. But this situation was a step beyond *quiet.*

I just . . . I didn't know how to peg the situation down.

"There's animosity between them," I murmured, more for my own sake than hers. "For being 'friends', they sure don't speak at all, do they? And Kimball is obsessed with time, for some reason. Supposedly, they came to the mountains to relax, but Kimball seems pretty wound up. And Steve? Has this guy ever set foot on a mountain in his life? No. So why is he here? Why did he challenge Kimball about stopping? Something is wrong."

She straightened, a full bag of stream water dangling from her right hand. "People who have never climbed mountains pay for guides all the time. It's *why* they pay for guides. Argument point invalid."

"Okay, in general, I'd agree. But that guy? No. He's not at all excited about this. He's acting like he's obligated."

She scowled. "You want me to cancel my first overnight guide because their situation is weird?"

Stated that way, my case didn't sound as strong. The incredulous tone of her voice certainly didn't help, either. The more I spoke this out loud, the less certain I felt. I sat in the grass next to the stream and sighed. Unfortunately, there was a chance I was being too paranoid. That I read into comments or situations too much to help keep myself and Ellie safe.

Life back from deployment got weird in strange ways.

"I don't know," I said.

The flash of irritation in her gaze faded. She hung the unfiltered bag off the branch of a nearby tree, then looped the other bag on a nearby branch next to it. Clean water trickled into the second bag while she settled next to me.

"I can't cancel the guide unless I have a real reason to believe that they mean us harm, or that all of us aren't safe. Just because their dynamic is a bit . . . off . . . doesn't mean anything about us."

The way she said *us* gave me too much of a physical thrill. I tried to ignore it, but I couldn't. There was too much hope in me to give up on us yet, even if she'd been as distant to me as Steve was to Kimball.

"You're right."

She sat next to me in the grass, close enough that our arms

almost grazed each other. For a moment, I could forget Steve and Kimball. Could just stare into the trees across the stream and remember when this was our every day. When the world always seemed bright and okay because Ellie was at my side.

So, how had I not understood then?

Why did it take a fellow Marine dying in my arms for me to see what should have been blatantly obvious?

There would probably never be an answer to that question, but a dozen possibilities rotated through my mind. Maybe I hadn't been ready to recognize my feelings for Ellie. Maybe it was only after leaving that I understood what she meant to me.

Even if young Devin hadn't known how much he loved her, at least he had recognized that we had to have a chance to be apart. Her reliance on me had been too strong. She had pivoted her world in whatever direction I took mine. Didn't matter what she wanted or thought. Even *then* I knew it wasn't good.

Now here we were. Me, a Marine, rotating through paranoid thoughts about safety and terrible men and the things they do when their mind is in the wrong place. And Ellie who was attempting to create her perfect life . . . without me in it.

She'd certainly stopped her dependence on me.

"I won't retract my suspicion," I said when those thoughts shuffled away. "But I will at least concede that it may be too early for me to say we need to call the trip off and get back." My gaze met hers. "I want this to be successful for you, Ellie. But I also need you to be safe."

Her gaze held mine for a long moment, then she nodded.

"I'll keep my tent close to yours, just in case," she said. "We'll be far enough away they can't eavesdrop on us speaking, and we can put our tents in the brush where you can hear their approach."

Relief rippled through me. "Thank you."

While the wind shifted through the trees, we enjoyed the calm meadow. This moment was probably the best I'd had since being home because we didn't say a word. Just like old times. The water trickled from the dirty bag to the clean one, so I let my thoughts roll out again. Just having Ellie sitting next to me changed the magnetism of the planet. Like everything else came into alignment with her at my side.

And it wasn't just a warm body that I needed; I wasn't lonely. Other attempted girlfriends had left me feeling empty. Like part of my body had been taken away. A segment of my soul walking around out there in the world without me.

A hole that only the Wild Child Ellie could fill.

She leaned back on her hands, the picture of casualness. "So," she drawled. "You asked me a big question on the canoe the other day. Do I get to ask it back?"

"What question is that?"

"What makes you happy now?"

I answered before my better sense got the best of me. "Being here with you."

"Oh."

A beat passed while she soaked that up. In an attempt to recover the amiable air that had come with the question, I continued. "But I'll take the mountains as a close second and hiking as third."

"Can you do those things where you're stationed?"

"In LeJeune?" I shrugged. "Not really. It's on the east coast of North Carolina, so it's great if you like the ocean, but terrible for the mountains. I've driven across the state to Asheville several times, but they're not the same. Helpful, but there's no replicating this."

She smiled gently. "Yeah, there really isn't. Do you like the ocean?"

"I do."

Her pitch increased, as if she were scandalized. "Better than the mountains?"

I laughed. "No, never. Of course not."

"Right answer." She grinned, then sobered a little. "None of the things that make you happy are there, then?"

Although she strove to keep her tone neutral, her attempt failed almost dramatically. There was something probing and searching in her words. If any part of *my* Ellie lived under the steel plates she'd formed since my absence, she'd be worried that I was depressed, lonely, or bored.

Boredom wasn't an issue, but the others were.

"It's fine. Livable. I love the guys, my brothers, for the most part. But it's not my place. It's not where I belong."

"I can understand that," she murmured. "But I'm sad your everyday environment doesn't fill you with joy, like mine."

My thoughts filtered back to my parents.

"It's worth it."

She nodded, then shivered as a breeze trickled past with a cool breath. I nudged her with an elbow.

"When did you become such a wuss in the cold?"

She sent me a casual glare, and I laughed again. Her faked annoyance faded into a smile of her own.

"I'm just teasing. You're killing it, Ellie. You're doing a great job up here."

"Thanks." She sank her teeth into her bottom lip, then shook her head, as if to get out of her own thoughts. "I . . . I really want this."

"You'll get it. Do you need a long-sleeved shirt?" I asked. "You can borrow one of mine. You look cold."

For a half a second, I could have sworn she considered the offer, but then she shook her head. "No, thanks. I have my own. I'm not all that cold."

A sound from behind us drew her gaze back and she sighed. "I should go check on Kimball."

I straightened up, righting the tubing that had twisted up between the filtered bags. The water was cool in the bladder, and I couldn't wait to drink it. Everything tasted better up here.

"I'll get a fire ring going," I said.

"Thanks."

She hesitated, then started back toward the tents. I watched her go, unnerved by a pair of eyes that peered out of a small pup tent across the meadow. Kimball looked up, saw me watching him as he studied Ellie, and disappeared inside with a little wave.

* * *

"So," Kimball drawled. "About that map?"

Firelight flickered on Ellie's face that evening as she looked up from an empty rehydrated meal package. She tossed it onto the fire, and the edge of the package curled on itself. White formed around the edges as they shrank and collapsed in. Lines of crimson flared beneath it on the coal bed.

"You want to see where we are?" she asked.

"Can I show you the meadow that a haunted cabin is supposedly located in?" He scooted closer to her on a fallen log that doubled as a bench. "Maybe it's not too far away from where we are now."

"You saw it on a map?" I asked.

Kimball didn't look my way. "Yeah, the guy showed it to me."

"And you'll remember?" Ellie asked. "Maps are complicated, especially the mountains. We may not look at the same map."

"Sure." He shrugged. "How hard can it be?"

Ellie refrained from commenting, and only her professional career kept me from laughing out loud.

"What was the story behind this cabin again?" I asked and eyed his closing proximity to Ellie. He kept a short inch or so between them and I had to physically calm the rising hair on the back of my neck.

"A guy died there," Kimball said. "Said it had buried treasure."

My neck tightened. Buried treasure? That's not what the story had been the first time he mentioned it at the beginning of the hike. Steve's gaze flickered to Kimball, then away. So, he caught Kimball's blunder as well. Interesting. I poured water into a tin bowl and used the pad of my thumb to wipe residual rice and teriyaki chicken off the sides.

"Oh, right." I cleared my throat. "I thought you said it was haunted."

Kimball paused. "Oh. Yeah. That too. You know, the ghost guards the treasure. The same old story."

Ellie rummaged through her backpack on the other side of her log, then extracted a folded map. Overhead, stars popped out of an impressive sky. Steve finished eating his second rehydrated meal and tossed the bag into the flames. For all their weird tensions earlier, Kimball was eager to pitch food Steve's way.

Ellie swallowed a bite of her protein bar as she unfolded the map. After a few moments perusal, she tapped on one spot. "We are right here."

Kimball's obsession with this cabin had been weird this morning, but now that he was lying about something, it was my business. I finished wiping the bowl down with my fingers, tossed the water away, stood up, and sat next to Ellie on her other side. Kimball glanced up, but didn't meet my gaze.

"Here's Pineville." A subtle sense of hesitation lingered in her voice. Ellie tapped the map, then drew her finger along a canyon road, through a mountain, and into a very small meadow where we lingered. "This is where we came today."

Kimball made a thoughtful noise, his brow low as he perused the many lines. Finally, his expression brightened.

"I recognize this!"

He tapped to a canyon with lines almost on top of each other, indicating steep walls. Rock and shale, likely, and a stream cut through it. More of a gorge than a canyon, I would bet, but there was some sort of meadow-like place possible in between the lines. Ellie's lips bunched to one side of her face, a sure indication of deep thought.

"I've never been up there," she murmured. "It's pretty out of the way. I believe I've seen that canyon, but never traveled through it."

Kimball flicked the map. "Let's go there."

Ellie turned to him. "You want to go *there* instead?"

"Yeah! Looks awesome."

"But . . . it's two miles out of the way. Miles that don't have a trail. It'll be brush beating and rock climbing and . . . difficult."

"It'll be fine."

Annoyance slipped into her tone. "Why did you have us start this way if you wanted to go there?"

He shrugged. "I don't know. This is pretty and I like it, but I'd like to chase something a bit more . . . challenging. I wanted to give your route a chance first."

Somehow, he'd edged closer to her, and the side of his arm pressed into hers. Ellie glanced down at the space where their skin touched, then back to him in a pointed glare. He scooted away with a murmured, "Sorry," and pointed back to the map.

Atta girl, I wanted to say, then lock my arm around her shoulder and pull her into me. I refrained, however. The last thing Ellie wanted was an overprotective friend, even though I wouldn't mind.

"It's not that big a deal, right?" Kimball asked. "We can find other places to hike around there after we find the cabin. It'll be the same number of days."

"Why?" I asked. I leaned my elbows onto my thighs so I could meet his gaze. He met mine, and despite the flighty personality I'd seen so far, there was something hard as stone in his gaze now.

"Because it's an adventure."

"What if I say no?" she asked.

Kimball's mouth opened to respond, then closed again. He blinked three times before he responded. "Well, of course, I'll defer to your expertise, but I thought you knew this area. We were told we were getting the best guide from these mountains. If a little detour like this is so dangerous . . . well . . . maybe the trip isn't worth the money we've paid."

A lingering note of challenge in his tone drew my spine up, and he pointedly ignored me to stare hard into Ellie's eyes.

Her gaze tapered.

"Are you challenging my professionalism and attention to safety?" she asked in a low voice as hard as granite. "Just because you want to follow an idea that may not even be real doesn't mean I have to agree. I don't appreciate insinuations, so if you have something to say, then say it."

Atta girl! I wanted to say again. Then cuff this loser on the side of the jaw so he had a good, long sleep tonight.

Kimball lifted two hands, a look of contrition on his face now. "Of course I trust your expertise. I apologize if it came off as something else."

"*Do* you trust my expertise?" she asked pointedly. "Because I have my doubts for obvious reasons."

"Well, yes. I just . . . I think this could be kind of boring. We came to this alpine place for a bit of adventure."

"*I* came to make sure you're safe. If there is a course change, which I can be open to, it will be a safe one."

Kimball nodded and managed to look at least a little repentant. "Fair. I'm sorry if I overstepped."

"You did." Her tone softened. "It's your hike, Kimball and Steve. We can go where you want. But I will not be bullied, frightened, or manipulated into it. Are we agreed?"

"Agreed."

Steve met her gaze and nodded, even though he hadn't said anything. His reluctant gaze from earlier had a bit more curiosity in it now. For so many reasons, I wanted to throw my arms around her and kiss her like I never had before.

Ellie turned back to the map, all rigid professionalism now.

"The place you want to see is about two miles from here, but we'd have no trails and would have to cross a couple of ridges. I know them. I've been to the top of most of them before, but it'll take most of tomorrow with terrain like that, because you can't always go in a straight line. There's ups and downs and unknowns. We could get there in the evening at the pace we took today."

Kimball clapped his hands together. "Sounds great! Isn't that better than a boring trail?"

"No. There are shale fields that get slippery and hold mountain lions, not to mention thick brush and forest to move through. A broken ankle isn't unlikely. Do you really want to do it?"

"Yes."

"Steve?" Ellie asked.

He shrugged.

She stared hard at him for a moment, then back to Kimball. No doubt she was torn between the common sense of sticking to the plan and known routes, where Daniel would be aware of her movements, versus abandoning them to a whim. But how to please the customer? Particularly when he proved to be a wild card. For a moment, I wanted to ask to talk to her. To pull her aside and convince her out of this utter madness. The deeper we trekked into difficult territory, the harder to extract—or get away from them. But that would make her lose respect and she was the decision-maker here.

"Can I see the map?" I asked quietly.

Thankfully, when my arm pressed against hers, she didn't give me a dirty glare or move back. If anything, she'd scooted closer to me now. Whether subconscious or not, I felt grateful she didn't shy away. Our legs pressed together. Her stability against me was more powerful than I expected.

Just like old times.

"This spot?" I asked Kimball to verify. He glanced at the map and nodded.

"Yeah."

"Probably has a shale field above it," I murmured to Ellie.

"Doesn't seem like a safe spot for any house," Ellie said, more to me than him, her brow creased in thought. Her finger touched a line. "We can make it to this ridge, I'm just not sure how to get down."

"This person you spoke with about the haunted cabin with treasure," I asked Kimball, "what was their name?"

"Can't remember."

"When did you talk to them?"

Kimball shook his head, his gaze on the fire in a should-be relaxed pose that didn't fool me. "A few days before we came."

"Huh."

Another silence fell on the group, burdened this time with questions. Of course there was no person that he talked to. Ellie and I knew everyone in town, which is likely something he didn't bank on. The holes in his story would make his boat sink because now I was onto him.

There was *something* at that cabin, all right. But I doubted it had anything to do with ghosts or treasure. Even Steve kept his gaze away now and I wondered what he'd have to say if he cracked that thick shell and came out a bit. Maybe if Kimball wasn't around, I could get the big guy to open up.

Tomorrow, there may be a way to do that.

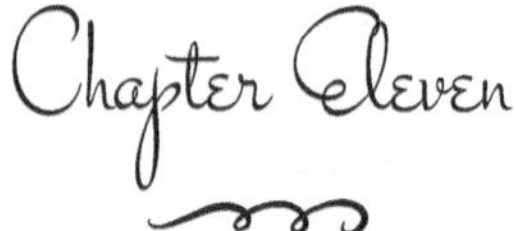

ELLIE

A distant rumble of thunder accompanied us to bed.

The thick, rolling sound felt eerie against the hiss of Devin dumping water on the fire and the rolling clouds of smoke that billowed out of it. Embers winked out, leaving darkness in the wake of warm light. I reached up to turn on my headlamp but stopped to let my eyes acclimate to the dark first. When I could make out what I needed to by starlight, I left it off.

Devin moved next to me but didn't say anything. I felt his presence like a band of warmth at my side. Although I didn't entirely acknowledge it, he made me feel safer.

"Steve," I said and broke the quiet. "I think it's safe to say that we should expect rain at the very least. More likely hail and lightning. I'm not comfortable with you sleeping outside without any protection."

"He'll be fine," Kimball said.

I ignored Kimball.

"Steve?"

Steve shifted, a mere shadow in the night. "Thanks," he said. "I'm fine."

In the darkness, they were only blurry lumps. The extra cover of night seemed to give Kimball even more courage to speak on behalf of his friend, which I didn't like. The whole evening had been odd and sent me for a bit of a loop. Why was their dynamic so weird? Why did Kimball want to get to a supposed haunted house so badly? My instincts told me there wasn't a house there, but there could be. An old trapper's cabin, dilapidated and in pieces. I'd stumbled on them in the back mountains before. Besides, mountains were tricky. They didn't give guarantees.

A crack of thunder growled overhead. Lightning streaked through a bulkhead of clouds moving in from the west. It blocked out the stars in the distance. For all its size, it didn't seem to be in a hurry.

I made my decision in the split second when the light illuminated Steve's face, and I saw uncertainty there. One could even call it fear, and I had a feeling he hadn't meant to let me see it.

"My tent is yours," I said. "Devin and I will share one."

A moment of dumbfounded quiet followed.

"What?" Steve asked.

Devin didn't say a word, and I realized that I'd held my breath and wondered if he would. No sound issued from him, so I took it as a good sign. Thankfully, he'd brought more than just a pup tent, or this would be a *very* cozy night.

"The choice is yours," I said in Steve's general direction. "I can't force you to sleep in it, but I won't be in it. I would be annoyed to find out you endured hours of hail and cold rain when an empty tent awaited you, particularly because we may have a challenging day tomorrow."

An edge of reluctance—and relief—colored his reply.

"That's . . . very kind. Thank you."

Kimball said nothing.

Devin stayed right at my side as I headed toward his tent, which he'd put near mine. Would Kimball balk at being left on his own side of the tree line? We'd pitched our tents at least fifty feet away to give them privacy. Devin had chosen well, in a copse of sturdy quaking aspens that would provide some shield from the inevitable wind. Their leaves would soften some of the hail if it fell.

Once I approached the tent, I flicked on my headlamp and pulled my sleeping bag and pack out. Wordlessly, Devin grabbed my pack and ducked into his own tent with it. My sleeping bag soon followed. I couldn't help but wonder if Steve felt relief at being away from Kimball for the night.

For some reason, I did.

As soon as I emptied the tent, I paused to think through my next move. Devin seemed to read my mind as he flipped his headlamp on.

"Go ahead and grab your toothbrush and stuff," he said. The beam of my headlamp angled away from his face, illuminating his hands as he gestured to the tents. "I'll check the tie-downs and the rain covers. Then I'll stand guard while you change at the creek."

I hesitated, shocked that he'd remembered. Then I felt silly. Of course Devin remembered. I liked to clean up in the stream before I climbed in my sleeping bag. He'd only teased me endlessly about it our entire teenhood together. *Can't be dirty when you sleep, Ellie? You'll still smell like a hibernating bear afterward.*

My lips twitched with the memory.

"Thanks," I said.

Darkness hid his expression, and his voice was perfectly neutral, leaving me to wonder if he was annoyed at me volunteering to share his tent without permission. Our earlier conversation left me skeptical that he'd care, but we would be cramped together all night.

The rolling thunder continued noisily in the distance while I grabbed my pajamas and a small toiletry bag. Devin rustled with the tents, setting mine farther away so Steve wouldn't sleep so close. The rain protectors were latched firmly on the top when he flipped his headlamp down, grabbed a bundle of things near his tent opening, and gestured for me to take the lead.

Behind him, Steve climbed inside my tent and zipped it shut without even taking off his boots.

My mind spun on Steve and Kimball while I headed to the stream. Near the gurgling water, Devin's beam flashed around to see the trees across the way.

"I'll keep watch while I brush my teeth and wash my face." His light went out. "But don't take your time. That beast is headed this way."

Behind him, light flashed across the sky, filling the thunderous bulk with electric bolts of light that turned the edge of the sky a vivid purple. At this high altitude, that kind of storm was a definite lightning hazard. On previous hikes from our high school years, we'd felt a charge in the air so strong the hair on our arms stood up. I shuddered with the memory and turned to my task.

My toes sang with freedom when I ripped my long wool socks off and dunked my feet in the water. Devin didn't make a sound, but I could see his dark silhouette against the few stars that remained.

While I wet a bar of soap and rubbed it into a small washcloth, my mind wandered to this Devin. Devin the soldier. Devin the *deployed* soldier. He acted so even-keeled. Once emotional, energetic, and extroverted, I now sensed a far more nuanced and sharp undertone in him. He hadn't lost that Devin magic . . . but he did seem *tired*.

Was this Devin without me?

I turned that thought away, because down that path lay a dangerous game. A game of wondering whether he mourned me as much as I mourned him. Whether he felt as incomplete as I had— did—and if he thought about it. Those thoughts gave way to hope, and hope wasn't something I invested in.

Not now.

Not when there was an actual chance.

Inside my head, all of my boxes rattled.

The cool water of the stream on my arm reoriented me in the

moment, and the lightning provided ample motivation to finish my quick wipe-down and necessities. Devin splashed a few steps away, but not too far. Lightning brightened the woods when Devin reached back and pulled his shirt off. A quick silhouette of his flexed arms and shoulders came with the streak of light, and my stomach bottomed out. *This* Devin was certainly different from high school.

When I finished, the angle of Devin's silhouette meant he watched the sky.

"Going to be nasty tonight," he murmured as he gathered his bundle back up, flipped on his light to check the stream bed for anything we left behind, and we headed back. A few steps before my beam illuminated the orange tent, the full realization of what I'd done settled in.

Ten hours of no-avoidance-contact between me and Devin.

His tent was a two-man tent, but with our packs and those new shoulders of his, there'd be no space. Unless we wanted to put our stuff outside and let everything get drenched in the downpour, of course. We'd have to lay back to back or . . .

Worse.

With a gulp, my steps slowed. What could I do now? Nothing. Wind started to stir the trees with a sweet, balmy breeze that smelled like incoming rain. The lightning inched closer with every passing minute. Thunder grew in volume, like a giant punching the slate rocks overhead. Half the sky was overtaken now, the stars replaced by a dark mat.

Devin slowed behind me. "Climb in," he called over one particularly loud percussion of thunder. "We'll figure it out inside."

Wind stirred my hair as I climbed in. My sleeping bag had been hastily thrown in next to his. On top of it, my pack. I dropped to my knees, removed my shoes outside, and shook the dirt free. Devin climbed inside after I pulled my shoes in and flipped on a small, battery-operated lantern. Wordlessly, he hooked the lantern onto a little tie on the ceiling. Light flooded the area and lent a sense of normalcy to the surreal evening.

For several minutes, we quietly shuffled around. I replaced my toiletries in my pack. He riffled through a bag, mumbling to himself. The small lantern cast erratic beams through the tent. I could almost pretend that we'd stepped back in time. That high school passed the way I planned. That he hadn't lied, I hadn't chickened out, and a mere miscommunication hadn't separated us for three years and turned us into different people.

Pretending a false dream gave my heart one quiet reprieve before I had to escort it back to reality all night long.

The gentle, sporadic *pat pat pat* of rain sounded on top of the tent. The drops plunked loudly, separated by long hesitations. At the same time, we finished our busy work. I settled back onto my sleeping bag. A rock stuck into my shoulder blade. He pulled his headlamp off and set it aside. Neither of us seemed to know what to do next.

He reached for the lamp. "You good?"

I nodded. He flipped it off and plunged the tent into a thick black. In the utter darkness came a moment of relief. At least I didn't have to stare at those broad shoulders. The strong jaw chiseled in his new life experience. The edge of something in his motions now. I stared at the top of the tent as he wiggled right next to me and began to wonder.

Would I sleep better because I could smell him?

Would our friendship come back quickly?

Like riding a bike, maybe. Instinctive. Something that you just did because you always had. You didn't have to think about the *how* or even the *why*. You just did it.

Hadn't it already started to do that?

Would I really be able to be acquaintances with him?

I almost scoffed at the idea, but to scoff would be to admit defeat already. Besides, that answer depended on him. If he deployed all the time and lived in North Carolina, doing who-knew-what else, would he want to stay friends with a wild child like me? After so many years away, he wouldn't be likely to hold onto Pineville.

Maybe that's what hurt tonight. We were supposed to see the world together and he took that away from us. Pineville had never been big enough. I'd wanted more, and Devin had been my ticket out. My *safe* ticket out.

No, I thought, suddenly confused. That couldn't be true. After three years without him, I'd proven I could do anything alone that we did together. Mountain hikes. Rugged terrain. Exploring new places.

Did I *need* him to get out?

No.

So why hadn't I left yet?

Uncomfortable with the implications in that line of questioning, I turned my thoughts to Steve and Kimball. This guide wasn't as fun or adventurous as I'd hoped. Nor did it seem all that safe. Before now, any guide I had done was fulfilling enough—I spent time outdoors, taught people how to appreciate mountain life, and received money for it.

Yet, that hadn't been enough. Despite the freedom of it, there had always been a gnawing sense of *this isn't it. There's something else out there.* Which led me to overnight guides. Bigger challenges. Mighty trajectories.

But this didn't feel good either.

Certainly not safe, for one. The mountains had always been a haven for me. Perhaps I'd wrongly assumed that I'd still feel safe with other people up here. Second, I didn't like catering to people and their whims. Was I a control freak, or did I just want to dictate my mountain experiences?

My thoughts felt like an unsteady lurch, as if I'd missed the last step on a staircase. A big realization hovered in the distance, just out of mental reach. Too exhausted to grapple for it now, I shoved it away after one final, lingering thought: maybe Devin is what I'd been chasing all along.

Adventure. Excitement. Fun. Laughter. Connection.

Memories.

Devin had left, disappeared like a ghost. The mountains were *our* place. The place where he came alive. The place where I could find him everywhere I went, and it didn't hurt as much.

Was guiding a poor attempt to chase ghosts?

Tonight wasn't the time to question all my hard work. Now I had to focus on two strange men with a plan of their own. Two men that, by all accounts, weren't on the up-and-up. All of a sudden, I was inordinately grateful that Devin had come. A mere canvas tent in between me and Kimball would never be enough. If not for Devin, I would have been up all night, concerned but not able to articulate why.

In the midst of my deep thoughts, Devin stopped shuffling around. Without his thick arms or warm smile every time he looked at me, the night would be far less claustrophobic.

"Thank you," I said quietly.

The plea-like words encompassed so much more than letting me sleep in his tent. He chuckled, smooth as the roar of thunder in the background. "No problem. I'm relieved to have you here. I wouldn't have slept well with you in the other tent."

A spiral of warmth, then the unsteady feeling of falling through the air, followed his words. "You moved my tent right next to yours," I said with the hope that practicality would bring me back to earth. "You would have been sleeping on top of me."

"I did."

A forbidden question surfaced and I tried to blink it away. The temptation wouldn't be denied, so I pitched my voice low. I had to ask or I'd never sleep.

"You still don't think we're safe?"

He hesitated only a moment before he said, "I think they're hiding something. Both of them."

The sleeping bag rustled when I turned to face him, the edge of my jaw brushing a bent elbow. He lay on his back, I'd bet. Arms stacked behind his head with a ruffled expression as he thought something out. Just like he always used to. His arms had doubled in size with his shoulder span, so I'd be in danger of an elbow jab to the eye if I wasn't careful.

"Kimball," he murmured contemplatively, and I would have given money for his thoughts then.

My mind churned for a moment. "Yeah, I haven't really been comfortable with it either. Let's see how tomorrow goes. We'll call it from there, okay?"

"Okay." He let out a long breath. "Just . . . don't hold onto this as your career-maker, okay? One bad overnighter doesn't doom you to abject failure or a poor reputation. Or anything, really."

No, I thought, *but it does mean something else.*

What that *something else* was, I had no idea.

"Of course."

Another crack of thunder ripped by, this time right overhead. Lightning illuminated the tent outside. Mountain storms had always rolled through my life, but I couldn't deny a sense of comfort with Devin at my side through this one.

The words I *needed* to say thickened my throat. The temptation to leave them unsaid flitted through my mind, but I ignored it. We had too much experience with the unsaid nature of important things.

"I'm grateful that you're here. This wouldn't have felt safe without you."

A warm hand found my wrist and squeezed. My breath stopped. I paused all thoughts and waited. Would his hand move? Would he keep his fingers tight around my skin? My eyes fluttered closed. I breathed the feeling of his skin against mine like missing oxygen.

"I'm glad I'm here too," he said quietly.

The roar of the storm unfolded around us while we fell into

silence. The silky touch of his fingertips against the delicate skin of my inner arm didn't change. He kept his hold, and my heart thrilled to it. His shoulder moved against mine as he shifted, grunting with the effort of adjusting in such a small space. Alone, this tent would have been just right for his massive body and penchant to sprawl in sleep. Together, I felt like we tried to squeeze two feet into one shoe.

Unable to help myself, I asked, "Do you still sleep like a star?"

He laughed under his breath.

"Always. I always will."

The rain picked up overhead, falling twice as fast.

"Do you still hum in your sleep?" he countered.

In the darkness, I smiled. "It's not a hum," I muttered, but couldn't keep the amusement from it. "It's . . . a reverse snore."

Devin barked a laugh. His grip didn't give away. "Call it what you will," he murmured, "but it's definitely a hum."

"Are you sad to go back to North Carolina?"

The question blurted out of me like it wanted to squeak its way out. My heart sped up in response, a dull *thud* against my chest in the burdened air that followed. A hint of vulnerability lay in the question, like a little girl inside of me that really wanted to ask, *do you really want to be away from me?*

"I wouldn't be," he said quietly, "if you came with me."

The storm shattered the silence with a percussive roll of thunder that made my bones shake. Instinctively, I shifted closer to him. He released my wrist to wrap an arm around my shoulder and pull me close. Right now, I had no answer to give him.

Except, in some ways, this one.

My eyes fell closed. My heart slowed. Devin's smell escorted me into a calm, dreamless sleep.

* * *

The thunderstorm left a wet world behind.

Sparkling sunlight slanted down from the clouds when I emerged from the tent in the morning. Drops of water slid down the rain fly, jostled loose from the opening teeth of the zipper. The air felt crisp in my lungs. Birds twittered nearby in a strange dichotomy of sound after the crash of thunder in the night. The bowl of the mountains echoed each blast of thunder for hours.

My arms spread in a long, silent stretch as I studied the meadow, the smell of dew and wet grass thick in the air. Steve's tent remained shut, but Kimball's flap lay open. Steps through the calf-high grass led all the way into the trees across from us, and I thought I saw a flicker of movement not far from the stream. When I shoved on my boots and hastily tied them, my eyes caught onto the fire ring Devin had made last night. The charred logs lay saturated, not a hint of smoke left behind after torrents of rain.

The muscles in my legs were cramped from being so tightly bundled against Devin all night. The sensation was familiar, one from my childhood. Having it again came with a reassurance I hadn't expected.

Perhaps we couldn't avoid the return crash.

Like pieces of a puzzle that just fit. Could time change our edges so drastically that we couldn't return? Maybe time hadn't changed *my* edges. Maybe I was still the same person, interlocking with the same Devin. Or maybe we changed in the same ways because we'd always fit.

Kimball appeared out of the forest with a wave. "Morning!" His greeting rolled across the open meadow. I waved and made my way to the creek as he shoved something into his back pocket. A radio? No.

Or was it?

Something like an antenna stuck out of his pocket before he pulled his shirt and jacket over it, hiding it completely.

"Sleep okay?" he called with a bright smile that belied my suspicion. In the light of a gorgeous day, I felt sheepish for the thought.

So what if he *did* have a radio?

"Good sleep," I said. "You?"

His grin widened. "Like a baby."

I gave a smile and kept going, but my thoughts remained uneasy. Normally, I wouldn't have thought twice about my hikers having a radio with them. Backups to mine were always welcome. Technology could fail right when we needed it most. Besides, there was no inherent issue with them having access to our route or the outside world.

Yet, something about Kimball having a radio—and not saying anything about it—set my teeth on edge.

By the time I returned, Devin had shuffled out of the tent, still half-awake and tousled. His hair stuck up just a little on one side of his head, and sleep lingered in his expression. He gave me a lopsided smile that made my stomach flip. I wanted to walk right into his arms. Instead, I mentally shoved the urge away and gestured to the fire ring.

"Want to attempt it?"

He shook his head. "Better to have a quick breakfast and get going." He yawned. "The grasses and wood will dry through the day again as we hike. We can make a fire at lunch if we need to."

Minutes later, we had hot water boiling on an instaboiler I'd packed and dry oatmeal packets ready in bowls. Steve groaned from within the tent when he woke up. Kimball eyed the tent and chuckled to himself over a mug of instant coffee.

Meanwhile, I tried not to think about last night. Or the way I woke up with Devin's gentle breath near my ear. I crouched next to my bowl and dumped steaming water onto my dry oatmeal. My mind still drifted to the warmth of Dev at my side. Or the way both of us had been curled up on our sides, him at my back. Such a cozy night conjured up daydreams I should leave dead.

But maybe I was tired of that, too.

The cry of another voice rippled through the camp from the corner of the meadow. "Hello the camp!"

My head jerked up. Devin turned to look over his shoulder in the direction of the sound. Kimball stopped mid-sip and stared. A male figure trudged through the grasses toward us, clad in familiar, dark green pants and a gray shirt that indicated a forest ranger. Pale hair shone in the budding morning light, shielding light eyes. He wore a heavy pack on his back. The moment I recognized him, I smiled and straightened up.

"Neils?"

Neils paused, then his white teeth flashed in a grin. One hand raised.

"Ellie?"

I set aside the oatmeal. "Good to see you again! Come on and join us. We're just scrounging breakfast together after that downpour."

"Who is this guy?" Devin asked quietly, suddenly at my left side.

"One of the backcountry rangers for the area," I said. "His name is Neils. We've seen each other a lot the past couple of years. He's . . . sort of a friend, I guess. Very kind whenever I do see him. Which is more often than you'd think, actually."

"You run into him a lot?" Devin murmured. "Seems odd. Most people never see them when they're back here."

I shrugged. "He's really nice."

"Or he has the hots for you," Devin muttered. I laughed.

"Yes, Dev. He stalks me and comes out on hikes just to run into me. You're right."

Stated that way, Devin gave a good-natured eye roll. Kimball's tension increased as Neils approached with a bright smile on his face. His eyes darted around, encompassing the whole camp quickly, before he came to my side. Neils shook my hand, and I felt a rush of relief. I'd never been a hugger.

"Good to see you again," I said. "It's been a while."

"You have been avoiding the mountains?" he asked. He had a distinct, Nordic accent that tilted his words in a charming way. I laughed, gratified to see him again. We'd eaten several breakfasts or dinners together when we ran into each other.

"Never."

Neils winked at me, then glanced over my shoulder. He adjusted his pack with a nod to Devin, then to Kimball, who studied the bottom of his coffee mug.

"Oatmeal?" I asked, then lifted the mug. "We have extras, if you'd like something warm."

He graciously shook his head. "No, thank you."

"You're up early?" I ventured.

"We've had reports of grizzly trouble on the back trails," Neils said with a head jerk away from the mountains. "I started up here late yesterday and camped just about a mile down the trail. Thought I'd get an early start after the rain and heard voices. Thought I'd check in."

Neils had eyes that crinkled around the edges, but his expression appeared more haggard than usual. We'd run into each other on the trails now and then. He spent most of his summer—and some winters—in the backcountry mountains. I suspected he had a place he hid away and hadn't told anyone, but I could never get him to admit it.

Devin stuck out a hand. "Devin Blaine. Good to meet you."

"Neils. Same. You're a lucky man if Ellie is your guide." He smiled at me. "She is the best in these mountains."

"You know them far better than me, Neils," I said.

He waved that off. "No. You are a true natural here."

Neils had become one of the few friends I'd found once Devin left, and I wanted Neils to like Devin. Devin would, of course, like Neils. At least, the old Devin would have. *This* Devin seemed oddly similar, but still different. This Devin was far more wary around people than before.

The merging of my old life into my new one felt like bumps on a lake.

"Where's the bear?" Kimball asked as he tossed the dregs of his coffee into the weeds. Neils studied him for a beat, then nodded to the west.

"Reported around a canyon out that way, somewhere near the Alpine Crest trail."

I froze.

"Oh?"

Neils eyes jerked to mine. Confusion registered on his expression. "You're going there?"

"We're heading that way." When his confusion deepened, I rushed to explain. "We were originally heading to Nightingale Peak, but they requested a course change for a bit more adventure. Have you heard of a cabi—"

"Is the grizzly dangerous?" Kimball asked. Anxiety lined his usually happy features now. The empty coffee cup that he clutched with white knuckles lay at his side, dripping coffee onto his shoe.

"They all are," Neils said.

Devin made a noise in his throat. "The Alpine Crest trail isn't far east of where we want to go," he said. "We should be safe if the bear doesn't travel lower, which seems unlikely in this heat. Is it a mama grizz?"

Neils shrugged. "Not sure. We think it may be guarding a carcass. I'm spreading word on the trail for people to avoid it before I do some investigating."

"From over here?" Devin asked.

"Yes. It's where I started when I heard the news."

Devin's confusion wasn't misplaced. If Neils wanted to spread the word, starting this far south did strike me as strange. There was no direct route from here. Like us, he'd have to haul across open country, but he hiked so fast I had no doubt he'd get there in no time at all.

"Any attacks?" Kimball asked.

"No attacks yet, but it charged a hiker three days ago. Another report came in yesterday afternoon of a charge. I headed out shortly after to investigate."

Wildlife was certainly something we always planned for, but I dreaded grappling with now. Kimball and Steve would be wildcards in those situations. Devin and I had hiked the Alpine Crest trail years ago. It ended on a lacy, snow-run-off waterfall that faded near the close of summer. Worth the hike, if you appreciated wild beauty. I had my doubts Kimball would care about it.

"We'll keep an eye out," I said to Neils, but sent a meaningful glance to Kimball. Kimball nodded with only a hint of reluctance. Unlikely he'd fight me on this point. Steve stirred again in the tent, and Neils glanced over as he stumbled out. His tousled hair and stubbled face lent an oddly dark appearance. He ignored all of us and headed toward the creek with a bumbling stride.

Neils turned back to me, a warning in his gaze. "Careful, Ellie. The predators are unusually agitated this spring. I don't want to answer a search and rescue call with your name on it."

I nodded. "Thanks Neils."

He gave a chin lift to Devin, sent one last, searching look to Kimball, who gazed away with a troubled expression on his face. With a wave of farewell, Neils turned and headed back toward the main trail again.

Chapter Twelve

DEVIN

Kimball whistled while he hiked.

The high-pitched, incessant sound droned in my ear like a mosquito. Within an hour, I wanted to push him off the ridge we skirted. Then he began to walk next to Ellie as she broke our path across difficult terrain. Every now and then, he'd reach over and touch her. His grating charm and loud voice irritated my already sensitive nerves. At that point, I *really* wanted to get my hands on him.

When he didn't whistle, he chattered.

"Money is power," he said as he finished a particularly nauseating story about a successful business transaction, or something stupid like that. "The old saying is true. More is better."

Ellie nodded, but hadn't spoken a word in over thirteen minutes. She kept her gaze ahead, her eyes roving. The Alpine Crest trail area lay firmly northwest of where we stood, but only by a few miles. Her eyes lingered in that direction enough for me to know that she had a new stressor. Steve puffed along behind me. This far into the forest, Kimball seemed to lose his weird attention on his "friend."

For hours, we'd cut across terrain I would have rather not dealt with. Long grasses gave way to scraggly, knee-high brush up rolling mountain slopes. Mixtures of rocky ground and thick vegetation in the low parts slowed us down to a dusty crawl, just as Ellie predicted. The adventure of it would have been fun if it were just me and Ellie and Thor, or if Kimball had an off button. But the novelty of the new hike had worn off when I saw the flowing, rocky ridges that awaited us.

Scraggly brush, impossible ups and downs, and an endless supply of intense alpine sunshine that never let up.

Meanwhile, Kimball had never seemed happier.

Neils' warning ran through my head while I hiked, bringing up the rear, near Steve. The only benefit of Kimball's running mouth was my chance to get to the bottom of this strange situation. While Kimball and Ellie scrambled ahead of us, I purposefully hung back with Steve. We faced a hand-over-fist climb up a steep slope. Despite his long legs, he struggled with the increasing altitude and had slowed.

"You good?" I asked Steve.

He hiked half-bent over as we scrambled up a hillside, attempting to gain another ridge. The afternoon sun lay heavy on my back, clearing the morning humidity haze. Now, everything felt hot and dry. Rocks baked in the sun as we scrambled past them. Their heat expanded into my shoes, my pants, my skin. Most of the last hour had been two steps up, one slide down. Steve often looked as if he didn't move a step, even though he tried.

Steve nodded.

"This kind of hiking can really suck sometimes," I said.

No response.

Right. Might need a new tack.

"You're a quiet guy. Is that why Kimball talks so much?"

He glanced ahead of us, but didn't say anything. There probably wouldn't be another chance when Kimball wasn't watching Steve like a hawk, so I leaned into the quiet. Time to press my luck.

"You and Kimball good friends?"

Steve looked at me from the corner of his eye. He wiped a meaty arm across his brow and stopped.

"No."

Finally, the truth.

"Did you really want to come here? I mean, it's no secret there's weird tension between the two of you. And he's a lot more excited about this than you."

Steve squinted ahead of him, then bent back to his task. Rocks scrambled beneath his feet as he started back up. Beneath the sound, I heard a quiet, "Yep," before he returned his attention to the hillside. Dust coated his arms and legs. He walked like a tired donkey. What pushed him so hard?

Why was he here?

I remained a few steps back and to the side in case he plummeted down the hillside. Clods of dirt and small pieces of rock plunked behind him. At the top of the little rise, near clumps of thick bushes and some trees, Kimball glanced back for a moment. Seeing us separate and not far away, he turned back to speak with Ellie. I quelled a rush of jealousy. Kimball had no real hold on her attention, even if he wanted one.

Still, I didn't like him that *near* her. Too skeevy.

Their conversation drifted toward us as we closed in. I readjusted my pack across my shoulders, gratified that my left shoulder hadn't struggled with the trip so far. The pack was heavy, but all the work I'd put into recovery seemed to pay off so far. Later, after a few days, it might be a different story.

"Seems like a great place to live." Kimball had his thumbs hooked into his backpack straps. "Adventure awaits, and all that. Mountains. Exciting stuff. Are winters bad here?"

He strapped on a huge smile when Ellie looked his way, but her expression didn't change. She murmured a response. When she turned to look to the north, his amiable brightness dimmed. His tone had a bit of strain in it, like he fought for something to talk about. Ellie never spoke out of obligation, which meant he probably struggled to know what to say next. His conversation reminded me of a nervous tic. A compulsive effort to stop the silence.

The whole damn thing was a moving puzzle, and I didn't like it.

It didn't take a genius to realize that Ellie's jaw was tight, shoulders pulled back. Even though they'd stopped hiking, she didn't take off her pack. She studied the ridges in front of her with a ruffled forehead like she'd missed a clue.

Something wasn't right.

Steve grunted when rocks slid beneath his feet, sweeping him farther down the mountain. This time, he recovered quickly, and with what seemed to be the last of his energy, he pushed himself up the last few feet. Explosively landing at the top, he dropped to his knees on a clump of grass. His chest heaved from the final exertion.

Kimball hardly spared him a glance. I gained the ridge and put myself closer to them. The sun had long been sinking toward the horizon, and I guessed we had an hour or so left of daylight, with the dredges of light for another hour after that. Full dark would descend soon enough, and I wanted dinner.

Ellie looked my way with a little twitch of her lips that resembled a welcome smile, and it sent a thrill of victory through me. Might have been nothing, but I'd take it as progress. Just like sleeping in my arms last night.

Baby steps.

Kimball pulled me from my thoughts. "We're close?"

Ellie pulled her bottom lip through her teeth. "I think so," she finally said. "This ridge should be the final one before we drop into the canyon where you think the cabin is. Which means the cabin is likely somewhere down there."

Her hand made a vague waving motion. Kimball's expression brightened, but Ellie's darkened like a thunderstorm.

"But?" I drawled.

She looked at me and I saw the trouble in her gaze, even

through her sunglasses. "But I don't think we can get down right here." She pointed down. "Check it out. The rocks are a straight drop right here. The cabin should be just that way." She motioned to the left, where a spur of rock and trees blocked half of the canyon from view. Wouldn't take long to walk the ridge and see if the cabin was there or not.

So why did she hesitate?

I stepped up to her side and gazed down. The rock face that unfolded below was straight down and daunting, but not impassable. If we had the security of ropes and if it were just the two of us, I'd attempt. For Kimball and Steve, it was an absolute no. To our right, the ridge ran at a steep slant down, but curved in a sort of elongated bowl. Uneven, thick woods cluttered the ridge tops, with sharp mountain spurs jutting all the way down to the bottom of the canyon like stone roots. Somewhere down there should be a creek.

In other words, it was as dangerous and impassable as expected.

Kimball had already started to venture down the ridge to the left, where Ellie expected the cabin. When he was out of earshot, I quietly asked, "What's wrong?"

With hesitation, she shook her head. "We could get down there, but it'll take a while. Not enough light for it today, but Kimball has told me at least six times that he wants to sleep in the cabin tonight. He's determined."

"Because it's haunted?" I asked incredulously.

Was Kimbal *twelve*?

She shrugged. "I don't know. He's just insistent it's tonight. I told him he could sleep there tomorrow but he won't listen."

My gaze drifted northwest. "Meanwhile," I muttered, "we have a cranky grizzly bear just a few ridges over."

"I haven't forgotten," she said quietly, with a quick glance to Steve. He sat on a rock now, his body doubled over as he rifled around for food in his pack. "Besides, it probably wouldn't be safe up here anyway. We're too exposed. We have to go down this ridge and find a spur that isn't so treacherous. Might add more than a few hours and it won't be fun."

"You sure you don't want to camp here?"

"No." She shook her head as she glanced around our immediate area. "Too exposed. What if another storm came through at night?"

She made a good point, and the thought gave me a shudder. Last night's lightning storm on this ridge would have been utterly open to the thunder and electricity.

A death wish.

"What else?" I pressed after she hesitated again. Her gaze fluttered to mine, but I saw relief in there.

"I just . . . I don't know. Something is off."

"If you want to end this guide now, say the word," I murmured quietly. She tensed, so I hurried to continue. "We don't have to leave them behind, I'm not suggesting that. But this path is stupid. Take back control, E, or it'll be dangerous for all of us. If there's anything I learned from the last three years," I added with the painful bitterness of experience, "it's not to ignore your gut."

She frowned, but nodded. The words sank in, I could tell. While I'd support any decision she made, I certainly wanted her to make the safest one. She fell silent, so I gazed around again. The feeling of being in the open swept through me, no doubt exacerbated by the constant uncertainty of the past two days.

I'm back in the States, I told myself firmly. *This isn't Afghanistan.*

This is under control.

And yet . . .

A whoop caught my attention. Ellie and I looked up at the same time. Kimball beckoned for us, barely visible off to the left. Steve didn't even move. He lay down near his bag now, an arm thrown over his eyes.

"Found it!" Kimball called. "It's right down there."

Ellie drew in a deep breath, her shoulders expanding. She sent me a look that I couldn't interpret, but thought meant *this isn't going to be pretty.* Dirt and baked grasses crunched under our feet as we picked our way over, leaving Steve behind. Kimball pointed down, exultant.

"See?"

Indeed, a dilapidated building waited at the bottom of the canyon, near a dried-out creek that clearly hadn't seen much water this year. The roof had caved in on one side, and primitive logs crossed each other at the corners in ninety-degree angles. One end slumped to the right. For a moment, I swore I saw a flicker of movement inside, but figured it was a bird when it didn't repeat. Late afternoon shadows slanted over it, casting it in darkness.

"Wow." Ellie's eyebrows lifted. "You're right, Kimball. The weird, haunted cabin of your dreams does exist."

Kimball beamed.

"Now, how do we get down there?"

* * *

"It'll take a while to safely work our way down that slope," Ellie said with a ring of authority that took me back to our childhood, "but we *can* make it down. We'll have to be very careful. If we hike as a group, we can make sure that rocks don't dislodge and fall down the slope onto someone else. No one can twist an ankle, though, because going down this scree field with an injury is a recipe for disaster. Got it?"

She stood at the top of a shale field of rocks that looked daunting enough to me. The three of us stood back a few paces in a half-circle that faced her. After locating the cabin, she scoured a bit further and found this scree field to take down. With every word Ellie said, Kimball nodded eagerly, hands rubbing together with eagerness to crash down the volley of rocks ready to bruise our bodies. The cabin waited at the bottom.

We were at least forty-five minutes away, at best. The ridge hovered so high over the canyon below it already started blocking out daylight. Shadows crept up in the crevices. Steve's pale expression meant he wasn't too excited about our foray down the rocks either. With all that brawn, he'd fall hard.

Ellie readjusted her backpack and nodded. "Then, let's go. Everyone with me."

She started down the slide, nice and cautious, and nobody spoke. Each of us kept close to her tail and focused on where to step next. Not even Kimball had a word to say. All our attention focused on a path to boulder down, stop for rocks, hold our breaths, and eventually crawl toward the weird cabin. Any attempt to keep track of our surroundings was nearly lost. I stopped a few times to keep an eye out overhead, but someone would inevitably slip and draw my attention back. Whether it was Kimball's strange excitement, or Steve's even greater withdrawal and apprehension at every step, something wasn't right.

That cabin wasn't *just* a cabin.

But I couldn't stop our descent now, nor could I rule out massive paranoia after my deployment. In my mind, enemies waited at every shadow. Ever since I stepped off Afghani soil and back onto the terra firma of the US, I wasn't sure what part of my instinct was real. I'd honed my instincts to the sandbox of Afghanistan, but now I had to figure them out again in real life.

Ellie kept pressing toward the cabin and I could always trust her. Last night, the affection and the warmth in her tone *had* been real. No denying that. Ellie never falsely represented herself.

We inched our way down the scree field with quiet, painstaking care. The occasional call of birds rang through the air, followed by the shudder of rocks as they skittered by. Even I felt the eerie silence all the way to my chest.

Finally, an hour later, the four of us fanned out in a line. We slowed to a stop on dirt ground again. A great sigh of relief slipped out of Ellie as she glanced around. The black ends of hair swept her shoulders as she regarded me.

"We good?" she asked.

I nodded. Kimball didn't respond. His gaze had turned nearly feral with excitement and fixed beyond the cabin. He issued a high-pitched whistle. The hair on the back of my neck stood up when the quaking aspen trees behind the dilapidated structure started to rustle. *Only* those trees. No movement near the neighboring pines. Nothing else even gave a sigh. A shot of color caught my eye. To the right of the cabin, where a small, circular clearing had been made, lay a shiny, foil wrapper.

A candy bar wrapper.

Next to it lay a small, folding camp chair that almost blended into the bush where it had been hastily shoved. The lines in the dirt beneath meant it had recently been pushed there. A few things clicked together in my mind at that very moment.

Kimball's incessant chatter up the side of the ridge, like he wanted to make noise all the time.

His loud whoop once we arrived.

His obsession to get here.

Movement in the cabin.

Signs of people here now.

This had all been set up, and something was about to get really ugly. Just as I made a move to close the distance between me and Ellie, Steve tensed. Ellie's eyes grew wide, then panicked. A second before I heard her shout, a rustle came just behind me. I turned a second before something slammed into the side of my head.

Everything went black.

Chapter Thirteen

ELLIE

Devin crumbled like bits of paper.

Before I could so much as scream, a pair of arms wrapped around me from behind in a vise-like grip. The moment I felt the muscular hold, I started to kick, scream, and thrash. Wild fear had her grip on me, and I let her roll.

"Calm down!" Kimball shouted right in my ear. "You're only going to make this worse. I don't want to hurt you, but I will."

"Let me go!" I shrieked.

My cries echoed off the cliffs, bouncing like an erratic bouncy ball. I gathered my thoughts together to stomp on his foot, but stopped. Several other male bodies advanced out of the trees. I could get away from Kimball, but not from them. Two of them, like Steve, had thick necks and arms as wide as trees. Steve's upper lip curled when he saw them. He took a few steps forward next to Devin's limp body, which he ignored.

Tension tripled through the haphazard circle of men that had formed. Including Steve and Kimball, there were five of them, and they all had nasty snarls on their faces.

"Calm down," Kimball muttered, his breath hot in my ear. "Or they will kill you. Let me emphasize to you that they have done so before."

Common sense replaced my sense of rage. Although I didn't relax, I stopped fighting. Instead, I eyed the four other men with a sick feeling in my stomach. Two of them looked like hulks, just like Steve. The other two, like Kimball, were smaller men. More wiry. Unlike Kimball, who could have been considered handsome, the others were more intense than attractive. Lowered brows. Sharp lips. One of them had white-blond hair. The other had coppery brown hair that probably appeared red in the sunlight. Here, it looked like muddy water.

The two strapping men with clenched teeth and dark gazes seemed to take stock of Steve. Just when I thought the simmering rage in the air would explode, Kimball shattered the quiet.

"Gentlemen," he called. "What kind of welcome is this?"

The two smaller men stepped forward. Each of them stood next to one of the burly men, as if each had been paired off with a behemoth. "You brought outsiders," called the small redhead, then looked to me and Devin.

"You say outsider," Kimball replied easily, "I say practice."

"The girl?"

"Creator's wish."

Interest sparked the redhead's gaze. He glanced at the behemoth of a man next to him, then to me. The behemoth leered at me through a fire-scarred expression. I growled, my teeth bared. Whatever Kimball meant by *practice* or *Creator's wish*, it couldn't be good. The behemoth's sickening stare didn't leave any questions about what *he'd* do to me.

The redhead snorted with amusement, then lifted his gaze back to Kimball. He gestured to Devin with a nod.

"The other one?" he asked.

Kimball shrugged. "Practice. Warm-up. Whatever."

"Do they know?"

"No."

"And the Creator?"

"Always watching." Kimball tsked. His gaze darted to the tree-tops. "Always watching."

"What is this?" I hissed and attempted to wrench myself free. Kimball increased his hold until pain shot through my arms, like he wanted to squeeze the bones until they broke. His raw strength surprised me. After seeing him at the gym, I never would have thought he could overpower me.

I stopped fighting with a frustrated grunt, unable to budge an inch. I could smash his toes with the heel of my boot, but there were five other men ready to attack. If the way they knocked Devin out was any indication, they wouldn't hesitate with me either.

"This," he said silkily in my ear, "is Survival Club. And you, my dear, are our new prize."

* * *

Twenty minutes later, my heart rate still hadn't slowed.

It pattered under my ribs like a wild thing trying to fly. They'd tied my hands in front of me and my ankles together, then shoved me in the old cabin and met back outside. Gathering darkness made it difficult to see, but I could make out some flurry of scurry of movement through the aged slats in the logs. Steve and the third behemoth, a man with biceps like hams, gathered wood into a large pile near the edge of the clearing. Bonfire, I'd guess. But why not put it in the middle?

The fire-scarred man who gave me the lusty glance with a promise of terrible violence dragged stones in a circle around the edge of the small open space.

Some sort of ring?

With a shaky breath, I forced my mind to focus on something else.

Not far outside the cabin, but far enough he wouldn't be able to hear me, lay Devin. He hadn't moved. They'd left him there without a backward glance. He lay on his back, his left arm thrown wide and knees bent. I hadn't torn my eyes off him much, afraid of what his stillness could mean. Would he wake up soon? Ever? My throat felt thick with fear for several reasons, but the greatest was for Devin.

Would we make it out of this?

There's no way I'd ever leave here without him, even if that meant I had to haul his limp body away. Hopefully, he'd wake up soon, and we'd have more options.

The three smaller men stood in a huddle not far away, speaking quietly. Fire behemoth squirted lighter fluid on the bonfire pile. Steve rummaged for a lighter, struck it, and touched it to a nearby branch. All of them recoiled away when fire raced over the saturated branches, then exploded in bright, yellow flames. A wave of heat rolled past the cabin, and the flicker illuminated the canyon walls. Steve tossed the lighter and lighter fluid aside as I tried not to panic. Those kinds of flames could set this whole ridge aflame, then there'd be *no* escaping for anyone.

My thoughts flittered around, unable to land, not fully aware of the ugliness of our new situation. As though I wanted to comprehend the whole picture, but didn't truly dare. Still, I forced myself to take mental stock. Facts were easier to work with than emotions. If there was anything I had practice with, it was bottling emotions away to deal with later. So I bundled up my terror and worry and anxiety and pushed it into a box at the back of my mind. The way I had when Jim came at me with a stick. Or when Lizbeth and I walked through the mountains to find Bethany.

Or when Devin left.

I had a lot of boxes.

I turned my mind to this moment and everything I knew about our situation. Clearly, Devin was passed out. Whether waking up would be a good thing or not, I wasn't sure yet. They could have plans for him. Hadn't Kimball said *practice*? If Dev didn't wake up, that would likely indicate a severe head injury.

Hope of getting him out of here intact dwindled with every passing minute. Now, I just hoped to get him out alive.

Men with nefarious purposes and obvious physical brawn surrounded us, but their motivation remained unknown. They'd taken my pack and Devin's and put them . . . somewhere. Probably out of sight, in the woods, where I couldn't easily locate them if we stole away. Our radios and any hope of communication were out of reach. It was unlikely that we'd be able to use them for anything and we'd lose time looking. Daniel wouldn't expect us to return for several more days. I checked in with him every night via satellite text message. If I didn't for tonight, he probably wouldn't worry. Maybe after two nights he'd feel some concern, but that would be far too late.

So, all told, quite bleak.

The words *Survival Club* ran back through my mind. Was it an actual game? A competition? Did all of them participate? If so, Kimball and the other two idiots had no chance against the monsters they'd brought. Likely, the big guys were going to fight. Maybe with fists.

But why fight?

And why *here?*

While most details remained murky, my position in this horror was abundantly clear. The inevitable victim of someone's disgusting lust at the end. Whatever game they played, the winner got *me*. And wasn't that just peachy? Because underneath all his layers of alcohol, that's all Jim had really wanted: my innocence. Ultimate power over me, the object of his wife's affair. Karma had somehow brought me back here.

All of this in the middle of a forest where an alleged territorial grizzly roamed not too far away. If given the choice, I'd take the grizzly.

But I wouldn't call our chances impossible yet. Their ropes weren't impressively tight. With some determination and pain and blood, I might be able to wiggle my hands out and spring my ankles free. Binds notwithstanding, I knew the forest. They clearly didn't. If I could just *get* in the trees, the wind would be my only competition as I hauled out of here. Even if I had to hustle at night.

Except, Devin posed a problem. Perhaps I could sneak out of here alone easily enough, but I refused to leave him behind. I started wriggling at the binds, using my teeth to tug them loose. The idiots, distracted by whatever they were up to now, had tied my hands in front of me.

Devin wouldn't like my plan. He definitely wouldn't agree with it. He'd tell me to run fast, far, and get to safety, then send help.

Forget that.

My days of leaving Devin when he needed me were far behind me, and so was my plan to keep him an acquaintance. No. There was too much between us. All that shared history bolstered me now and made me brave. Devin had always let me lean on him. Now, it was time for me to fight for Devin.

The decision to stay with Devin no matter what gave me something firm to hold onto, and I clung to it with renewed tenacity. Courage, fueled by my determination, followed.

My gaze darted around the cabin to map my options. Fallen boards, dirt, and a piece of a broken beer bottle littered the floor inside. Some charcoal along the dirt floor meant someone had lit a fire in here at some point.

I wiggled to the left and managed to grab a broken piece of beer bottle in my right hand. Small enough that it fit in my palm, the edges poked the sensitive skin there, but it was still large enough to draw blood. If anything, it would give me the element of surprise. I'd need something more, but I tucked it into my palm and kept working at the rope. The rope was tight but it had just enough give that I had a chance.

In between tearing at the rope with my teeth and the edge of the beer bottle, I turned my attention to the growing bonfire. The heat flared out so thick I could feel it through the slatted logs. I tilted my head to the side as I regarded the smaller men. They stood around now, shoulders slumped, voices quiet, talking not far from the fire. The three behemoths stayed away from each other. Each had surly glares and heavy brows.

My plan populated one piece at a time. Get out of the bonds. Find Devin. Wake him up. Grab one of the sticks that wasn't completely engulfed with flames to fight them off and haul out of there. The moment we could disappear into the darkness, we'd have an instant tactical advantage.

A weak plan at best. What if they attacked all at the same time? What if I couldn't grab a log? But at least it was something. I'd have to improvise as I went. Right now, I needed *something* to do, or else it seemed like we'd both endure torture before being murdered.

"Forget practice," a rolling, deep voice said.

My head jerked to look through the nearest gap in the wood. The behemoth with the burned face cracking his neck by canting his head to the side. "Let's get this over with and get the dust distributed."

My thoughts stalled.

Dust?

"Eager beaver?" Kimball asked, but it was acerbic at best.

The behemoth glared through slitted eyes. Kimball's false smile dropped. He cleared his throat and looked away. Not far from him, Steve growled in his throat, but the recipient wasn't clear. Kimball avoided him as well by canting to the side, giving Steve a shoulder.

The other two smaller men separated, each standing near—but not too close to—one of the behemoths. With any luck, they'd forget I was here, and I could sneak away. Devin was within the ring of firelight, which meant I couldn't pull him to safety, slap him awake, and get us both out of here without being detected. My mind ran back through my plan uneasily, but I shoved the reservations aside when Kimball raised two hands.

"Then let us begin! Gentleman, welcome to the second Survivor Club fight."

He reached into his pack to extract a plastic bag filled with what appeared to be two stocky bricks of something pink. A powder, perhaps? Night had started to fall, making the flickering shadows from the bonfire erratic and sketchy. Everyone in the camp became a bit more fidgety when the bag appeared. Kimball gestured to it with his free hand.

"Behold, a stash of pixie dust, given by your generous Creator. Creator shall, of course, remain nameless and faceless, as always. But know they are watching."

Kimball motioned around with a sweep of his arm, and I had an inkling that whatever unfolded next would be broadcast somewhere with a video camera. Through a live feed, perhaps? No, it was unlikely they could get a video feed to work up here. Perhaps the Creator person watched from somewhere nearby with binoculars. Did that mean Kimball had direct contact with this Creator person? If they could speak and this person saw me escape, that would significantly slow my plan to rescue Devin.

"There are two bricks of pixie dust available. One for you and one for your sponsor. You can distribute after the fight however you want," Kimball continued. "Keep in mind that this is the only opportunity for you to gain pixie dust for distribution. The next round of Survival Club will be announced to all sponsors before next quarter."

Already nauseous, my stomach rolled even further as the pieces clicked together. Memories of news clips solidified everything else.

Pixie dust was the street name of the unknown substance that had been circulating Pineville here and there for the last couple of years. The same drug that had driven three druggies to attack Serafina, a barista at the Frolicking Moose, and almost killed her brother from an overdose. A woman under the influence of pixie dust had once held Dagny at gunpoint.

Kimball must be "sponsoring" Steve in a fight to access the

drug. Maybe Steve would be a dealer. Though it was possible Kimball would deal, too. Kimball had apparently brought Steve this far, and Steve would fight for a massive load of the drug. Maybe the only way for him to get it. Then I'd wager they would both get a cut, turn around, and sell it for exorbitant prices. The lack of availability likely made it a gold mine.

And, as for the Creator . . . they must have stayed behind the scenes and watched the mayhem unfold. Made it available only every now and then. Forced brutish men to fight for the right to sell it and drive up demand.

No wonder pixie dust remained so hidden, yet wreaked such havoc.

Hernandez, the local sheriff's deputy and Dagny's husband, had been working tirelessly to find the ring *and* the source for months. Whoever the Creator was, they had been distributing it in the bowels of the forest. Probably moved from place to place, I suspected. Had they brought me with the *plan* to use me as an additional prize? Kimball mentioned I had come at Creator's request. Did I know them? The thought nearly made me vomit, but I forced myself away from that line of thinking.

No, I had to focus. Details could come later.

But, the more I understood their game, the more my panic grew into a greater fever pitch. Pixie dust was known for turning any user into a freakishly strong brute. Any one of these men would kill us without even thinking about it.

Kimball tossed three small bags to each behemoth as he continued, and I shook out my thoughts.

"You know the rules. Each of you snorts, each of you fights. Free-for-all. There will be one break when the first fighter drops out, and then the final fight between the two remaining men. The man who remains standing at the end is given a brick. The sponsor of the winner gets the other half. Then, it's game over until next time. The losing fighters and sponsors are not invited back."

The urge to vomit nearly overcame me yet again, but I forced it back with a deep breath. *No,* I reminded myself. *Don't think about it. Do something.*

My gaze fell on a bright yellow bottle of lighter fluid discarded not far from the fire, toward the edge of the ring of light.

And suddenly, my plan became a lot more feasible.

Desperate now, I used my fingers to work the piece of glass farther out of my hand. It slashed my palm, and warm, sticky blood touched my skin. I ignored it and turned my focus to working on the ropes. If I didn't, Devin would die.

And he'd never know how I really felt.

Chapter Fourteen

DEVIN

My head throbbed.

It pulsed in a slow plod, like a heart trudging along slowly. Unfamiliar voices swam in and out of my mind. In the time that passed between consciousness and comprehension, I didn't move a muscle more than breathing required. I wasn't entirely sure, in all those eternal seconds, whether I had lived or died.

For a terrible twenty breaths, the sands of Afghanistan seemed to surround me. I knew I'd never left. That choking dust and the smell of burning rubber mixed with scorched skin filled my nose. Screams still rent the air, even in my mind. My shoulder throbbed in time with my head, a tandem pain. My ears rang in my head, and somewhere in the blur of it all, I knew I was probably a dead man.

And Ellie still didn't know how I felt.

That thought anchored me out of the moors of my mind and put me back into reality with a firm shove. Just like she had in Afghanistan.

Ellie. Ellie, Ellie, Ellie.

No, I wasn't in Afghanistan. I hadn't dreamed of returning home to her wary gaze. To the feeling of her so near me last night that our breaths mingled.

Consciousness returned slowly. My brain sorted through the voices to remember a cabin. The forest. Ellie flitted through the memories like a fairy until everything cemented itself again. My heart took off at a gallop. Ellie had been alone with Kimball and Steve and . . . someone *else* all that time.

They could have—

The unmistakable sound of fist hitting muscle broke the air. With it, the guttural shouts of animated men.

My eyes flew open.

A bright bonfire illuminated the dusky mountain canyon. At least an hour must have passed because night had already fallen. Beyond it lay mostly shadows, but the pulsing pain in my head likely accounted for some of my inability to see. Or to make sense of what I *did* see.

Three massive men grappled in a stone circle like wild things. Heavy fists flew with dull thuds, flashing in the firelight. None of them moved quickly, but every punch seemed deadly. One slam of a fist into a pair of ribs resulted in an audible crack, then a howl of pain. A slap to the face echoed through the night, eliciting shouts of delight from two other faces I didn't recognize. Kimball stood with two men that didn't fight. That meant six men in addition to me.

Or were there others?

My head didn't move as I swept the space with my gaze, attempting to find Ellie. No sign of her. A good or bad thing? Hard to tell. Had she run away? Broken free to go for help? She damn well better, but even with a head injury that made my thoughts like liquid, I knew it was an impossible hope. That stubborn wild child would never leave me here. That meant she likely waited in the cabin, or in the shadows. Bound, probably.

Whatever they did here clearly had nefarious intent, and I didn't need to linger around and figure it out. Right now, I had to find Ellie and get out of here. My sole objective was to keep her intact and safe.

If my body would stand.

With the three smaller men focused on the fight, and the three other beasts beating the hell out of each other, I carefully shifted to the left. My eyes went to half-mast, as if I were still asleep and I kept my body contorted in the same position. Carefully, I tried to shift my whole torso all at once. The awkward bend of my knees gave me some leverage to move, but not much.

No one seemed to notice at first, but it only took a few inches to know this wouldn't work. It would take forever to get out of sight, and by then some of those idiots would be dead. Their attention would turn back to us. My head throbbed just thinking about it, and my stomach curled in on itself, ready to vomit at my first opportunity, but I forced it back.

I let Ellie down once and I would not do that again.

One deep breath in.

Out.

I rolled.

The ground bumped into my shoulders, elbows, and hips as I rocketed away from the fight and spun into the shadows not too far away. Bushes cracked beneath me, louder than fireworks. My shoulder blade hit a log and jarred the old injury, but I kept going. I forced my body into the shadows where bushes and brambles awaited. The shouts continued to ring out despite my escape.

Dizzy from the movement and my aching head, I let my body stop. Three seconds passed while I tried to gain my equilibrium back before I shoved to my hands and knees, then up to my feet.

The world shifted beneath me the moment I straightened, and I sagged back down. By willpower alone, I managed to stay in a crouch instead of dropping like dead weight. Darkness crept over my vision, layered with white stars. A breath away from unconsciousness, I leaned on my fingertips and blinked rapidly. When I forcefully ground my knee into the slate rocks below, the pain woke me back up.

Ellie, I thought. *Get. To. Ellie.*

Flashes of bonfire gave way to a sandy landscape. I blinked as the rock walls of the canyon shifted, transitioned to a desert at night. A familiar, Afghani desert.

No, I thought desperately. *I can't go back there.*

The hallucination carried more feeling than vision, but I recalled stars spattered high overhead. An overturned Humvee with fire crackling out of the engine. A body lay out the side of the broken Humvee, coated with dust. Blood dripped down limp fingertips. The ringing in my ears became a dull whine and occupied my thoughts for too long. Shouts came from the distance, interspersed with the *ack ack ack* of hostile rifles.

Not there, I mentally screamed. *I'm not there. I'm in Pineville again.*

But my brain didn't understand, and it slipped back in time. My mind didn't work here in the desert. In Afghanistan. Somewhere in the back of my head, I felt pain, but wasn't sure where it belonged. My ribs? Shoulders? What happened to my guys? Where was I? Where did the blood on my hands come from? My left arm wouldn't respond to my command.

Ellie, I thought desperately. She was the only reality that made sense, even here. The only thing that mattered while I stood on the precipice of death in such a hellish world.

Ellie.

Ellie.

Ellie.

Her face swam before my eyes, concerned. Frightened, even. My mind registered fear in her gaze. Why was she afraid? Why did she look at me like she'd never see me again? I fell back to the desert floor, unable to hold myself up anymore. Gritty dirt pressed into my cheek as I hit the ground with a dull *thud* and passed out.

With a hard shake of my head, I broke the hallucination and returned to the present. *I'm not there,* I told myself firmly. *I'm here.*

The mountains returned. The smell of burnt hair receded,

giving way to smoke instead. Blinking hard, I slowly straightened. My thoughts fluttered away like feathers in a breeze.

"Break time!" a male voice called and broke apart my hallucination. "Joe is just about dead. Get these two some water. Collins, take your loser and get out of here. No pixie dust for you."

A dark silhouette appeared between me and the bonfire, but I didn't dare move. My body still *wouldn't* move, like it was locked back in Afghanistan, my left shoulder pinned under a piece of the shattered Humvee. The person approached. My upper lip curled. The fingers of my right hand tucked into my palm. The flash of a familiar, white-toothed smile set the hair on the back of my neck up on edge.

"Well, well," Kimball drawled. "The conquering hero awakes."

He grabbed my shoulder and shoved me toward the fire. Too weak to fight back, I stumbled that way. The blood threatened to drain from my head again as I tried to keep my feet underneath me. The pounding headache became a vice around my skull. I leaned to the side and vomited.

"Time to make you useful," Kimball muttered, then shouted, "Collins! Hold up. Let's give your boy Joe a chance to redeem himself."

* * *

The pressure of a hand squeezing the back of my neck drew me out of the hazy tunnel that threatened to take me back. Back to Afghanistan. Back to that night, the worst of all the most horrible days of my life. Back to where rage had been my only ally.

My only ticket home.

Rage had been my friend in Afghanistan. The source of grit that fueled my survival. It brought me back to life and threatened to consume me every day that I reclaimed that life. With a forced, deep breath, I glared at the other men in the circle. Maybe that burning rage would save me again.

Because these men might be massive, but I was *pissed*. Not just about Ellie's safety and their betrayal, but about everything. About my fellow soldier Trixie dying in my arms. About endless fear. Scratching out survival and a weird return home.

And I was ready to let it out.

Kimball shoved me into a circle of stones that clearly outlined a fighting ring. Two of the burly men sat on the ground off to the side, chests shiny with sweat. One of them was Steve. He glared at me through a split lip and a swollen left eye. His shoulders heaved up and down. Dust lingered around the edge of his nose and on his upper lip. Five yards away sat another beast of a man, his face scarred by what looked like fire. On the other side of the ring was the first fighter, Joe. His head lolled around on his neck while a smaller man slapped him and shouted in his ear.

And the anger grew inside me with every passing second.

"Where's Ellie?" I cried. Maybe she'd hear me and know I was awake. Kimball snorted but stayed out of arm's reach. I swayed on my feet but tried to hide it by stepping to the side.

"Your girl is safe, don't worry. She's ready to be the honored prize. If the Creator will allow it, of course. He has in the past, as long as he gets them first."

The rat of a man that stood next to Kimball snickered. I vowed to get my hands on him, but held myself back for now. Functionality slowly returned to my limbs. My muscles. I felt my body reorient within itself, and my stomach settle.

Safe, Kimball had said.

But his eyes had darted to the cabin.

Take my distraction, I silently begged her. *Take it and run.*

I studied the two fighters on the other side of the ring while the throbbing in my head eased off a little. They still looked amped up. Their eyes were bloodshot. Were their pulses fast? I couldn't tell in the shadows. Looked like they were hopped up on something. Cocaine, if the dust on their noses meant anything. That definitely changed my odds.

"Here's the deal," Kimball said to me with a careless wave of his hand. "We love a good match, you know? And, frankly, Collin's boy Joe was no match for Steve or Rick." Kimball gestured to the man with the burned face when he said Rick. "But Joe might be a match for *you*. So I'll make you a deal."

Kimball stood with his hands on his hips now, a superior expression on his face. Clearly, he enjoyed the power of a spotlight. Perhaps a bit too much. Every eye was riveted on him. Just to make sure of that, I shifted to the side. All their eyes caught mine next. Seconds later, a gentle, slight rustling sound came from the cabin.

"What's your deal?" I asked.

My voice rang through the night—too loud for how close they were—but no one turned a suspicious eye to the cabin.

Kimball studied me, then gestured to the trees. "Win against Joe and you go free."

"And if I don't?"

Kimball shrugged. "Dunno. He'll probably kill you. If he doesn't, we won't be taking you home. So you'll have to figure it out from there."

"Different proposal," I countered. "I win, Ellie goes free."

"If you lose?"

"I won't."

Kimball laughed. On the other side of the ring, Joe rose back to his feet. Next to him, the smaller man named Collins hissed like a snake, indecipherable. The crack of the bonfire created too much noise for me to hear words, but the bright gleam of Joe's eyes meant he thought I didn't have a chance. Even with his groggy steps and struggle to stay conscious.

Maybe that rat-like little man was right.

Maybe I didn't have a chance against Joe. Joe who already glistened with sweat and blood. Joe who weighed at least fifty pounds more than me and had shoulders like a tree. His eyes held that same bright, stiff expression, like he'd snorted something. Fists like his could topple a brick wall. Their whack on my head when we first arrived made certain I wasn't in great shape either. When I didn't have a walloping headache that could be a head injury, I'd barely have a chance with this guy.

But my anger was back—and it was ready.

Ready to throw fists. Ready to vent the building aggression that had been simmering under the surface since I hit American soil again. A life or death situation would be the excuse I needed to vent the truth that haunted me every night.

I shouldn't have survived.

The guy with the scarred face looked as if he were going to protest my new terms, but Kimball spoke before he could.

"Fine. Ellie goes free."

Kimball lied—he'd no sooner set Ellie free than he'd let me live. All of this was sport, and he'd probably try to kill me by the end of it. The back-and-forth was only an attempt to buy time for her to get away undetected. But when I *did* beat Kimball's meat-head slave, then they'd all be scared. I'd have the upper hand. Frightened men made terrible decisions, and that might be the only edge I needed in order to get us out of here.

No further sounds issued from the cabin, which hopefully meant she'd cleared it and was on her way out. I needed to stall more, because I didn't know if Kimball would follow her or not.

How badly did they want their prize?

I had to assume they'd follow.

Although I had no idea what they'd done to her—if they tied her up or knocked her out or drugged her—I felt in my bones that she'd get away. She'd fight, somehow. The cat-like young girl that had flown into a rage against her step-father and choked him to unconsciousness to save her sister's life flashed back through my mind.

Ellie would fight.

And she *better* get out of here.

"Step up to the circle, Joe," Kimball cried, but he backed out of reach like a frightened cat as Joe advanced. Warily, I watched Joe's every step. He walked heavy-footed, but certain. I'd guess he would be slow to pivot, but he'd punch hard.

A flood of uncertainty filled me when he stopped a few steps away. His too-long stare trained on me, but I couldn't tell if he saw me or not. Was he with it? One of his cheekbones had taken a hit, the top skin scraped off to reveal a bright red underlayer. A purplish bruise bubbled up from underneath. The same gentle dusting of powder showed around his nostrils.

I shoved my lacking confidence back and shook my head, the pungent smell of lighter fluid filling in my nose. Whatever drug they'd given these men, I had to hope it slowed them down, because my only tactical advantage here was speed. Adrenalin rocketed around my veins in anticipation of the fight and alleviated my headache. I honed in on Joe, who tilted to the side and caught himself just before he fell.

Maybe this would be simple.

Then Joe let out a bellow like a livid ape. Blood vessels popped out on his forehead when he bent at the waist, flexed his arms, and charged at me like a bull.

And suddenly, I knew we were utterly screwed.

Chapter Fifteen

ELLIE

The sound of flesh hitting flesh made me choke.

Frantic, I tripped over my own feet for the tenth time and barely kept from jostling a bush. Blood freckled my hands and wrists. I'd narrowly missed cutting an artery as I sawed through the ropes to freedom. Smears of crimson decorated the lighter fluid container that I'd been clutching for the last sixty seconds. Sneaking out the back window had been treacherous. The entire cabin threatened to pitch over with any jostle. Thanks to Devin's loud conversation with Kimball, I freed myself without drawing suspicion.

Now, I had mere seconds to save Devin's life.

He looked pale and fierce as he engaged in the ring with the monster of a man that ran at him. Winces occasionally crossed Dev's face. Headache, I'd bet. Traces of vomit lingered on his shirt. He held up for now, but he wouldn't make it long. Nor would he survive any attack from Joe for much longer.

The deep bellow of Joe slamming into Devin for a second time rang through the canyon, setting fire to my fear.

I hastily squirted the last of the lighter fluid around the dark edge of the firelight. Kimball and his minions had been sufficiently distracted, and they didn't notice me circling them. Didn't seem to smell the lighter fluid or hear the *hiss* of it escaping the bottle. Nor the crunch of my feet on dried pine needles as I passed.

A guttural sound from Devin pushed me to ignore the pain in my leg as I stumbled over another rock. I crouched on the other side of the bonfire. Fortunately, these men were idiots. They hadn't even checked on me, and they all clustered in the same space on the other side of the fire. No one would see me back here.

Devin ducked a blow to the face, then drove a fist into Joe's stomach. Joe gasped, his heavy body carrying him to the ground before he could right himself. Devin shoved a knee into Joe's neck as he fell.

I forced myself to look away.

Sweat broke out on my forehead as I crawled to the fire. My fingers burned from trace amounts of lighter fluid which seeped into the cuts from the broken beer bottle shard. With a rock from nearby, I nudged a piece of wood out of the fire. Two fist-size lengths of it stuck out, untouched by the flames so far. I yanked it free. Bright orange ashes flared in the sky like discarded glitter.

Dreams of walking up to Kimball and setting *him* on fire clouded my mind for only a moment before Joe let out a cry of pain and jolted me out of them.

Time to end this.

I drew the stick close, studied the white-hot center for only a second, then turned and slammed it onto the dry pine needles where I'd just emptied the last of the lighter fluid.

Fire shot out of the bracken and raced through the darkness in a quick, fast line. The dried leaves underneath the continuous circle of lighter fluid illuminated hot flames. Yellow light filled the air in a bright blaze. A cry of surprise came from the cluster of men not far away.

Blinded, Joe turned away, arms thrown over his face.

Devin paused, looked around him, then turned toward the cabin. The flash of brightness seemed to stun him. A bruise already started to form on his left cheekbone. I bounded across the space, grabbed his arm, and tugged him away. He followed, stumbling over the line of fire.

"Follow me!" I cried quietly.

Behind us, Kimball screamed. Fire leapt out of the ground at his feet, where I'd silently squirted extra lighter fluid as I made the circle. His two scrawny friends darted around, attempting to extinguish the fire on their shoes. Twigs and bracken illuminated to a bright orange as the greedy flames sped quickly through the dry understory of the forest and toward the cabin. Within moments, the entire fighting circle was nearly consumed. Flames already worked their way to the outside of the cabin and climbed up the side of the dry, aged wood.

Devin glanced back. In the firelight, I could just make out his wordless question.

"What—"

"Later!"

He stumbled over a rock. I tugged him upright again and threw his arm around my shoulders. He sagged against me a little when I wrapped an arm around his back. "We need to get out of here, now. Hang on, Dev. We've got this."

* * *

We plunged into the darkness.

Tree branches whipped at my face as I pushed through clusters of trees that would take us down the canyon, away from the fire and the rocky canyon walls. If we didn't move quickly, that fire might end up being the very thing that killed us. With any luck, it would take out or at least distract all those idiots.

Devin followed with only a few grunts here and there. His steps were uncertain, but he moved faster than I expected. He leaned on me more than he probably realized and sometimes he mumbled unintelligibly. But he didn't make much noise, and his legs kept moving.

"Stay with me, Dev," I panted as we pushed out of a particularly dense cluster of trees. Moonlight overhead remained minimal, but enough to give me a vague direction of where to go. If we stayed at the bottom of the canyon, we'd make better time. If the fire caught up with us, we'd have to scramble up into the scree fields.

"Ellie," Devin said.

"Yes."

"You're here."

His tone was a statement, as if he said it to make it real. An unusual sort of haze, almost like he was in another place, had overcome his expression. I held onto his wrist and tightened my hold around his back. The fast staccato of his heartbeat against my fingertips.

"I'm here, Dev. I'll always be here, now."

"Ellie. Here. You're real?"

He reached out with a shaky hand and I paused. The moment his fingertips touched my face, he sucked in a sharp breath.

"You're not afraid," he whispered. "You're not saying goodbye?"

"Never."

Something in my fierce whisper seemed to bring him back to himself. He blinked several times, then shook his head. His gaze darted around, encompassed the night, then dropped to his left shoulder. The fingers on that arm opened and closed.

"Dev?"

"I'm okay." It came out firm. "Sorry, I . . ."

"You okay? Does your head hurt?"

"Fine." He swallowed and shook his head again. A grimace crossed his face, but the haziness left his gaze. "Yeah. It hurts. I'm fine. You're brilliant. You . . . the fire?"

"Yeah."

"Let's keep going."

I steered us toward the old creek bed. Spindly bushes, dry and cracked from the heat, loomed on either side of us. Rocks littered what used to be the stream, but held no water now. It would be easier to navigate in the moonlight than the bracken, at least until the canyon walls opened up. When I glanced back, light from the fire brightened the rock walls in the canyon. It had to be spreading.

Stupid, I thought. My plan had been desperate *and* stupid. This place would go up like a tinderbox . . . but a fire like that would also get resources here fast. If Neils were still in the area, he'd see the flames and investigate. He'd have a radio to report it, too. At least, that's what I told myself. The thought of burning up my own forest was too much to think about.

Devin, I thought. *Think about home.*

With a deep breath, I forced my thoughts back to the moment. Relief that we'd gotten away gave me a moment of hope, but there was no time to mull over the victory. We had a fire and six drug-addled pursuers to evade. With any luck, Kimball had caught on fire or his shoes had been destroyed. The others would be disoriented, at best. Maybe they'd even try to put the fire out, or just get away. Whatever they did, scattering seemed most likely.

And that gave us a chance.

"Dev," I said through a heavy breath. "We're going to get out of here, okay?"

"Got it."

"That's our sole focus right now. We need to get out of this canyon in case the fire spreads. If we cut back to the south once we're out, there's a creek with water and a trail that we can follow down the mountain. We'll be miles from the car and I have no idea where my pack ended up, but at least we can get onto an open road. It'll be safer to walk near it. Maybe we can flag someone down."

He nodded vaguely, and somehow I could tell that he attempted to work it out in his mind. With every step, he grimaced. His body had to ache after the battering ram of a man slammed into him several times. How he'd held his own, I'd never know. A trickle of blood appeared at the end of his nostril, staining the skin red.

The sound of my plan in the night comforted me, so I kept speaking. "We'll take a break in a little bit, okay? I think we can get out of this in forty-five minutes if we push hard. Once we're on the other side of that stream, we can relax for a little bit."

"I'm with you, E."

Despite my terror, my heart thrilled. The voice, the nickname, the words. All of them were from *my* Devin. I pushed away every other thought. Ignored the possibility that Kimball could be on our heels. Of what they'd do to me if they found me, because I'd made sure that the spot where they'd dropped their precious bricks of pixie dust had also gone up in flames. Devin was in no position to stand against them again.

Instead, I focused on us moving through the forest.

Together.

* * *

Moonlight hung overhead as we hobbled through the woods. Time seemed to pass in weird stretches.

The farther we moved south from the canyon, the stranger the night seemed. Darkness loomed everywhere. Branches caught my hair. The *hoot* of an owl and the shuffle of feathers sounded overhead. I did my best to ignore all of it and focus on our goal, but we slowed when the distance out of the canyon was greater than expected. Mountains had always been tricky. Tonight, they were downright deadly.

By the time we shuffled free of the looming rock walls, I almost collapsed.

When I turned back, a dancing light lingered in the black smudge of the forest. The fire seemed to have calmed. The still night without a hint of wind, and the cool moisture palpable on my skin, worked in our favor. The heat faded enough at night that I doubted the fire would advance now. Neils would have time to phone it in. Likely, they'd get a smokejumper crew out here if it flared back up.

My body ached with fatigue. Devin's weight on mine felt greater with every passing moment, but I forced myself to stay upright.

"We need to turn south," I whispered. "I'm not really sure where we are, but I have a good idea of where we'll end up. There should be a creek eventually. We're not safe here. If we fall asleep and the fire advances, we'll be right in its path."

Bleary-eyed in the moonlight, he nodded, his face drawn. No doubt his headache persisted, and I feared the depths of his injury. His arm tightened around my shoulder again. Ever since he'd returned out of his weird haze, he'd fallen quiet. But he hadn't let me out of his reach. I tightened my hold around his waist.

More slowly this time, we turned to the south.

Trees and a few rolling, gentle ridges made movement easier than the clogged brambles of the canyon. We moved more quickly without all the rocks. Knee-high grass swished against our legs as we walked from moonlit-spot to moonlit-spot. My mind blurred with the movement of my legs until my thoughts resembled a rocky crag instead of a meandering trail. I didn't recognize that we'd arrived at a creek until I heard the splash of my foot in the water.

Both of us stopped, startled.

Moonlight glinted off the top of the creek as it rushed by. At least fifteen feet across, it cut down the mountain in a hearty artery that should lead to the reservoir at Pineville. The comforting sound of tinkling water wiped away the unnerving silence. How long had we been walking? My gut told me it was well past midnight, maybe 2:00 am. That meant almost five to six hours. The darkness gave me no idea where we were, or how far we'd gone.

"There." Devin pointed to a particularly dark spot, surrounded by what appeared to be bushes. "Let's try it."

We moved out of the open area and toward the greater protection of the trees. Bushes cluttered the riverbank, forming a natural kind of barrier. The dark spot was a portion of streambank that had crumbled away and sloped into the water, leaving a place below level ground that we could sit on. Bushes on top would shield us if anyone walked by, which I doubted. Most likely, Kimball and the others would head straight west, staying at the bottom of the canyon until they hit a road or something.

I hoped they walked right in front of a semi.

Still, I couldn't shake the fear that they had followed us. That they wanted revenge and would find us here to finish what they intended to do. The night was too cold, the dark too deep, and my fatigue too great for me to know whether my thoughts even made sense or not.

We slipped down the dirt slope, which was wide enough to sit side-by-side. Dev dropped to a knee, plunged his hands into the water, and brought it to his face. He gave a little gasp from the cold, then did it again. He rubbed down his face, his neck, his hair, then drank until I settled numbly next to him. The water cleared the dirt and blood from his face.

Thoughts of Kimball and the fire-scarred man retreated to the back of my mind again while I worried about Devin.

I sat back and stared at the top of the gentle creek as it slid by. Moonlight illuminated the top in white slivers as the water bumped over rocky rapids. Thoughts spilled all over my mind, just like the creek. They flowed with equal parts relief to be away from the reach of the fire, euphoria that Devin was still with me, and utter terror that Kimball would somehow find us. All the courage that buoyed me up at the abandoned cabin fled from me now and left me weak in its wake.

"Ellie?"

Devin's voice cut through my mind and stopped what had

become a fast spiral of thought. I shook my head, blinked, and registered that he was staring at me. The moon illuminated enough of his profile that I could see the angle of his cheek, softened by his swollen cheekbone. The urge to reach up and touch his face nearly overcame me. He seemed oriented now, as if the water had woken him up.

"I'm okay," I said quietly.

Unable to endure the intensity of his stare, I scooped up water and drank from my cupped palm. The moment my lips touched the cool liquid, I drank hungrily, scooping six or seven times before my thirst calmed. The water had a mossy taste and slid with cool relief all the way to my ravenous stomach.

"Probably past midnight, you think?" I asked as I shook the water droplets off my hand.

"At least. How long was I knocked out?"

"Not sure. Half an hour, maybe."

He frowned.

I didn't know what to say, so I remained quiet. To acknowledge what he said would force me to acknowledge our position, and I wasn't ready to do that. My brain needed to keep all emotions in their respective boxes. That way, I could push through and not let my love for him get in the way. Nor would the fact that I'd almost lost him again slow down my judgment.

My battered mental boxes trembled tonight.

Devin reached over and grabbed my shoulder. The solid grip made me suck in a sharp breath. I tilted my head back to look at him, limned in starlight. Concern lay evident on his features.

"Are you really okay?"

I nodded, even though both of us knew I lied. Right now, I was fine. All of this would spill out later, once I let the emotions out. For now, I'd stay buttoned up and in control.

"Are *you*?" I asked.

He shook his head, then grimaced a little as he stretched his body around. "No." He scoffed, and it could have been a chuckle under different circumstances. "Joe was a friggin' wrecking ball. At least . . . not really bad. I can walk off the mountain."

"Your head?"

"Messed up in so many ways," he murmured.

Before I could ask what that meant, he repositioned. His left shoulder leaned against the wall of dirt behind him. Our knees pressed together. This little nook of dirt and rocks would hide most of us for the night, but we wouldn't be able to lay down. Sitting upright made it feel as if I were ready to react to anything that came along. Dev grabbed a pine needle that stuck out of the dirt near his face and began to methodically split it into pieces.

"I had a flashback." He met my gaze. "Back there. That's why I acted so weird. It's been happening pretty often after this last deployment. Based on the intense circumstances tonight, I think it's gotten worse. Like my body recognizes when I'm back in that fight-or-die position and runs back. I'm sorry."

I recalled the haze in his eyes and his attempts to reiterate my existence. The word *flashback* helped it click back into place. Hearing the confirmation sent a shudder through me. He looked over the stream, then shook his head softly.

"I'm not sure what my triggers are yet," he continued. "I've seen a professional to help get myself out of the flashbacks, but only had a chance for two visits before I got my leave. They still rear up despite some initial work to keep them at bay. Mostly in dreams. Sometimes in situations like this. I still can't peg exactly what starts them, but . . ."

He trailed away and I wondered what he was going to say, but prevented. A thousand questions filled my mind, starting with, *what happened to hurt you so deeply?* And *when were you going to tell me?*

If we hadn't experienced this horrible night, would he have let me in on his secret? Would I have ever known that he suffered? Maybe not, because Devin and I didn't owe each other that anymore. The silent give-and-take ended when he left and our friendship stopped so suddenly.

But did it have to continue like that? Couldn't friends pick back up where they left off? *And they always leave,* Mama whispered, which engaged the real question.

Did I trust Devin?

"I'm sorry, Dev," I whispered to silence the other voice. "That's . . . I'm sorry it's happened to you. I would never wish that on anyone."

"Thanks." He swallowed. "Me too. It might happen again tonight, which is why I wanted to tell you."

"What can I do?"

He let out a breath. "It's called grounding. You already kind of did it back there, or helped me do it. When I'm in the flashback, it feels like I'm back at a few specific moments of the deployment. I say things to ground myself back in reality. Things that remind me where I am. They reiterate that I'm not there so I can eventually work out of the confusion."

"Like when you asked me if I was real?"

His nostrils flared and he nodded. For a moment, he looked as if he would say something, but his lips sealed shut. Finally, he said, "I'm not ready to tell you everything about that deployment. Maybe I never will. But it was hell over and over again. One of the most difficult postings we've had." His fingers curled into a tight fist and bitterness edged his tone. "Over forty men died there before the government finally agreed to leave it so we didn't have to fight and die anymore."

Unable to say a word, I just reached over and took his hand. The touch seemed to give him courage. He looked over at me. His gaze dropped to my lips, then skated away. His voice returned to the melodic singsong of before.

"Although every day had a question mark on it over there, there were three times I really thought I would die. Those are the flashbacks I have now. They haunt me the most, although sometimes I have memories that surface out of nowhere. Like pictures in my mind, when I'm walking or in line at a restaurant. It's unpredictable. Each instance when I thought it was my last day, I . . ."

He faltered. A troubled expression crossed his face and he tightened his fingers around mine. I wanted to pull him close. My heart longed to draw him into my arms and soothe all that frustration from his eyes. But I froze because I knew Devin. He needed to get this out and he wouldn't do that unless he could look into my eyes.

"I saw you."

My eyebrow rose. "Me?" I whispered.

"Each time." His voice became strained. "Each time I thought I might die, I saw you. You just looked . . . worried. Concerned. Angry, even. Like you came to say goodbye. But you never spoke to me. That's why I was confused when you said something tonight."

His fingers felt hot against my suddenly cold ones. The words played over and over in my mind. *I saw you. I saw you.* Devin and I had always had a more intense connection than most people expected, but this was something else. I licked my lips, speechless for several seconds.

"Wh-what did I do?"

Devin let out a long breath, then faltered. "I . . . You . . ."

I put my free hand on his arm. "You don't have to tell me, Dev. It wasn't a fair question. Keep going."

His eyes closed in relief, which only deepened my desire to know. "So far, you haven't been in my flashbacks. It's how I ground myself. If I don't see you, then it's not real and I'm not there. So when I saw you tonight, you sort of mixed with the flashback and I was . . . confused. Worried. It's like a strange merging of past and present. Sometimes I feel the danger and the fear, even though I know I'm not at that place. Sometimes, I can see the memory play out in front of me, like a movie. That's why I asked if you were real and whether you were *here*. Because at that place in Afghanistan, when I thought I was about to die, you didn't speak to me. Tonight, you did. It convinced me that it was just a flashback."

The crack of my heart would have been audible if my heart had words. I didn't move my gaze off of his. He pushed through.

"If it happens again, which I hope it doesn't but it probably will, do what you did. Help me ground and get me back to reality by telling me where I am. Tell me what we're doing. Give me concrete details until I'm fully back. In those moments, I need to know what's real and what isn't. If you don't," he added quickly and with a spurt of fear, "I might get too far into the memory. I could hurt you. I haven't yet, I can normally get myself out of it." Agony etched into his features. "But I *could,*" he added softly.

I squeezed his hand. "You won't, Dev. You never would."

He leaned forward until our foreheads touched. So many questions filled my mind, but not even they could distract me from the smell of him. The warmth of his body next to mine. Without him, I would have been out here alone.

"We need to get some sleep," he whispered. "We can huddle together, in case it gets much colder, and doze. I won't sleep deeply, I hope, but if I get into a nightmare, try to wake me up."

"I'll ground you."

He smiled gently, then pulled away. There wasn't far to go, so he wrapped an arm around my shoulder and we leaned back into the stream bank. I wiggled closer and put my head on his shoulder. Like missing puzzle pieces, we slid together. The boxes in my mind jangled with an ugly reminder of how full I'd filled them tonight. Devin's whispered confession, so darkly vulnerable and stark in the reality of his new life, created more boxes.

More emotions.

More uncertainty.

"Thank you for telling me," I whispered.

He squeezed my shoulders and I slid into a reluctant and fitful sleep.

Chapter Sixteen

DEVIN

Dawn edged the sky when my eyes fluttered open.

Darkness still lingered in the trees across the stream, but the sky had started to lighten in the east. For the first time in my life, the presence of light in the mountains wasn't a comforting thing.

We'd make better time and would hopefully be able to haul off the mountain today, but so would Kimball and Steve. There was more to see in the daylight, and we were included in that. Without knowing their motivations and whether or not they wanted to come back at us, I had to assume they were still hostiles. Particularly this morning, after time allowed reality to set in. I'd seen the pink bricks of powder burst into flame before we stumbled away. Men killed over lesser insults than lost drugs and money.

A gentle sigh drew my gaze down. Ellie's head remained tucked up on my shoulder, her breath warm and gentle on my neck. Her arm lay limp across my stomach. Dew had descended overnight, dampening our clothes. Her skin was cool where she wasn't touching me. I wanted to curl her all the way into my arms and wrap her in a hold that pressed my heart on hers. Maybe she wouldn't even protest. We'd always cuddled and touched more often than most. But that didn't necessarily *mean* anything.

I shoved those thoughts away. Practicality demanded attention, not dreams. No matter how hard I tried to get rid of them, they returned.

Besides, Ellie wasn't mine. She never really had been. She *felt* like mine in high school when our worlds intermixed so easily. When I could keep an eye on her and also have other friends. That life wouldn't have lasted. The adoration I saw in her eyes for her best friend was part of the reason I knew I had to leave, at least for a while. Because Ellie was, for all intents and purposes, *mine*. Totally under the spell of what friendship we had. She'd hold herself back in all elements of her life because of her loyalty to me and never think twice about it.

At least, not at first.

Resentment would have built over time. I'd seen it in my sister and my parents and wanted better for Ellie and me. I tightened my hold on her without thinking about it and she stirred.

The gentle twitter of birds overhead drew my thoughts back to our surroundings. The stream bubbled by, soft as a sigh. No other sound interrupted the lazy woods, but my gaze darted around anyway. Nothing was ever *this* peaceful.

Yes, it is, came the thought. *You've just forgotten.*

Flashes of deployment in Afghanistan and the *brap brap brap* of hostile fire jolted me. I shook my head to get rid of the intrusive thoughts.

I'm here, I told myself and forced myself to draw in a deep breath. The fresh scent brought me back. *That world and that life aren't real right now.*

Except it was for someone else, and that made me just as sick to my stomach. With intentional mental force, I turned my mind back to where I wanted it for the third time: our plan to get out of here.

A popular, even wider creek should have waited at the bottom of another ridgeline, set to the south of the one Ellie almost set on fire last night. But we hadn't found it yet. We'd crossed over this stream yesterday, but farther up. At least, I thought we had. The ridges and valleys were unclear without the absolution of a map. Any attempt to recall it met with uncertainty. I *thought* I knew where to go, but couldn't be sure of it. My stomach growled as if it sensed my lack of confidence.

We couldn't wander forever.

The ridge wasn't as high here and had more forest cluttering the hills, but I hoped it would intersect with the well-known trail near the bottom, where the stream dumped into a lake that people often hiked to. Once we hit the trail, we could move quickly and get out of here.

My head pulsed lightly with pain, but it felt dull and thick instead of torturous thuds. I'd need to get to a hospital sooner than later, but, for now, my focus would solely be on getting us out of these mountains. If Kimball did follow, they'd expect us to stay near the stream. We'd walk high, following the creek in the trees if we had to.

"Dev?"

The quietly spoken word stirred my chest. I glanced down again to see Ellie blinking up at me. She shifted away, gazed around in panic, then sagged back in relief. She returned to the same spot and snuggled in more deeply, her forehead pressed against my neck. I held her tight against me and tried not to feel annoyed that I smelled like blood, dirt, and vomit. Instead, I let the deep intensity of hope from her touch fill me. Like I could draw all her power into me and stuff it into all my broken places.

My voice came out a scratchy burr when I asked, "Sleep okay?"

"Yeah. In and out."

"Same."

Her eyelashes fluttered against the column of my neck as she blinked. I rubbed her cool arm with my palm and she shivered.

"It's cold this morning."

"It'll warm up fast." My gaze darted up to a cloudless sky. "Should be a hot day."

She nodded. "How long have you been up?"

"Just a few minutes."

"Already mapped out our escape?" she quipped and her face moved into a little smile.

Despite my own pessimistic thoughts regarding the onset of daylight and Kimball's likely deep desire for revenge, I heard optimism in hers. The sky had turned blue overhead. To the east, rays of sunlight had started to break. Birds sang in a wild cacophony of sound. It would be another hour or so before the sun would be visible over the craggy mountains, but light reached the world all the same.

"Had some ideas."

"Follow the stream?"

"Yeah, but in the trees." I tilted my head toward the bank of trees that reached up to the ridge. "Even those idiots could figure out that following a stream might be the easiest path out."

Her face moved into a smile that I could feel. "You have good ideas," she murmured. "It's what I was going to suggest."

She pulled away again, and I felt her missing pressure and heat like a removed limb. With her fingers, Ellie picked a hair band out of her hair and let her locks spill free on her shoulders. My throat tightened at the sight of her, rumpled from sleep, her eyes bright, and crinkled hair unbound in a wild mess over slender shoulders. I turned away and wondered how I'd ever be able to walk away and back to North Carolina.

"Is your head okay?" she asked as she combed through the hair with her fingers. A twig dangled off a few strands near her left shoulder. I reached over and plucked it free, flicking it off my fingers. A smile twitched my lips as I pulled another bramble out of another lock of hair. She snorted.

"My head hurts," I said, "but fine. You ready to hoof it out of here? I want to get started now that we can see."

"Yeah, let me just get a drink."

Ellie slowly straightened, arms stretched overhead. I diverted my hungry gaze so it didn't rove over the elegance of her arms and the shape of her shoulders. Then she reached for the water, drank several times, splashed her face and arms, and turned to me. Her eyes met mine for the first time this morning with a clear, sparkling curiosity. Brilliant as the thick greenery around us.

"You ready?" she asked.

For you? I thought. *I always have been.*

Instead, I dropped my gaze. "Just about." I couldn't tolerate her this unbound and in her element. The depths of unfiltered Ellie affected me too heavily to articulate. This is what I'd lived for. The hope of these sort of moments again with her is what kept me alive. Now that I lived them, they scared me more than anything.

How would I live without her easy grace to look at every day?

With her away from me, I slowly stood. Both of us roved through the forest with our eyes, but no movement or sound unfolded. We seemed, for all intents and purposes, alone here. My head pulsed with the movement, but it passed when I paused. The lingering headache still ached, but I'd deal with that later.

"You need more water," she said. "Drink it while you can. Dehydration will only make your headache worse."

I nudged her with an elbow. "Thanks, Mom."

She smiled reluctantly. "I'm hoping this stream leads to Red Lake, remember?"

"Yeah. We went there all the time."

Another fleeting smile brightened her face. "Yeah, and we won that game of chicken against your sister and her boyfriend at the time."

"That guy was a total jerk."

She giggled. "He was so angry. Anyway, Red Lake is miles from the truck, but maybe we can find someone, borrow a cell phone, and call Maverick?"

"Hernandez, too."

The edge came back into her gaze when she nodded. "Yeah.

Him, too. It'll take most of the day," she murmured with a sigh, "but we'll get there."

After I'd rubbed my face down and drank until my stomach hurt, I motioned downstream, where it narrowed through a little gully, then opened back up. "Let's cross over there and stay on that side. If they come upon us later and have to cross, it could slow them down."

"Sure."

"Then, let's get this over with. I'm starving."

* * *

My body warmed up fast once we started moving, even though my stomach protested every now and then. At least we'd been able to fill up with water. If we stuck close to the stream, we'd be fine. If not, dehydration sets in fast at these altitudes in the summer. We would only decline from there.

We moved back out of the immediate view of the stream, then picked our way through the forest. Boulders appeared here and there to narrow our path options, but we stayed out of sight and mostly quiet.

"So," I said after a long stretch without speaking, my voice pitched low, "tell me what college was like. You covered the vague stuff when you said you didn't like it, but I'm curious about the details."

The question had lingered on the tip of my tongue for months after Mom told me that Ellie went to the state university, then returned a few months later. Ellie tightened a little as she considered my question, but didn't clam up.

"Isn't much to say," she murmured as she stepped over a log. Her gaze darted to the right, where the creek cut through the trees out of sight. Seeing nothing of concern, she relaxed a little. "I hated it."

"Why?"

Her brow furrowed. "Are you going to get high-school-Devin-level protective if I tell you?"

"No."

"Oh."

"I'm going to get Marine-corps-deployed-soldier-Devin-level protective. Some asshole put his hands on you?"

Her lips twitched and some of the humor returned to her gaze. "I took care of it."

My feet stopped of their own accord. Wait, what? She took care of *what*? Warily, she slowed and glanced back. My brow rose and I had a sick feeling I wasn't going to like whatever story came next.

"Ellie?"

"Let me explain."

She spoke quietly, but with the same tone she would have used even if we weren't hiding from rogue drug dealers that wanted to kill us. I nodded back to the forest to indicate we should keep moving, and she followed suit.

"I didn't get along with my roommates," she continued. We walked side-by-side through a more open expanse of trees. "They were too loud and in my space. I think I got assigned some particularly rowdy people, I guess. I don't know. They had boyfriends over all the time and they didn't really respect boundaries. I didn't expect them to *not* drink alcohol, I just didn't want them and their drunk friends in the apartment. That seemed fair."

My entire body tightened. "Tell me how this ends first," I said, "then tell me the details. I don't want to wait through all of this until I know how whatever you're going to say happened."

She snorted. "Dev, I'm obviously alive."

"Say it, E."

"I kneed him in the groin, then almost broke his nose, and he never came back."

The conclusion of the story only made it worse. I didn't relax. Instead, I felt more troubled than ever.

"Tell it."

She sighed, but let the story roll off her lips more quickly. "One night, my roommates and their boyfriends were drunk. One of the boyfriends stumbled into my room and wouldn't leave. He . . . he got belligerent, so I kneed him in the groin. That made him angry, so he tried to come at me again. Naturally, I shoved an elbow into his face. Noses bleed like crazy," she finished on a mutter, and my anger at the image of some hulking, drunk man in her bedroom made my rage at Afghanistan look like party glitter.

"I don't like that," I said, shaking my head. "I don't like that. I don't like that."

I should have been there, I thought.

Her hand found my arm, and the touch soothed my rattled nerves. "I know, Dev. I didn't like it either, which is why I never went back. I packed up the next morning after barricading myself inside."

"Do you think you could have gotten different roommates?"

She shrugged. "Maybe. At that point, I didn't care. I had already been miserable and didn't think it was worth it to roll the dice. I hadn't really found a major that I wanted to do, and I missed home. It just . . . it wasn't a good fit."

Her ending wasn't satisfactory to me, but I nodded anyway. She gave my arm a little squeeze, then her fingers slid away. Trails of fire lingered in their wake, and I wondered how it would feel to interlock our hands.

Never mind that her lips would probably start my heart ablaze.

"There were a few other close calls," she said breezily, as if that could be so simply dismissed, "but all my self-defense classes had paid off."

"Self-defense?"

She nodded. "Yeah, I took classes with Benjamin and Serafina after you left. She's been helping with them every few months. I didn't . . ." She hesitated, met my gaze, but then gave me the full dish of honesty that I deserved. "I didn't feel safe without you by my side all the time." Her tone brightened just a little, but not enough to feel inauthentic. "The classes ended up being a good thing, particularly when the three guys approached me on campus."

My stomach twisted in a sickening way. I stopped. She stopped. Then she turned toward me with a hesitant, almost apologetic look.

"Three guys?" I whispered.

She swallowed, the sound audible.

"Dev, it's—"

"What happened?"

Troubled now, she spoke quickly. "It was a few weeks before I left college. I had a study group that ran late and had to leave after dark. When I walked across campus, a group of three guys called for me to stop. Said they had a question."

My questioning glare could have burned through brick. She hurried to finish. Although she played a tough game, I could see the trouble in her gaze. This event, whatever it turned out to be, still bothered her.

"I didn't trust them, particularly because they approached too fast and tried to push me against a building, where there were shadows."

"What happened?"

My tone remained steady, but the agitation was evident. Her voice became a bit more distant. She nudged her toe at a clump of fading wildflowers and focused on a spot in the distance. Deep grooves formed between her eyebrows.

"I kicked one in the throat. The other two advanced. I had my car keys between my fingers and slashed one in the face. I stepped back to prep a kick, but the third ran away. I took off."

"Did you report it?"

"I did."

"Did they find those assholes?"

She nodded.

"You pressed charges?"

She nodded again. A long breath of relief rushed out of me. No *wonder* her form had been so excellent at the gym.

"Good."

I regarded her with an entirely new set of fears now. Once Ellie had returned to Pineville, I hadn't felt as concerned. Clearly, I still needed to be. Her beauty, so wild and untamed, was too much by half. The disinterest she gave most people only made it all worse.

She chewed on her bottom lip, but didn't look away. The weight of the last three years sank into my bones. Not only had ghosts, injuries, and memories torn apart the fabric of my life and put me on a different path, but they did that to Ellie too. My sudden departure had rocked her world as much as it had mine.

I would have left no matter what—I had to help my parents and make sure both of us knew ourselves without the other. This had been the right path. But maybe it wouldn't have been so jarring if my pride hadn't been so great.

"I'm sorry," I whispered.

Did she feel the weight of what that encompassed? Could she know, in just two words, how deeply I meant what I said?

She blinked and studied me, then she said, "Don't be. You did the right thing, Dev. Your parents needed you."

Her exoneration didn't feel as good as I'd hoped.

"I should have told you about their debts."

"I wish you would have," she murmured. She looked away first, then kept walking as if she didn't know what to say. The slow crunch of twigs and grind of rocks beneath her feet was the only sound for several heavy moments. I followed, lost in her footsteps and my thoughts.

"And you're happy now?" I asked.

The slightest hesitation came before she said, "Yes, of course."

"If I hadn't left Pineville and we went to college together according to our plan, would you have stayed in school?"

Her brow wrinkled. "I don't know. If you'd stayed, Dev, everything would have been different. We could have found a place together. Gone to classes together. I wouldn't have been in that apartment or—"

"Exactly."

"What do you mean?"

My heart beat firm against my chest now, as if I'd been running. For three years, I'd wanted to make this point. For three years, I'd wanted her to see my side of this whole dilemma. Now it was my chance, and I prayed she'd come far enough into adulthood to understand. Or to at least consider my angle.

"If I had been at the university with you, would you have taken self-defense classes?"

"No."

"Would you have ever been on your own?"

"Well . . ." She hesitated, then shook her head. "No."

"You might still have finished college because *I* was there. Even if you were miserable, you wouldn't have left, would you? Even if it wasn't right, you would have stayed because I stayed."

Her mouth remained partially open for several seconds. Finally, she gave a reluctant nod. Her honesty filled me with hope.

"You would have stayed for *me* no matter how much you hated it. Never would have gone to the Outfitters and played in the mountains and learned all of this stuff about yourself. Right?"

Storms built in those beautiful emerald eyes and I let them build. Something charged the air between us, intense and hot and building like a thunderstorm. Ellie licked her lips.

"Maybe."

"I had to go, Ellie. We had to do something apart so we could come back together." My voice thickened with intensity. "We relied on each other too much. We would have resented it at some point. Somewhere in the future, we would have broken apart because of that resentment, but then it may never have been repaired. *We* may never have healed. I could see it. I wanted us to find ourselves first."

Her eyes had gone wide and a little distant, as if she reviewed things in her mind. Did memories and circumstances play through her mind the way they had with mine? Because they had haunted me at almost every step of my adult life.

Did she see it all so differently now?

"I'm sorry," I said again. "I should have told you my thoughts, my parents' troubles. If I had been transparent with all of this, those terrible years would have been easier on both of us. But I was weak, Ellie. I didn't have the strength and courage to do that. So I took the coward's way out and I didn't say anything. I just . . . disappeared because I thought it would be easier."

My chest tightened with the power of finally letting that out. Now, she had to decide what to do with it, and I wouldn't blame her if she hated me a little.

"It wasn't an easy path," she said.

"I know. Because seeing what happened to you as a result of my decisions totally sucks. Without knowing what you went through, I still hated it every moment of every day. But it felt right at the time."

Ellie's wide eyes remained frozen in muted disbelief. Finally, she nodded. I could see the implications and layers of what I'd just said slowly settling in, and I didn't want this pleasant part of the mountains to stay in this odd tension. I started to walk again, and she followed at my side. Silence followed for several minutes before I couldn't stand it anymore.

"So," I let out a punctuated breath. "You came back to Pineville after college. Then what happened?"

"I came back," she said with finality and a little relief. "Started back at the Frolicking Moose. Hired on at the Outfitters. Eventually cobbled together the idea of guiding and working outdoors. It was much easier here. Much . . . safer."

"And you like it? Guiding?"

She laughed. Despite our circumstances, there was real levity there. "Not sure anymore." She hedged for a second, then added, "I don't really know. Being outside is great. Getting *paid* to be outside is great. But . . ."

"It's not what you thought?"

"No."

A real sense of defeat lingered in her words. I slipped around a tree stump in a cluster of rocks while she gathered the words in her head. The easy flow of her responses and lack of hesitation was like a balm. Ellie wasn't holding back out of mistrust this time. That felt like a step forward.

"It just . . . hasn't been as fulfilling as I expected," she finally said. "I mean, this is my first overnight guide, so that's probably not a fair measurement. The day hikes were fun. Just not . . ."

"Not what you thought?"

"Right."

"What are you hoping to get from it?"

"I don't know," she said quietly. "Maybe something I used to have."

The words rang with something else, but I couldn't puzzle together what she meant. Not with the low pulse of a headache through my neck and my thoughts cluttered with men that tried to hurt her. Men I should have been there to protect her from. But that wasn't realistic. We'd been together for days now and I hadn't been able to protect her from these men. Our current circumstance was proof enough.

"I'm jealous."

Her head lifted up. "What?" she asked.

"I'm jealous," I said easily. "I'm jealous of all the people that came into your life that spent time with you. Time I didn't get. It's . . . weird that you have all these experiences I wasn't a part of. That was hard when I left. Knowing we'd have parts of our life that we didn't share."

To my surprise, a quick smile lifted her lips. "I know the feeling."

"Yeah?"

She nodded, her hair waving around her shoulders. I wanted to reach out, take a fistful of it into my hands, and lay a kiss on the lips I'd studied every day of my life from the time I was a kid. The moment I met Ellie was the moment I fell in love with her.

"It . . . it seemed so weird that you'd be in the world without me," she said. "I didn't know how to say it, but it does feel like jealousy."

"Did you date?"

The question rushed out of me. If I'd known it lingered there in the shadows, I wouldn't have let it free. But once it came out, relief followed. Ellie snorted again, but something like a wall had appeared in her eyes.

"Not really. A few dates, but no serious boyfriend."

"Couldn't find anyone?"

She shrugged. I glanced to the right and then behind us, feeling an obsessive pull to be certain we were alone. No signs of others lingered, so I motioned forward again. With the mostly clear ground, we moved quickly. Hilltops built up behind us as we angled down the mountain. Once we moved closer to the popular Red Lake, we'd grapple with what came next. For now, I felt content just to be with her.

"How about you?" she asked and pulled me out of my thoughts.

"Me, dating?"

She nodded, her lips pursed together. Her gaze remained ahead as she picked a path for us through the pines and brush.

"Nah. Too busy. Went on one or two dates but wasn't really interested."

"Oh."

She kept her gaze ahead. Did I see new tension in her body? Was there a glimmer of hope for us after all? If Ellie had any sign of jealousy, maybe it meant something else. Then again, maybe it didn't.

Although tempted to reveal all, I set that thought aside and let the lulling forest speak in the gentle sough of leaves overhead. This weird moment of revealing ourselves was *not* the time that I'd tell her how I felt—how I'd always felt—about her. Running from druggies in the mountains after almost dying several times just didn't ring with romantic drama. At least, not the way I wanted.

Or maybe I was still just too chicken.

The crack of a stick and a muffled noise sent me to the ground. Ellie followed. I lay in the bracken, my heartbeat in my ears, for ten full seconds before the splash of something in the stream came next. A dark figure moved not far away. Before my mind registered what it was, Ellie cracked a wide smile.

"A moose."

I straightened over the brush I'd ducked behind. A lanky, hulking shape hovered in the middle of the stream. Loose lips nibbled over mossy rocks that stuck up out of the stream and collected greenery and sticks. Bone paddles at least four feet wide stretched from either side of its head, and a dark waddle dragged in the stream at its feet. I grinned and whispered, "It's been years since I've seen one."

"They certainly don't frolic, do they?"

A giggle bubbled out of her as the moose advanced one slow plod forward. His ear twitched when I laughed, but he just shook his giant head and kept searching the water. The laugh echoed in my chest until we both lay back in the sun-warmed earth, clutching our sides.

For the first time in a while, things didn't seem quite so bleak.

Chapter Seventeen

ELLIE

My legs and feet moved as if numb through the forest while we walked. The break of speaking after so much being said felt like a reprieve. Whatever burden Devin had gotten off his chest now felt like it lingered on mine.

His ownership over his decision to leave stirred me up. It didn't surprise me—Devin had always been reliable and straightforward that way.

But it did *affect* me.

He moved into his emotions so easily. Like they were always present and entangled and he didn't mind holding them up and saying, "Look what I found!" Meanwhile, I kept mine boxed away, locked up tight, in a place I didn't like to go. And maybe that was part of the problem.

His visceral response to the story of my roommate's boyfriend also didn't surprise me, but it did warm me. Also, it made me frustrated. *Why weren't you there?* I wanted to ask. *You should have been.*

At the back of my mind, Mama kept whispering.

Men leave.

Love dies.

You take care of yourself.

But what if they came back? I asked, and her voice pieced away into nothing.

Besides, it was one thing for Devin to hold an opinion on what we *should* do, and another thing that he took matters into his own hands. Why couldn't we just talk about the potential for resentment issues? Resentment built when people didn't communicate, not just when they disappeared without explanation.

Which, consequently, meant we didn't communicate and resentment had built after all.

Men were dorks.

Then again, he'd been eighteen. On some level, he seemed frightened of something at the time. Like he'd been running away from something instead of running toward something better.

But what had he run away from?

Devin's comment about finding ourselves made me roll my eyes at first, but the idea had been slowly puzzling together the more my feet moved. Was it Devin's job to be my security guard? It had been in high school. We'd both accepted his protection as part of our relationship and that had meant so much. But would he have wanted to do that forever?

Would I *want* him to?

No, of course not. I held my own power, and isn't that what I found? When the security left, I created my own. What if he had found a girlfriend—what would have happened then? The idea of Devin dating another girl had never really taken root in my mind because I'd always seen him as mine. My Devin. My escape. My safety.

But his departure made it very clear that he wasn't mine.

Devin belonged to Devin.

Perhaps that had been the hardest lesson of all. The one that was the most difficult to accept and the hardest to articulate. Best friends or not, Devin always had his choice at the end of the day. He could choose me, or he could choose his own life.

If he'd just chosen me, I thought, *we could have been . . .*

That thought died away too, because I saw what he meant more clearly now. We could have been *something,* but for how long? The dependence would turn to resentment. Hadn't that been Mama and Jim? Jim relied too much on Mama. To get rid of him, she'd cheated on him. Used him.

Resented him.

The truth lay in ugly paths before me. But I couldn't face this now, so I swept it all into its own box and set it aside to think about later. Later, when I wasn't so hungry and wildly emotional. Later, when a drug dealer and his cronies weren't hunting us down in the forest. Or maybe they weren't, and we were just that far gone to fatigue and hunger.

If nothing else, catching up with Devin in such an easy way had been a gift. I missed just *being* with him, and it seemed like we sidled closer to that easy dynamic every day. Now wasn't the time to grapple with what we would be after this. Best friends . . . from a distance? Friends that reunited when we could, but lived our separate lives?

As good as it felt now to pick back up, what would it feel like when he left again? And again?

And again?

Bigger questions lay behind all those. Questions I'd been stuffing back in the boxes they kept sneaking out of. Questions like *when will I see the world?* And *If not guiding, then what will I do? Who am I if not this?*

I turned my attention to our destination to get my mind off the heavier weight of Devin and Ellie. Of adulting and decisions and futures. Right now, we needed to get home. The rest could unbox itself then.

The ridges overhead shifted every now and then, revealing new rock formations or wooded hills. Canyons funneled here and there, hiding behind other mountains as we approached. In general, the landscape didn't look familiar, but I hadn't hiked this far up this stream before. Besides, a mountain looked distinct from one direction and completely different from another. The most familiar places could be completely changed in the space of only a few steps.

Still, I couldn't help but wonder if this was the *right* stream.

My footsteps were slower today, held back by hunger. We slipped to the stream several times to keep drinking, but my empty stomach became more offended. The water slipped away from my belly too quickly and left me ravenous. Not only that, but the stream narrowed in size.

"Dev," I said with a croak. I cleared my throat. How long had I been lost in thought? "I'm not sure we're in the right canyon."

He paused. "Me either."

That troubled me more. "Why didn't you say something?" I asked, and it came out sharper than I intended.

"I wasn't sure."

I rubbed a hand across my forehead. So much for him taking a backseat and letting me control this ride. "Maybe I didn't understand the ridges the way I thought. I could have sworn . . ."

In vain, I tried to draw up a mental picture of the map, but it was too complicated to pull from memory. My instinct told me to head south a little more, maybe circle that way to get back to our original campsite, and then the truck. But what if we were too early? We couldn't have gone *that* far south the night we'd escaped.

Could we?

Devin glanced overhead, then crouched down, braced a stick between two rocks, and marked the tip of the shadow with a rock. Mac used to make a shadow compass in the same way, as a method of gauging what direction was north and south. Dev straightened again.

"Let's make sure we're still heading the right way," he said. "Might be a good time for a break, anyway. We'll give it thirty minutes, then make sure we're in the right direction."

"Good idea."

We took a moment to rest. Sweat dried on my arms. I brushed off the gritty white powder that remained on my skin and tried not to think about how delicious a box of crisp, salty fries would taste right then. My legs ached. Despite frequent drinking, my head still felt dizzy and my mouth was dry.

Devin grimaced every now and then if he moved his head too quickly, and I wondered if he'd have lasting effects from such a nasty blow to the head. I leaned back on a rock and closed my eyes. He put a gentle hand on my shoulder that jolted me awake a few minutes later and gestured toward where the shadow had moved on the ground.

"We're still heading west."

I frowned. Then why did this look so unfamiliar? Perhaps I didn't know the mountains as well as I thought. Our options weren't great. If this wasn't the right stream, at least it headed down. But where we'd land, I wasn't quite sure. Some streams just disappeared into the ground, and then we could really be stuck. Others kept trickling through the mountains until they dried out. Eventually, if we kept walking to the west, we might run into some ranches or farmlands. But if we were too far south, we'd just keep walking into the forest.

That couldn't be right, either.

If we were that far south, we should have been walking all night to make up the same distance we'd covered all that day. I couldn't recall we'd hiked that long. No, we just needed to keep going.

"Well." His forehead ruffled as he glanced up at the sun. "We're definitely not heading farther into the mountains east of here, which means we have to intersect with *something* else eventually."

I pointed behind us. "Not *those* mountains. But this range winds around a lot. We could skirt basins or inadvertently turn up the wrong canyon. It would take us deeper into the forest."

He nodded reluctantly. "True."

I sighed and pushed my frustration back. This wasn't Devin's fault. My short temper was probably more hunger and dehydration than anything else. Still, it rankled me that we couldn't find our way. Me, the adventure guide. Him, the Marine.

"Keep following the stream?" I asked.

He shrugged. "Let's see what happens. If it's the right stream, we may be able to find another hiker by nightfall."

* * *

The onset of twilight—and a dwindling stream bed with no lake or familiar landscape to be found—brought the simmering grumpiness in both of us to an ugly point. Cool air descended as the sun disappeared. My sweat-soaked clothes would be miserably chilly in no time at all.

Dried sweat, salt, and dirt made my shirt stiff as the sun melted beneath the trees and pulled darkness in her path. No longer did I fear Kimball or Steve. They were long gone from my mind, because who could have followed us here? We were in the middle of nowhere. Now, I feared only myself.

Had I been arrogant enough to think that I knew *all* of these mountains? That I was ready to be an adventure guide at twenty years old? All the quiet trudging and silence had given me more than enough time to think about why I insisted *this* be my life. I still hadn't figured it out, and that seemed like an uglier conclusion.

What was I trying to prove?

Mountains had always been tricky. Terrain that looked familiar could change within a few steps and a different angle. Ravines were always deeper, or ridges higher, or summits hid other bigger summits. But getting knocked down a peg didn't feel great—not on an empty stomach. It spurred bigger questions I wanted to answer even less.

Did I *really* want this for the rest of my life?

Devin stood at the edge of the narrow stream we'd followed all day, hands on his hips. Deepening lines of concern cluttered his face now. At some point, it seemed like one of us should have pointed out the obvious—this stream wasn't going to empty into a lake. Looking back, I couldn't pinpoint a single moment that seemed like the best time to make that call.

"We're going to run out of water," I said.

My throat felt dry from the hot air all day long. It baked off the rocks and surrounded us in a sticky, hot embrace. We'd slowed significantly the past several hours, and I tried to convince myself it was to conserve strength, not for utter lack of energy. The last time we'd eaten had been at lunch yesterday, so we wouldn't die of starvation soon.

It just *felt* like it.

Devin didn't say anything, just changed his gaze to stare out at the trees. Usually, by now, we could expect to see some sign of the reservoir in the distance. That alone would tell us where to go, but all we faced now were hills of craggy rocks and a thick forest.

Where had we gone wrong?

The question lingered in the air between us, which had grown with tension the last several hours. Perhaps he blamed himself while I blamed myself and, meanwhile, neither of us really knew where to go. While we didn't argue, our friendly questions and banter had long since quit, and we spoke in single-word replies more often than not. Devin's occasional mumble to himself set me on edge. Was he slipping into a hallucination the way he warned me? But when I tuned in, it always ended up a mutter about a shoelace that wouldn't stay tied.

"I think we should stay here," I said as I struggled to sit on a boulder. I put my head in my hands and relished the lack of movement. "We sleep and recover for the night, then make the decision on what to do next in the morning."

His jaw tightened. "That is one option," he said in a diplomatic tone that meant he didn't like it. "But if you can push through, I think we should go farther. There's a chance . . ."

He faded away. A chance that we'd find something other than *this*? The same backdrop we'd stared at for days now? Not knowing what to say, I let the conversation drop. We sat there for several more minutes before he dropped next to me on the boulder like a bag of rocks.

"I just want to get out of here," he said.

"Me too."

"Then let's keep walking on this path and see where it takes us."

I groaned. My feet already felt like splitting apart and so did my legs. Sleep would at least take me away from the gnawing hunger and anxiety of our unknown location. Another hour of walking would only take us into the exact same terrain and hopelessness we'd wandered into all day.

"Disagree," I said with equal firmness. "We're tired, lost, and I don't think we should make decisions right now."

"We're going to be tired *and* hungry in the morning."

"We're hungry now," I snapped.

He let out a forced breath. I gritted my teeth and closed my eyes. "I'm sorry. I shouldn't have snapped. We're both tired. I just . . . I don't know what to do anymore. We should have backtracked and found our original camping spot. It was the freshest path in our mind and might have been the smartest."

"That way didn't have water, and we wouldn't have been able to do that in the middle of the night while running for our lives. We couldn't have scaled that ridge. The path we took was our only option."

His voice remained tense, like a thin veneer of politeness held him together and threatened to break at any moment.

"It had some water," I said. "But mostly it had familiarity. We could have been back to the old campsite by now where there's plenty of water."

"Without *water* on the way," he ground out. "We have no containers to hold it in, like we did yesterday."

All my patience evaporated in a heartbeat. I shot to my feet. "Yes, Dev," I retorted. "Without as much water *on the way*. But at least we would have enough water *and* a path back to the truck now."

"With no keys! Remember? You kept the keys with you."

The words *Instead of leaving them hidden in the truck* remained unsaid between us. I recalled our conversation before we'd left with gritted teeth. Growing up, we'd always ditched the keys near the truck just in case we did something unexpected—like jumping off a small waterfall—and lost them. But as an adult and a professional guide, I hadn't expected a posse of drug dealers to steal our stuff after tying me up and almost killing Devin.

My mouth opened to reply, but snapped shut because he was right. The truck keys were in my bags. Which could be burned to a crisp for all I knew, along with hundreds of dollars of camping equipment—some of which I'd grown very fond of through the years. The thought sent another frisson of annoyance through me.

"I did," I replied. "I took my keys with me and now we're locked out. But the truck had a road and a road leads to something and it's far easier to walk through than *this*."

He closed his eyes, his face a mask of frustration that I under-stood. But heat rolled through me now and I couldn't have tempered it if I wanted to. After keeping my boxes stowed away all day while our *known* path dwindled into territory we'd never seen before, the boxes hummed with the force of my frustration.

They were about to explode.

"Well, it's too late to backtrack now," he said evenly, with an obvious attempt at patience. "I think we should just keep going while we have light. We might run into someone or something and not have to stay here."

My mind spun as I attempted to cobble a plan together. We *could* backtrack, but we'd lose almost all day getting to the point where we could resume our previous trail to the first campsite. We'd have water access, but no food. No animals except for rodents and skittish deer found us today, but every hour we remained out here increased our odds of an encounter. If we did make it back to the right spot easily, we'd still have to cut farther south through rough terrain, with little water, and find the campsite again.

It wasn't a great plan, but neither was his.

"I want to sleep on it and decide in the morning," I said through gritted teeth. "That's my proposed plan. Unless you can tell me where we are and exactly where you want to end up tonight?"

His expression hardened, and I hated myself for being more attracted to him than ever. "You can't tell me where we are either," he replied.

"I never said I could."

"Then why are you putting that on me?"

"Because you want to keep walking in the dark and I think that isn't wise. If movement is your desire, it's responsible enough that we prove the plan out first."

"We don't have time for this!" he cried.

"We don't have time for *anything,* Dev!"

Our voices rang through the trees in an unnerving way. We'd spent the whole day being carefully quiet just in case Kimball did follow. Now, it seemed absurd. No one could have followed our erratic trail, and we'd given up trying to be sneaky long ago. We'd trekked next to the stream for the past four hours.

Neither of us had truly shouted just now, but the intensity was far greater than our usual conversations. His cheek twitched like an errant tick. I couldn't fathom what must be running through his mind right now.

"I just . . ." I hesitated. "I don't think it's our best plan, Dev. Not when we're this tired, even if there's still daylight to burn."

"Fine." He threw his hands in the air. "We sleep here. We wake up in the morning. We backtrack and try to map our trip home. Then when you find out that we were going the right way all along and just needed to give it more time, you'll feel really dumb."

"That's not going to happen! We would have found Red Lake by now." I gestured to the stream, only two feet across now and burbling in a shallow run of rocks that was hard to even get a cupped hand underneath. "The stream is dying! Even if we keep going, we'll lose our water then, too. We need sleep, Dev. Will you just trust me?"

The words escaped me before I could stop them, and once they broke free, I couldn't pull them back. I held my breath when a startled expression crossed his face. An interminable seven seconds passed while he considered his response. What would he say to such an audacious question after all I had—and hadn't—done the past three years?

Trust was not something either of us had earned.

Not lately.

"I want to," he whispered with a heavy frown. His eyes met mine, then dropped. "I want to."

"You don't?"

The question came out of me in a dying whisper. It slipped free with a quick stab in the heart as it passed. Of course, he didn't trust me. Why should that surprise me? It did surprise me—more than I would have ever admitted.

He ran a hand through his hair and turned away. I opened my mouth to say something else, but clamped it shut again. Wasn't his answer enough? I closed my burning eyes and stumbled a few steps away.

This wasn't our first disagreement. We had them all the time in high school. Some of them days long because neither of us would back down. One had lasted a week. We didn't speak to each other at all.

I'd never had this awful feeling in the pit of my stomach. Not then. Because *then* I knew that if he was angry at me, it would be fine. Dev always came back. Emotions were just emotions. Back then, boxes didn't exist and Mama didn't whisper to me from the depths of the grave. Now, I knew differently.

Men leave.

Love dies.

You take care of yourself.

They always leave, Mama whispered now and I didn't have the energy to shove her into the back of my mind where she belonged.

Emotions weren't just emotions. They were tidal pools deep enough to drown in. They were miasmas. Places to lose yourself. Things that swept you away on a current you never asked for. Emotions were better left boxed up because left to their own accord, they wreaked havoc.

My nostrils flared in a poor attempt to control the boxes. On their own, they started to unpack, spilling frustration, annoyance, fear, and panic. The chaos flooded my mind all at once and occupied most of my mental thoughts. Slowly, one at a time, I reined them back in. Tucked them into their rightful places until I had a better grip on . . . everything.

Go back, I told them. *Not now. Not. Now.*

Minutes passed while I got myself back under control. Eventually, I could judge my decision to sleep first through a different lens. Was it wrong to suggest we stay here? No, that plan was best. We'd only lose ourselves even more at night and risk another injury.

Devin had wandered close to the creek to drink and brood and stare at the rocks as if they held all the answers in their gray depths. Thick trees and bracken surrounded us until I spotted a place where I could clear out a hollow beneath quakies and have a spot to hide. Whether I hid from Steve, Kimball, or Devin, I didn't know anymore. Regardless, tonight would be a cold night. The chill already brought goosebumps to my arms. I felt so tired, however, that the cold may not matter.

With trembling, weary hands, I cleared out a place to lay down beneath a grove of saplings. Thick bushes cluttered their roots with foliage that created a little canopy. Two trunks rested against my back and provided a morsel of safety. Something firm behind me and close overhead felt like a wild cocoon, though still not as solid as Devin's arms.

Devin didn't return to the spot where we'd stopped or follow me. He just stood near the stream like an immobile statue. Had I pushed him back into an episode? I almost crawled out of my wooded nook, but I stopped. Not yet. He needed time.

We both needed time.

I lay on my side and watched his silhouette through the leaves. A thick darkness fell, bringing the quiet hum of nightlife. Singing bugs. Rustling wings. The distant tinkle of the brook. One muscle at a time, my body began to relax. Memories of our other fights passed through my mind. They were so long ago, the origins of the fights eluded me. None of them stuck in my head, which meant none of them mattered.

Except for one thing.

Devin had always initiated the apology. Even when I tried to get there first, somehow he beat me to the punch. After a disagreement over something when we were sixteen, he showed up with three pink roses just as I left to apologize at his house. He'd bummed a ride from a friend and beat me to it.

Do you trust me? I had asked.

I want to.

Sleep would be a long time coming.

DEVIN

How had I messed things up already?

The moment I snapped at her, I regretted it. The flare of fire in her eyes told me I'd crossed a line. Certainly not my first time making her angry, but when I'd done so before, it hadn't been this scary. High school Ellie had a temper, to be sure. But high school Ellie hadn't yet proven just how stubborn she could be.

Three-years-without-talking-stubborn carried a lot of weight behind it.

The thought that I may have just destroyed everything I came back to accomplish barreled through my mind. Ellie had cut me off before. She'd turned her back to me at prom and never once looked back. She didn't show up to my farewell dinner and managed to be out of town when I made it home.

Maybe I shouldn't have been so vague when I responded to the question of whether I trusted her or not. I could have reassured her that I did, that things were fine. I dismissed that thought as soon as it came. No, we both needed and deserved the truth. It had to be said. How could I expect her to trust me if I didn't tell the absolute truth anyway?

While I felt I bore most of the responsibility between what had happened with us lately, she had skin in this trust game too. She was the one who never gave me a chance to explain. Who worked hard for three years to avoid me. The only way any connection had happened again was because I surprised everyone.

That kind of avoidance determination scared the hell out of me.

My mind wandered back to my original purpose for coming home in the first place: to tell Ellie the truth. Never again would I walk into another deployment or day without Ellie knowing that I had loved her all my life.

But now that I tried to do the right thing, I realized that it wasn't so easy. I'd come out here with a heroic determination to have it said . . . but life seemed to thwart my every attempt.

Really, there may never be a "right" time to tell Ellie that I loved her. Maybe my hidden feelings for her would be the great secret of my life. The unexplored trail I would never conquer. Ellie would be the one that got away.

If I didn't tell her, we could eventually grow apart as friends and into her category of *acquaintances*. That process had already started, anyway. Might not be hard to finish. If I did tell her how strongly I felt, it might frighten her away forever, too. If I never meant that much to her, could she really be that for me?

The question haunted me sometimes. Especially when I realized those bleak Afghani nights, and how the hope of reuniting with her had carried me through.

Second only to that was the concern over her massive, hulking, unscalable mental walls. Everything she felt remained locked down so tight, I wasn't sure what she really thought. Did *she* even know?

My eyes closed on that question, and I wished I could open them onto a different scenario. Besides, she was right. I was too tired to make a wise decision, and the decision of what to do and where to go next needed to be a wise one.

We needed food. We were lucky to have as much hydration as we did today, now we had to make the most of it somehow. Stars popped out overhead. I shifted, my body tight with tension and fatigue. My stomach growled in protest again, and I dreamed of a steamy, hot shower. That thought, tangled so closely with my argument with Ellie, led my mind down different paths that I had to shut down.

I sighed, then turned to leave. Her voice stopped me in my tracks.

"I'm sorry."

I froze.

"I'm sorry that I snapped at you tonight," she continued quickly. "I think we're both tired. I'm sorry that we don't know where we are. I . . ." She let out a long breath. "I'm sorry that I've lost your trust. It's deserved. I . . . abandoned you right when you needed me the most."

She nearly choked on the words, and so did I. We hadn't faced each other yet, which seemed to make all of this a little easier. A tension deep, deep inside that I didn't know that I held onto released.

"You gave me a chance to tell you what my life was like when we parted." She exhaled softly. "Now I want you to tell me what it was like for you."

Had I ever expected to have this opportunity? To talk about *my* side of the last three years felt like a luxury. I'd been so focused on Ellie that I hadn't thought much of myself. Maybe that was part of our problem.

In fact, I wasn't even sure she'd see this situation the same way as me or if she'd see blame in herself. She had, though. Openly admitted she had been wrong too, which went a long way in repairing some of that broken trust.

Did I want this opportunity to be wholly truthful with her now?

A little bit, as frightening as it was.

In the days that followed prom, I'd oscillated through every emotion. Mostly, I just tried to stem the rage. I'd been frustrated that she ignored me, then stressed that she'd *keep* ignoring me. Anxiety over what it meant to be without Ellie in the world kept me up at night. Terror that we'd never reconcile or reunite haunted me during the day.

All the emotions had been a rolling, jumbled ball deep in my gut that I didn't untangle for years. Now it sat inside me like a heavy weight that I didn't realize I'd been carrying all this time.

Silence had fallen without me realizing it. So had nighttime. When I turned to face her, the dark made it almost impossible to see her features. Only a bright sliver of moon overhead set a gentle glow on her hair and brow.

"I thought a part of me had died," I said.

Her face fell.

"And I think it did. I felt betrayed by your silence. I knew if I could just explain my decision then you'd get it. You'd have totally understood and we could put all of that behind us. I wouldn't have had to go alone into that new world."

For a moment, I paused. Did I want her to feel the full weight? The words came fast once I let them flow. If I let them go, she'd know exactly how much it had sucked.

Yes.

We needed to do this.

"Although I never would have admitted it," I continued, "I was terrified. Freaking out inside. I wrote you letters, but it never felt right to explain it that way. Plus, I didn't think you'd read them."

Her eyes closed, her thick eyelashes a shadow against her porcelain skin. "I would have burned them, probably," she admitted softly.

The truth stung. I took a moment to process the intensity of her admission, and kept going with mine.

"When I did come home, you were gone. It sucked. Felt like you'd just abandoned everything we had experienced before for one single, fateful decision. I . . . I was scared by how intensely and how quickly you shut me out. How completely it happened.

There was no forgiveness in your actions. None. For so long I felt like I would have never measured up to you anyway, so maybe that was the best path. Even now, I . . ."

Although I didn't want to admit it out loud, I couldn't help but say it. The words came out.

"Even now, I wonder if you'll ever fully let it go. And if I don't trust you, it's because, at any moment, you could decide to shut me out again. I won't live those three years again, Ellie. And, to be honest, until you asked, I hadn't realized just how deep my fear of this happening again went. It's sort of new to me, too."

My own words cast a bleak pall on the night. Not for the first time, I wondered if there *was* any hope for us. Yes, I could trust her as a friend. Someone to catch up with when I returned to town. Someone held at arms length and consulted for the big times in my life.

Could we go back to the Devin and Ellie that lived and thrived in the details?

We had been strong because of the depth of our affection and trust. Now it had been shattered—on both parts—and the pieces seemed overwhelmingly too small to gather back together.

Only when my thoughts slowed did I realize that she'd made no response and several minutes had passed. She stood a few steps away, eyes luminescent in the moonlight as she swallowed back something.

"I went to your dinner," she whispered.

"What?"

"I watched the entire farewell dinner from the trees outside your property."

My heart sank further into my stomach. Back on that terrible day when I had to smile, act grateful, and pretend I wasn't dying inside, I couldn't believe she didn't show up. Some pipe dream of her appearing in the backyard with a wary, but apologetic, smile had kept me going. The shattered feeling after she didn't show up felt like drowning.

"You were there?" I asked.

She nodded.

I'd even considered the possibility that she might watch from somewhere else. Where else would she go but wild places? I should have looked for her. Maybe I could have just shouted it to her then. Told her everything. Blurted it out quickly so that . . .

No. It wouldn't have mattered.

When had Ellie ever allowed herself to be pinned down?

"The whole dinner," she continued with a thick voice. "I couldn't take my eyes off of it. And I couldn't bring myself to walk into that barbeque and tell you to be safe, even though I wanted to. I've hated myself for it for the past three years."

"Why didn't you come?"

She hesitated, lips parted. "B-because," she stammered. "I . . . I thought that I . . . I had always . . . After prom, I felt . . ." Her nostrils flared and her gaze dropped. "I lost my courage."

The feeling that Ellie had something else to say rattled me, but I couldn't fathom what it would have been. And I wanted to understand, because it felt like the real answer lingered in her words.

Ellie never just *lost her courage*.

I mulled over what she said for several long moments. History would never be erased. Certainly not by hashing it out like this and torturing ourselves with what we *could* have said or did. But there was some comfort in the truth. Regardless of what happened, she'd given me a chance to say my piece, and that meant a lot.

"Thank you," I said. "Thank you for letting me say it and for listening."

She frowned. "Why are you thanking me? I . . . I should have come. I mean, I get why you don't trust me. It's . . . it's fair."

"I wish you would have come. It does help to know that you did come, just not the way I wanted you to."

Ellie wrapped her arms around her middle with a frown. Both of us made concessions tonight after a long and grisly day. The time for emotions had passed. Pragmatism was ready for her spotlight.

"It's getting cold," I said. "We're sweaty and disgusting and probably smell like a bunch of nasty bears, but at least we're not alone, right?"

A hint of a smile played on her face. "You always smelled like this, Dev. I don't know what you're talking about."

I hooked an arm around her neck and reeled her in. "You like it, do you? C'mere. I'll give you a big whiff of it."

Her weak attempts to shove me off told me she wasn't really upset. She sobered when I pulled away, the lines between her eyes thickening.

"Maybe Daniel will be concerned," she said. "I normally check in via satellite text message every night. This will be the second night he hasn't heard from me."

"Can he track your location?"

She nodded. "My phone and radio are with my pack, though."

I shrugged. "Maybe. Doesn't change the fact that we have another night in the mountains, we're hungry, we're tired, our stream is dwindling, and we need to get some sleep. In other words, it's cuddle time."

A weary smile replaced the vague uncertainty in her gaze. She tugged me to a cozy little spot under quaking aspens and bushes. Spiny branches dug into my sides and back when I slithered inside, then pulled her back to my chest. We hid in the foliage where the lack of exposure might help us sleep better.

With Ellie in my arms again, I dropped into sleep.

* * *

The next morning, a bird fluttered through the branches overhead with a high-pitched squawk that brought me firmly out of a dead sleep.

With a groan, I stirred myself awake. I lay on my back, a rock jutting into my ribs. My right arm had fallen asleep where Ellie lay on it. She curled into my side as much as possible, her body tucked into my arm. The fan of her eyelashes opened against my neck with a gentle tickle.

Joe's repeated slamming into me, and a few well-placed punches, still kept me sore now. My stomach simmered angrily, sharp with hunger. I shoved away thoughts of breakfast burritos. Ellie untangled herself from my arm, her hair tumbling onto her shoulders as she surveyed our area through sleepy eyes. Early dawn unfolded around us a crisp, cool scent. We'd ended the day on a high, emotional level, but the cobwebs had cleared overnight.

"Sleep okay?" she asked.

I nodded blearily and rubbed the sleep from my eyes with the heel of my hand. "Yeah. You?"

She nodded. "Thanks for keeping me warm."

I gave her a roguish grin reminiscent of our high school days. "Anytime you need a man to snuggle, you know where I am."

She disappeared into the forest after a quick whack on my shoulder. I staggered over to the stream while my body attempted to wake up, and stared into the sky with a less emotion-cluttered mind.

Ellie had been right to stop us from making decisions while so tired, even if it had been frustrating. Now that morning had come, another plan hatched in my mind and unfolded slowly. When Ellie returned, her hair had been slicked with water and twisted into a braid that lay on her shoulder. She looked a little less disheveled, but her eyes were still bright.

"Thank you," I said. "Not deciding last night was the right thing to do."

Her lips quirked a little. "I know."

Her arrogant wink sent my heart into a whirl. If she did that too much, I'd kiss the breath right out of her, and then where would we be?

Right where I wanted us.

With a little mental slap, I shook that thought away and glanced overhead. "What if we find higher ground and survey where we are? Maybe we can see something that we recognize and go from there."

She nodded. "It's what I was going to suggest. I have no idea where we are," she murmured. The admittance seemed to cost her, because she winced. "There's a ridge over there that would get us high enough. It's a good plan."

She pointed to the west. A tower of rocks jutted through the trees with a daunting climb up the backside of it. That sort of ridgeline and ascent would surely take a lot of energy out of us. At least an hour of climbing up, I'd guess. Slipping, uncertain spots could be treacherous. Sleep had given me a boost of energy to take advantage of, so there was no need for both of us to waste energy.

"I'll go," I said. "You stay here. Conserve your strength."

She shook her head. "We do it together. You don't know what you'll find up there. Both of us should have our eyes on it."

I hesitated, but seeing the firm look of her eyes, didn't protest. Instead, I held out my hand.

"Then let's go."

* * *

At the top, Ellie frowned, panted, and then cursed under her breath. While I surveyed the greater view of the horizon and tried to gain my bearings, a sense of puzzlement settled over her. She glanced behind us, then to the north again. Before I could make sense of it all, she muttered in astonishment, "No way."

"What?"

Ellie shuffled closer so our shoulders touched, then pointed to the north. Her arm led out, gesturing to the northwest.

"That's where our original camp was."

"What?"

"I'm certain of it. See the ridgeline? We crawled over that, then went north there."

While her fingers traced an invisible path, my mind scrambled the location together with quick, sporadic memories. At the time of hiking it, I'd paid more attention to Steve and Kimball, but I'd still tried to memorize as much of our surroundings as possible. Although we viewed the route from an entirely different angle, I saw the path that she meant.

"We came too far south?"

A troubled expression creased her brow. She licked her lips, and I wondered if her mouth was as dry as mine.

"Yes. That first night, we must have gone farther than I thought. I think we sort of made a circle yesterday evening. We were heading south, but then we angled southwest, then west, and now we're looking to the northwest. Look at the river down there? It curls. It's subtle, but it winds a bit. See that glimmer on the horizon?"

My heart nearly stopped and I felt a rush of euphoria. Glimmer, indeed. That glimmer indicated the reservoir at Pineville, which needed to be in the north. Relief rushed through me as I clapped her on the shoulder.

"Ellie, my guide. You have saved us!" I held up both hands in an expression of surrender and said. "I fully admit that I was wrong, you were right. If we had gone with my plan last night, we would have kept walking into the woods and been totally screwed."

"Agreed, minion. Your subservience is accepted."

I laughed. She grinned, but eyed the path of the stream and canyon below. Indeed, it turned vaguely west/southwest around another mountain ridge, taking us farther from our ultimate goal. We would have stumbled all day for nothing.

She managed a wan smile.

"*Now* can we go back to our old campsite?"

Chapter Nineteen

ELLIE

The silky tops of grasses tickled my fingers as we slipped through a mountain meadow. We'd been hiking for several hours, and I guessed the time to be about noon. Wildflowers stirred as we passed, our gazes fixated on an open tract of the mountain that lay beyond this one. A familiar meadow appeared back there.

A very *familiar* meadow.

The place where we'd first camped with Steve and Kimball when the thunder rolled through.

Had that happened ages ago?

The relief that had flowed through me this morning when I recognized where we stood buoyed me up now. We'd be able to find our way back to the truck. We didn't have the keys, and Kimball and Steve could have beaten us back and slashed our tires, but at least we had a location.

Either way, we'd have to walk to Pineville, but it would be on a road far easier than this. Angry red scratches and scrapes filled my arms. Devin had one across his left cheek. A few holes littered my shirt near the bottom from branches and brambles that reached for us in the thickest bracken. I didn't want to see another gully filled with bushes ever again.

Our surroundings now were vaguely familiar. I was certain I had hiked them before. Maybe I had brought my dog Thor here in the past. We'd camped at that campsite several times. Seemed likely we might have ventured down here.

A quiet feeling lay over the mountaintop, like the calm before a rainstorm. Clouds scudded over the sky, keeping the temperature cooler. We'd moved away from water after drinking until our stomachs hurt, so the calm warmth felt like a gift. Dreams of a savory BLT dripping with butter and a crisp salad filled my mind as we walked.

"Is it really hot on the east coast?" I asked.

Devin snorted. He walked only a few paces behind me, the crunch of his boots on the ground a comforting sound.

"As hell. It's so humid. Not as bad on the coast, near the ocean, but still . . . it's not like this."

My thoughts ran over his reply. I'd never grappled with humidity before. Had never seen the ocean or other places. Mountains rarely battled moisture, particularly with how dry things had been this year.

"Do you miss it?"

He shrugged. "The humidity? Definitely not. The east coast? It's not so bad. I have a few friends there."

"Any potential girlfriends?"

The quick question startled me as much as it seemed to startle him, especially considering our conversation about this topic yesterday. Before I could berate myself for asking *again*, he saved my pride and laughed it off.

"There are women I work with, but none that I spend a lot of time with outside of the job. Are you jealous?"

"Yes."

He paused, then grinned in a loopy way. "Really?"

I tried to keep it light and shrug it off, but my tone gave me away. "I've missed spending time with you."

"Oh." Shock riddled his tone. "I'm . . . glad to hear that."

To salvage my pride, I kept walking. We neared the edge of this meadow and would only need to push through what appeared to be a band of trees before the next one opened up. Brush cluttered the floor at the base of a quaking aspen field. I pushed one large bush aside with my knee.

"Will you come visit me?" he asked.

"Can I?"

"Of course. Would you actually come?"

"Yes. As soon as I could."

"Really?"

The lilt in his tone indicated a deeper surprise than I expected. I glanced at him from over my shoulder.

"Really," I said.

"You just . . . I wasn't sure you'd want to come. Have you left Pineville since I did?"

My brow furrowed. "Not yet. Not beyond Jackson City."

"Do you want to?"

"So much."

A startled expression crossed his face, leading back to the goofy smile that I'd missed more than anything.

"Then let's do it. Come and see me. I'll let you know my schedule. Probably have a long weekend coming up, or something. Or you can just come and stay for as long as you want and we'll hang out after work. Things won't be quite as intense right after leave and we get put back together from deployment."

I smiled. "Agreed."

We turned our attention back to the copse of trees. The thick brambles forced us to wade through grasses high and thick, the thorns scraping our arms while the leaves trailed gently on my skin. My mind spun over the shock in Devin's voice. Did he think I'd be one of those people that lived and breathed Pineville and never left?

And . . . hadn't I been?

There was nothing wrong with staying in my hometown,

except that it didn't feel fun anymore. I wanted to see more of the world just as much as I wanted to anchor in the mountains when I returned.

So why hadn't I traveled?

No answer surfaced through the vague haze that had become my mind.

For the next ten minutes, we slowly worked our way through the young grove. Sunlight angled through the tree branches overhead and fell on my shoulders. I couldn't wait to get into a hot shower and scrub the grease out of my hair. Devin had fallen quiet at my back, only the gentle swish of his pants as he walked and the low, quiet thud of his boots.

I stumbled over a rock as we neared the edge of the meadow. Devin grabbed my shoulder with a little hiss, then yanked me the rest of the way to the ground. My breath rushed out of me, but movement out of the corner of my eye sealed my lips shut before I could protest. On our stomachs, Devin pointed to the northeast, not far from where we'd first made camp.

"Steve," he mouthed.

My stomach twisted with a cold fist of dread. We held our breaths to listen. At first, I heard nothing. Then a voice, which definitely belonged to Steve. And another voice.

Kimball.

With a deep sigh, I closed my eyes and pressed my forehead onto a rock in disbelief. No. Way. Somehow, they'd made their way back to our original campsite at the exact same time as us?

Devin had gone on full alert, his hands pressed into the ground as he occasionally rose up to see them, then lowered back down.

"They're thirty yards away," he murmured. "Not aware of us as far as I can tell. No signs of a new camp, but I can't be sure. They may have just arrived."

"Do they have our bags?" I whispered.

He hesitated, peered up again, then nodded. "Steve has your bag on his back. He's taking it off. Not sure about mine yet. No sign of any of the other guys, but I'd bet they split off from each other."

"I hope their shoes are melted and their feet are burned raw from the fire," I muttered.

Dev snorted.

We'd just been loudly tromping through the trees, talking about me visiting him. A promise that our life after this would be filled with each other. Now that was all thrown back into question again. The frustration set me on edge.

"What do you suggest?" I asked.

"We lay low. They're probably here to backtrack and get to their truck, just like us."

Their figures were distant enough we couldn't see all the details, but at least I could see that they hadn't moved. Steve seemed to lounge against a tree. Kimball, sitting on a stump or something.

"So why aren't they going already?"

He shrugged. "Not sure. Maybe a break."

"Can we tail them? Follow them down the mountain? If they have my bag, we can get my keys that way."

Devin's mind moved behind his glassy eyes, and I wondered if he shared my thoughts. My pack had the radio, my phone, the truck keys, water, food—if they hadn't eaten it all—and a permanent escape. Without that bag, we could still be another day or two from eating, depending on how long it took us to travel the road back.

We could skirt around them and get down the mountain first, but then what? If they had the truck keys and we had to walk, they'd eventually pass us on the road. Unless we walked in the trees and avoided the road, but that would only prolong our time out here. Now, they even blocked our water access.

In other words, we needed that pack.

Devin stared, gaze tapered into slashes. His fingers had curled around a clump of weeds and tightened in thought. I pushed off the ground to peer over the top of the grass. Two figures shifted along the far tree line, seemingly oblivious to our presence. Steve stood against a tree, my pack at his feet. Kimball regarded something in his hands. A radio, perhaps? Who would they speak to out here? I doubted they kept in contact with the other scrawny cronies.

I lowered back down. Just the sight of them made me want to throw up.

"Dev? We have to get that pack."

His hand released the grip around the grass. He turned to me, blinking out of deep thoughts, and said, "I have a plan."

* * *

Ten minutes later, my heart hammered in my throat. I crouched behind a chokecherry bush, then hustled behind another. I stepped carefully and swung a wide path behind Steve and Kimball. They spoke quietly and only intermittently, mere flashes of grubby color amongst the foliage.

Silently, I stalked through the forest on my hands and knees, close enough to see them, but far enough they wouldn't hear me. Based on their loud voices and lack of attention, they likely hadn't noticed anything. Heat rose from the ground, dampening the air from the dissipating morning dew. Not a hint of wind stirred to provide sound cover. My breath landed like bombs.

When I thought I'd found the right spot Devin told me to take, I paused. Their voices were still audible, though muffled. After a few seconds to ensure no one else crept up on me, I ducked down to crawl toward Kimball and Steve. Rocks poked the sensitive skin on my thighs, bruising muscles and skin as I hurried over them. Dirt coated my palms and stirred my nostrils with a dry scent. I dodged grasses and bushes as best I could to avoid jostling them and inched along in an excruciating crawl.

What felt like an eternity later, I stared at Steve's back from no less than fifteen feet away.

The pack lay on the ground next to him now. He slumped to the earth with his back to the tree where he had been standing. His profile glowered at the forest. In the bright light of day, he appeared pale. His eyes were drawn. Had the pixie dust before the fight aged him like this? Or had life been so unfair?

Whatever the answer, it didn't matter now.

I lowered all the way to the ground near a cluster of bushes. Steve and Kimball were still visible through thick branches that sprouted small, clattering green leaves. The stream we'd used when we first camped lay across the meadow, so they wouldn't walk past me to get water. Steve and Kimball shouldn't see me unless they walked closer and searched the ground. I fervently hoped they didn't.

Once settled, I waited for Devin to enact his part of the plan.

My heart thudded against my ribcage while the sounds of the forest filled my ears. This low to the ground, the dirt seemed to move. Tiny bugs crawled over mounds, roots, and pieces of rock at the end of the grass blades near the dry dirt. I turned my focus back to the two men. With concentration, I could make out what they said.

"He said noon," Kimball snapped.

"What time is it?"

Kimball threw his hands in the air. "How am I supposed to know? Not noon. The sun isn't high enough in the sky. I think," he tacked on.

Steve tilted his head back to scrutinize the sky, then frowned at the dirt again. Who would they meet *here*? Kimball turned to face Steve, which gave me a full glimpse of his profile. Dirt marred his face and fatigue lined his eyes. Clearly, they had a few rough nights also, which wouldn't make them more amenable to me if they found me. I couldn't bring myself to feel sorry for them.

"We wait as long as we have to wait," Kimball muttered, more to himself than to Steve. "Which . . . whatever."

Another silence fell. I lowered my chin so I could still see them if they moved, but didn't have to hold my head up. Minutes passed. A lazy sun fell through the trees in a lattice of light that moved gently across the forest floor. Warmth rose from the ground while I entertained myself with dreams of pizza with cheese so thick it dripped off the sides.

A huge splash broke the quiet.

Trees rustled near the creek like crashes of thunder, jostled so hard the branches knocked into each other. Steve turned to look over his shoulder. Kimball straightened, and his head popped up like a gopher.

A deep, rumbling sound followed that made the hair on the back of my neck stand up. A giggle threatened to bubble out of me, but I held it back by sheer willpower. Devin used that same growl as an imitation of a bear to play pranks on his sister, Kendra, when we camped with his family. He'd prowl around outside her tent and shake it with that sound in the middle of the night. Her shrieks of fear—then sisterly rage—echoed in my memories now.

"What was that?" Kimball hissed.

Steve paled further. I rolled my lips together and wondered if this wild desire to burst into laughter was a sign of lost sanity. I wanted nothing more than to laugh until my stomach hurt, despite the tension in the air. Devin and I had one shot to get those keys. I couldn't mess it up with amusement.

They paused, and another long silence followed. My levity faded as I realized just how many ways this patched-together plan may *not* work. Another cluster of trees rustled, these a few paces closer. Steve rose, then stumbled back.

"That damn bear!" he cried. "The one Neils spoke about."

"Shut up, you idiot!" Kimball muttered. "That bear wasn't real."

Kimball also rose to his feet and started to back away. Another guttural, rolling sound from the bushes followed. My stomach ached as I held back another laugh. It sounded like Devin grunted as he choked on a bone. But they didn't notice the awkward, strangled sound. Instead, they kept backing away.

Neither of them remembered the pack.

The same clump of trees trembled again. Devin lay on the ground, just like me, while he made it appear that something ominous stalked toward them. Steve jolted when his back ran into a tree. He let out a cry and scrambled farther away. I inched forward. The pack was at least fourteen feet away, but they retreated and I advanced with every second. Since it lay on the ground, I had a very vague hope of drawing it away before they noticed it was gone.

Kimball stopped, almost fifteen feet away from where they had been. He paused, gaze tapered, when Devin gave another low growl. I forced my body to continue to crawl. Disbelief that this had worked so far hurried me along. I doubted they'd fall into our hands this easily for long.

"I can't see it," Kimball muttered. "Can't be a bear. We'd see it . . . right?"

"Cubs?" Steve asked.

Kimball's expression darkened. "Hope not. Go take a look."

"You take a look."

"You want him to freak out if something happens to me? He'll blame you and kill you."

"Why would he kill me? He doesn't care about you."

Kimball muttered something while I closed another three feet between me and the pack. Eight feet left and they hadn't noticed me yet. Devin let out another growl, but this time Kimball's alert stare became more suspicious. When nothing jumped out to attack them, their immediate fear faded.

Steve pushed away from the tree where he leaned. "Something else?" he asked quietly.

As one, they moved closer to the sound. Devin had wisely positioned himself so they stepped away from the bag instead of returning. They slanted at an angle to where I lay, allowing me to crawl forward again.

Five feet.

The sound of bracken crunching under their shoes echoed through the meadow as they continued to advance. I scooted my body across the dirt with the terrible realization that they could probably see Devin now. He'd face a decision point soon: he'd have to reveal himself and draw their attention or stop acting like a bear. If he stopped the noises, they might abandon the search, which would possibly expose me when they returned.

Which meant he'd reveal himself soon.

As if they sensed Devin's hesitation, the two of them paused. Frantic, I scurried the rest of the way to my bag, clamped my hand on it, and pulled. Steve glanced up, as if he heard the pull of canvas against the ground. I froze, my breath held, as Steve started to scan. His gaze roved to the left and headed right for me. I lay in the open, sprawled on the ground. He'd be able to cross the space between us in less than ten seconds. There'd be no matching or dodging those giant fists.

The cry of a voice broke the air.

"Hello, the camp!"

Steve and Kimball jerked to attention and swung their heads the opposite way. A body appeared across the meadow, brought by a familiar pair of green pants. Neils! Sweet baby pineapple, but he had fantastic—and terrible—timing.

Indecision warred within me. Did I call out a warning to Neils, or finish the task? The rustle of bushes not far away reminded me why we were here. With a shake of my head, I turned back to the mission. Once I had the keys and the radio, I'd call out to Neils. Doing so before would doom all of us.

I reached for the outside zipper of my bag seconds before Kimball returned the cry.

"Over here."

Kimball and Steve tensed as Neils approached. I gently tugged on the zipper as Neils slowed to a stop a few steps away. He eyed each of them, as if he could also feel the tension in the air. My heart began to pound. Neils was only doing his job. What if they harmed him? This wasn't fair for any of us, but at least I'd signed onto this hike.

Steve stood with his arms at his side, the permanent glower more apparent on his face. His suspicious glare dodged back to where Devin's bush-shaking had now stopped. Silently, I slipped my fingers into the canvas material and felt around, hoping to feel cool metal against my fingertips.

"What took you so long?" Kimball asked.

I froze.

Did he just ask that question?

"I could ask the same," Neils replied, with his distinctive accent and crisp intonation. "I saw the fire. What happened? Where is Ellie?"

With a sense of deepening dread, I gazed over my bag in their direction. Their heads and shoulders were the most visible part of them from here. Did I have something wrong? Was it Neils that just acted so friendly to them?

Yes, it had to be. The slight accent in his words was a dead giveaway.

"Lost everything, including her."

"What?" Neils snapped.

Kimball sighed. "It was her fault. We started with the hike she suggested, just like you wanted, and then cut across the mountains to the cabin. They almost didn't buy the stupid treasure story, or whatever, but I figured it out. No one knew where we ended up, and nothing appeared suspicious, just like you demanded. When we got to the cabin, we subdued her. Just like you said."

"And?" he drawled, murderous.

A slight hesitation followed. "She . . . got away. She set fire to everything." Bitterness lined Kimball's voice. His words rang with halted frustration. "And by everything, I mean *everything*."

"The dust?"

His voice had hardened into an unmistakable rage that confirmed my worst fears. Neils was in on this. Although the details weren't clear yet, the fact that he had something to do with the pixie dust was abundantly clear now. What did Devin think of this development? Now, we also had to escape a park ranger who knew these mountains even better than I did and had *wanted* me there.

A shiver scooted down my spine and pushed me back to my purpose.

Radio.

Truck keys.

Get the hell out of here.

The gentle rustle of leaves sang behind me for a few seconds before I heard a low whisper.

"Behind you."

Devin lay there, a look of serious concern on his face. He tilted his head to the pack, then raised his eyebrow in silent question. I shook my head back and forth just once. My fingers continued to rummage through my bag, now almost empty. Steve had ditched most of my gear, probably to lighten the load. Maybe I could recover it later. I shook that thought away.

Nope. Didn't want to go back there.

"We gotta go," Devin murmured. "No keys. Let's just get out of here."

My fingertips grazed something cool and hard. I held up a finger from my free hand as shouting rose from beyond us.

"All of the dust and the girl? You idiots! You screwed up everything."

A combined litany of curse words from Kimball and Neils followed. My heart beat faster. All they needed was to glance over. They'd see my shoes or my hair or something distinctive in the trees, and then they'd realize that the suspicious sounds had—even more suspiciously—just stopped for no reason. If they stepped back just a few feet and looked *anywhere*, they'd see me on the ground.

Game over.

My fingertips closed over a jagged key. With a muted cry of triumph, I pinched it between my two fingers and pulled the entire key ring free with the light tinkle of metal on metal. Their rising shouts reverberated through the meadow as I scurried backward, abandoning my favorite bag and all the food and resources inside. We'd have to make it without the radio.

Dirt coated my arms and legs as I folded the keys into my fingers and hustled backward. My body left a clear path in the dirt, but we'd have to take the chance that they didn't follow it. Devin touched my back as I approached so I knew he was there.

"Nice work," he murmured.

"What now?" Neils shouted. "What now? You will repay every damn dime of what you would have made—"

"It wasn't my fault!" Kimball cried. "It was your idea to bring the girl. *You* should have made sure she arrived, not me. You're the one that wanted her. And Collins was going to take her first, just so you know. I wouldn't have touched her, of course."

The syrupy placating of Kimball's tone made me want to vomit. Kind Neils, whom I'd met countless times on the trail. Who acted like my friend. All this time, a diabolical member of a drug ring that destroyed lives and wanted to rape me. *Why* he'd wanted me at the cabin only made me sicker, so I forced the thought away.

"I don't care who was in charge of getting her there!" Neils shrieked. The crack of a palm hitting skin followed. I winced. "You ruined everything and I *still* didn't get my chance with her. You're not worth the risk anymore, Kimball. Maybe you never were!"

Devin looked to me from where he lay on his back. "You ready?" he mouthed.

I nodded.

Dev gazed past us to a thick canopy of trees that dropped into a steep hill. If we were careful not to jostle anything, we'd be out of sight in just a few steps and at the bottom in a few more. Once there, we could slip into more mature trees without so many bushes and be nearly undetectable as we escaped.

Dev looked back at me in silent question, then grabbed my hand and squeezed it. The touch gave me a rush of courage. I nodded.

"Let's do it," I mouthed.

With one glance around us, and as the fever pitch of Kimball and Neils' voices rose, Dev rolled back onto his stomach and began to crawl away, low to the ground. With my heart in my throat, I followed.

Dirt coated my lips from crawling so long on the ground, but I ignored the gritty texture and the taste of loam on my tongue. Instead, I focused on the weight of the keys in my palm. The reassuring texture of metal and freedom and hope against the tender, filthy skin.

We got this, I told myself. *We got this. We'll get out of this area, hit the trail at a run, get back to the truck, and then be home free within an hour.*

We got this.

Then a hand clamped down on my ankle.

And I screamed.

Chapter Twenty

DEVIN

Ellie's scream turned my blood to slush.

I whipped around to find one of Kimball's withered cronies standing over her, a booted foot planted on her back and a leering grin on his face. Ellie struggled valiantly under the pressure of his foot, her limbs flailing. He leaned forward on her ribcage with a guffaw. She grunted against the pressure. Her attempts to shove off the ground by planting her palms on the dirt failed when he kicked her arms out from under her.

Rage built in my body.

"Well, well," he called over his shoulder. "Lookee what I found here. A spy."

The shouting we'd left behind had turned into a fistfight about ten seconds after we'd turned away from the pack. A shot rang out, and the scuffle of fighting calmed.

I shot to my feet, crossed the distance in two steps, and threw myself on top of the man. He fell to the ground with a startled screech, dropping like melted butter under my weight. With jagged, dirty nails, he reached for my face. I grabbed his shirt, yanked him off the ground, and slammed a fist into his nose. He crumbled with a gurgled scream. I hit him in the face again, and he went limp.

Fog flowed into my vision, clouding what I saw. One minute I saw the ragged, graying face of a man that intended harm to Ellie. Blood flowed down his nose and stained his lips. The next I saw Trixie as he lay dying in my arms, skin stained with soot and dirt and blood all over his teeth.

Someone grabbed my shoulder and jolted me out of the hallucination.

"Devin." Ellie's voice rang through my ears. "Devin, let's go."

Go, I thought. *I can't go. We don't leave brothers behind. I have to stay with Trixie.*

I shook my head.

No, I thought. *No, I'm not in Afghanistan. I'm not there. I'm home.*

Despite my struggle against it, the hallucination gained ground and overtook my mind. Smoke clouded the air as I slipped back to Afghanistan. I could still smell the hazy scent. It wound like lacy tendrils past me. What was that smell? Something distinct, like burning rubber but . . . worse. Skin. That was it. Singed hair. Burned skin. Trixie. Trixie was in my arms, his lips moving as he tried to say something.

"Devin!" Ellie cried.

I dropped the body, and it turned back into the rat that wanted to hurt Ellie. My Ellie. Ellie. Ellie wouldn't be in Afghanistan. She didn't speak to me there. My head banged like drums from the inside while I tried to decipher what was real. *I'm not there,* I told myself. *I'm not there. This isn't real.*

I tried to clear the picture with a racing heart. The fog faded. Ellie stood in front of me, hair wild around her shoulders, face lined with anxiety. But she'd always looked scared when I imagined her in Afghanistan. Each time I almost died, she'd been there. Her face had looked so worried.

"Are you real?" I heard myself ask.

Her expression softened. "Yes, I'm real. I'm not a hallucination or a memory. Devin, you're with me." Her hand pressed over her chest. "I'm Ellie. Ellie, your best friend. Ellie, the girl you spent your life with." Her gaze darted away, and then back. "You're not in Afghanistan. You're in the mountains with me."

Mountains.

I tried to peel the haze away as I struggled to my feet. That guy wanted to hurt her. I remembered that. Running down a slope. A pack. Reality slammed back into me all at once.

Kimball.

Steve.

Neils.

She tugged on my arm, then swore under her breath. "We have to go!" she whispered. Shouts from the rise above us grew stronger. Two male figures appeared on the ridge overhead, only a few yards away. I recognized one of them, but just as I remembered his name, it slipped away. Instead, I could hear screams of pain that belonged to Afghanistan. They echoed in my ears and made them ring.

Trixie's choked pleas to stop the agony.

My chest felt tight and my head dizzy. *Breathe,* I told myself. *Breathe.* The command went unnoticed. I thought I saw Trixie lying at my feet in the forest bracken, his arm almost separated from his body, and blood pooling beneath him.

Afghanistan returned with full force again, filled with smoke curling around me and distant shots. Sand in my gums. Heat under my feet and the dust and smoke of a destroyed Humvee choking the air. A shot sounded overhead. I ducked when the sound of, "*Incoming!*" rippled through the air.

"Duck," I cried. "You gotta duck."

"Get back!" Ellie shouted to someone I wasn't aware of. She'd moved. She stood in front of me now. "I wasn't afraid of you before, and I'm not now."

I'm not in Afghanistan, I told myself again. *I'm not there. I'm not there.*

Reality slipped back into place as I frantically tried to catch back up. Forest. Ellie. Running. We had been running . . . but why? It's like I lost time. The flashbacks occurred and I had no idea how much time passed while I struggled to find my mind again.

"Traitor!" Ellie shouted. "You're a traitor, and I'll make sure you go down for this, Neils."

Neils.

Park ranger.

Danger to Ellie.

My mind snapped back into place. The sands of Afghanistan cleared out of my mental landscape. Within half a second, I had Ellie behind me, with my body between her and the men leering at her now with hatred in their eyes.

I'd seen that look before.

Hell, I'd *felt* that look before.

"Let us go," I commanded as Neils skulked closer. "We'll let you go. Mutual pass."

Ellie held onto my shirt behind me, like she didn't want to be parted even a little. It grounded me to know right where she stood.

Neils scoffed. "Right," he drawled with a dramatic roll of his eyes. "I completely believe that you won't tell anyone what you saw here, nor what you did. That the authorities won't be on me in half a second once you get back to your truck."

"Who says they aren't already?"

Neils scoffed, then reached into his belt. A black gun appeared with a flash. My instincts kicked in. I whirled around, bear-hugged Ellie, and threw us to the ground. The sound of shattered wood broke above us seconds later. Ellie let out a muffled groan as I rolled us down the hill, narrowly missing a sapling and plowing through a dense chokecherry bush that grabbed her hair. She let out a little mewl of pain when it ripped a lock of hair free on our tumble down. Gunshots rang behind, hitting the dirt just behind us as we rolled free. The hot ricochet of a bullet whizzed past my ear as I forced us over a crumbling log.

And I dropped right back into Afghanistan.

This time, I lay low in the sand. Night descended around us in utter darkness broken only by a thick band of stars. The whine of bullets sped overhead as we burrowed farther into the sand, plastering our bodies into the ground to get farther and farther away. The sand gritted against my cheek, painful against unwashed skin and the gritty beginnings of a beard. My heart thudded, heavy and fast, as the bullets whizzed by.

My thoughts pulsed like the drum of a heartbeat, an image of Ellie in my head.

I'm so sorry I left you. I'm so sorry I left you.

Amidst the focus and horror of the moment, when I tried not to think of bullets tearing hot through my body and what it would feel like to fade into death, Ellie appeared. Her laugh rang through my mind. Her green eyes regarded me with amusement that faded to concern. When we'd been together in Pineville, she'd always kept a hand near me, even though there'd never been anything implicitly romantic about it.

Always near.

Even before I died.

"Talk to me," I demanded. "Talk to me, Ellie."

"Devin!"

Shocked to hear Ellie's voice *here* in the boiling sands, my head jerked up. The sands melted away. I stared into her eyes with a verdant emerald backdrop of the forest behind and realized.

I'm not there.

Another shot rang out, followed by a scream. The memory stole me away again. This time, for good.

Chapter Twenty-One

ELLIE

His arm felt gritty beneath my fingertips when I touched it. "Dev, it's Ellie. It's me. I'm here. That isn't real."

He paused. "Quiet. They're shooting."

"Ellie," I whispered. "I'm real."

He looked beyond me, then shook his head. The scuffles and shouts from the other snivelly rat that now had a broken nose ceased after the last gunshot. Neils had stopped pursuing us to yell at someone else, which likely meant that the other guy was now dead too.

It gave us a few moments to get out of here.

Where was Steve? Kimball? Had they both already been shot? If that other man could appear out of nowhere, so might someone else.

My hand trembled when I put my palm against Devin's cheek and willed him to return to me. *Come back,* I begged silently. *Please come back.* Terror filled his eyes amidst a backdrop of war. He struggled inside, I could see that. I wanted to soothe it all away and bring him back. Wanted to melt these horrible men into oblivion and forget they ever existed. Devin had demons now.

Demons only *I* could fight.

"Dev, it's me. Ellie. I'm here in the mountains with you. You're not in Afghanistan."

He continued to blink.

"Dev! It's me, Ellie."

"Gotta get out of here," he mumbled, then searched around. He stopped, and his erratic movements paused. He stared around us. I grabbed his shoulder to shake him. "Dev! Please listen. It's Ellie. You're not really there. You're in the mountains."

He shook his head and motioned for me to be quiet, then pressed himself all the way to the forest floor.

"Devin Blaine," I snapped. "You will not go back to Afghanistan, do you hear me? You are here with me, and I need you. We have to get out of here *now!*"

Devin turned to stare at me in a haze of misunderstanding. The vague, distant expression had returned to his glazed eyes. He lay right in front of me, but he was worlds away.

"Stop. Talking," he whispered, then mumbled something about bullets and sand. He flinched and ducked.

Fear like I'd never known slipped through me. How did I get through to him? He wanted me to ground him, but what he'd told me to do wasn't working now. Would he go so far into the hallucination that he'd hurt himself? Me? Neils would catch up to us if we stay here. Kimball probably lay dead somewhere, I assumed, but the sound of fighting continued overhead. *Someone* had to be here still. The chaos of this moment was our only chance to get out. I climbed on top of him, then grabbed his arm and forced him to roll onto his back. He snarled.

I slapped him.

The crack of my palm hitting his cheek brought his eyes back to me. Shocked, he stared at me in wordless confusion. My palm stung like a thousand needles. The sensation frightened me. Had I actually just *hit* him? He gazed at me in blatant question now. I grabbed his face with both hands.

"You are *not* in Afghanistan!" I whisper-cried. "You are here, with me, in the mountains. Where you belong. Where we *both* belong. I need you, Dev. I need you to come back to me and help me here. I need you and I openly admit it. I want you to stay. And maybe you'll leave after all this. Maybe you won't love me the way I love you, but it's a chance I'll take." A suppressed sob weakened my voice. "Because Mama was wrong. Not all men leave. Love doesn't have to die. And I can always take care of myself—even *with* you."

He blinked. Some of the haze slipped away from his eyes.

"Ellie?"

His response was slow and sluggish. The blurry motion of two men grappling in the underbrush came out of the corner of my eye. Steve and Neils? I couldn't tell for sure. They were too close to be safe, so I swiped the errant tear off my cheek, grabbed his arm, and yanked him down the mountain.

"Come on," I whispered. "We have to go."

Devin followed my command, but I couldn't be sure why. My heart felt quick and light with the terrifying sensation of running away, all while my mind threatened to fall into despair. A guttural shout, then another shot, ripped through the mountainside. I flinched. Devin grabbed my arm and pulled me close.

"With me!" he hissed.

He skidded down another precipitous drop with his fingers linked through mine. Dev held me close as we slipped and slid down a slope slippery with thick, fallen leaves. Mossy rocks overgrown with lichen rushed past us as we hurried down another short embankment and came to a stop on hard ground. A waterfall of leaves and rocks fluttered past us when Devin pressed himself against the wall of the embankment and murmured, "Don't make a sound. They'll hear."

Was this Afghanistan Devin or my Devin? I didn't question it yet. My heart bruised my chest as we waited, not even the comforting twitter of birds overhead. Tender, exposed roots curled out of the dry dirt near my cheek. My heavy breaths sent them drifting back and forth, where they tickled my skin with their gentle touch.

Devin stared at me with seemingly lucid eyes, but I couldn't tell for sure.

"Am I about to die?" he whispered. His voice trembled just a little, and the fear in his wide eyes broke my heart. "Each time I almost died, you came to me the moment before I thought everything would end. You looked so scared, just like right now."

The words *each time* echoed through my mind. How many times had there been? They must have been utterly terrifying to still wreak their havoc now, and I hated the circumstances that put him through this.

I reached a trembling hand to his cheek. "No," I whispered. "We aren't going to die. I won't let it happen."

The lie was blatant. At any moment, a bullet could end both our lives so quickly we might never know what hit us. Neils could continue to chase us through the woods and stalk us until he murdered us in cold blood, like the most malevolent kind of predator.

But I had to believe it wouldn't be true.

"And if we do die today," I said in a fierce whisper, "we'll do it together. If I have anything to say about it, Devin Blaine, we will never be parted again."

He leaned into my palm with wide eyes, vulnerable in their ferocity. "Then you are real. You never spoke to me before."

"We won't die. Do you trust me?" I whispered.

"Yes."

His quick reply, without a beat of hesitation, filled me with courage. "Are you back to me?"

"I'm not sure."

"Then let me bring you back."

I grabbed his shirt and jerked him into my chest. He stumbled into me with a silent breath of surprise that I caught with my own. The moment my lips pressed into his, he melted. All the bones disappeared from his body and I caught his weight on top of me. He moved, pressing my back into the embankment, and planted his hands on either side of me to keep from crushing me beneath him. My hands on his face elicited a low groan in his throat. His lips parted to mine. They were warm, hungry, and filled with passion.

They were everything.

They were soulship.

My stomach dropped as he twined his arms around me. His hold felt tight and protective and encompassing and everything I'd ever imagined it would be. Our bodies molded together with the declarative kiss. And now, there was no going back. His hand touched the small of my back, my hips. He reached down and pulled me into his arms until my legs wrapped around his waist and he held all of me.

Sheer exhilaration became my heart.

All the while, my lips didn't leave his, even though my heart fluttered free for the first time. The distant sound of shouts brought me back out of the sky. I pulled away with a gasp. Tears had jolted out of my eyes when I pulled back to look at him. Hunger had overtaken the haze in his eyes. He blinked, peering at me through positively burning want.

"I love you," I whispered frantically. The raw, raspy words sounded in a world of utter stillness.

The anxiety left his face and bled into concern.

"What?"

"I've always loved you," I whispered. My shaking hand found his cheek again. "I love you, Devin. I love you. I love you. You are my best friend and always will be. I loved you in high school and I loved you through your deployments and I love you now. You have my heart. My soul. All of me. I want to spend the rest of my life with you. I don't want to be your friend, your acquaintance, or anything like that. I want to be your soul. I don't even want to be a guide . . . all this time I just wanted *you*."

A cracking twig sounded overhead, not far away. I leaned closer, frantic. Our foreheads pressed together. Pressure built up in my throat as all the boxes unbraided. They spilled every emotion I'd battled since he left and swept out like a tide. His kiss had unraveled everything inside of me. Boxes that were once as strong as steel were now wet cardboard. I didn't even try to replace that stoic facade of indifference that had saved me for so long.

My boxes broke, and I let them go.

Different words flooded free instead.

"I'm sorry," I whispered, gaunt. Tears blurred the dark vision of his astonished expression. "I'm so sorry. If we die, I wanted you to know. I'm sorry that I brought you on this hike and didn't turn us back. I'm sorry that I never gave you a chance to explain. The past three years . . . I've kept us apart. I was stupid and stubborn, and I should have trusted you. I'm sorry, Dev. I'm so sorry that I've loved you for so long and didn't tell you. That's why I didn't go to your dinner and it's why I couldn't talk to you when you came home. Because I loved you so much I couldn't lose you again."

Tears slipped down my cheeks as I gripped his face. Could he feel my wild desperation? The terror of revealing all and knowing I could now lose him all over again? Mama reminded me not to be a fool with a quiet whisper.

Men leave, baby girl, she said. *Love dies. You take care of yourself.*

They leave, my heart whispered, *but the good ones come back.*

Mama disappeared.

His arms came back around me like a steel trap to hold together all the falling pieces. "Ellie," he whispered gently. "*My* Ellie. I have always loved you."

A hot kiss sealed his response and captured my disbelieving sob. He leaned into me until I couldn't breathe, but I took his weight because I wanted all of him. All of whatever he gave. The feeling of being turned inside-out quieted when he pulled away. He leaned back and tucked a piece of hair away. The feeling of his fingertip across the shell of my ear, gentle as a whisper, sent goosebumps through my skin.

An unreadable expression crossed his face just as a trickle of dirt dropped onto his head. Devin flinched and tilted his head back to look up.

Neils stood overhead, pistol dangling at his side. Dirt smeared his cheek. Blood cut a line under his nostrils and upper lip. A dark feeling passed through me, and I imagined I'd just seen the last sight I'd ever have in this life.

"Well," Neils drawled. "You aren't very good at running, are you?"

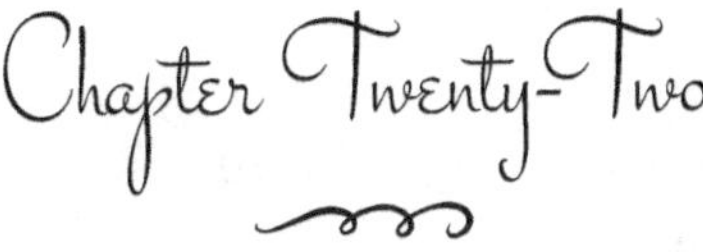

Chapter Twenty-Two

DEVIN

Every heartbeat that thudded through my body after Ellie slapped me brought me farther from the hazy tunnel of hallucinations. Recollections slipped back in a mad rush, reorienting me in the moment until full consciousness returned.

Ellie.

Mountains.

Kimball.

Neils, the park ranger.

With a blink, I forced myself entirely back to the present.

Neils jumped off the embankment and straightened in front of us. My lips still burned with our kiss as I met his gaze. My heart with her words. They wrapped around me like a soothing balm and the quiet reassurance that everything would be all right. Even if we both died, I'd said it. She said it. I shoved Ellie behind me with new power.

I love you. I've always loved you.

Only the gun that an increasingly unstable Neils waved so carelessly could detract my thoughts from their track of utter disbelief. I reached back for Ellie's hand. It slid in mine, and I gave her fingers a reassuring squeeze.

"So," Neils drawled. "You two got wrapped up in something, didn't you? Besides each other," he tacked on with a tasteless smile.

"So did you," I replied with forced nonchalance.

Neils scoffed.

"Tell me about the drug," I said.

"My drug," he corrected immediately, as if he'd done this before. A flicker of uncertainty followed in his expression like he'd just betrayed too much.

"Yours? Impressive."

He eyed me warily. At first, I couldn't tell whether he trusted the question or not. His eyes darted around, and I wondered if he thought I was stalling. Did I have someone on the way? Unlikely, considering how desperately we tried to get the bag. We wouldn't have fought for the pack if we had someone to back us up.

His eyes moved quickly. This man appeared intelligent enough. If he claimed a drug, did that mean he made it? Had his job as a park ranger been a cover? A way to hide his addiction? Maybe he had some sort of hidden place out here in the mountains. People with that kind of evil drive did all kinds of weird things in secret.

Although I didn't know why, I had a suspicion this guy didn't want to hide anymore. Why else would he correct me and claim it? Pixie dust had flown under the radar for several years now, only popping up here and there.

"I call it pixie dust," he finally said. "Because it's so pretty and pink."

"You made it?"

He shrugged. "Found it. Experimented into it. I'm a chemist, it's what I do. Whatever you want to call it. It's *mine*."

"What is it?"

"It's a miracle." A wide smile crossed his face. I inched closer to Ellie. "A modern marvel. Not only does it produce a lovely little high to make your day better, but it also gives you energy and a freakish strength for hours after ingestion. Who doesn't need that?"

"Perfect for anyone that you want to make you money in a fight?"

He smiled slowly. "Perfect for *anyone*."

"Kimball included."

A shadow passed over his eyes, like a sun crossing the cloud. "Kimball is now another unfortunate story. If he would've *listened* to me and stopped arguing, we might have worked through this. But he didn't." Neils's lips tightened. "It's his own fault that I had to kill him."

Ellie tensed behind me.

"What about Steve?" I asked.

"Steve acquired some a few months ago, thanks to Kimball. Now, he'll do anything for it. At least . . ." Neils glanced above us, where he'd appeared like a ghost and jumped off the embankment. "I thought he would."

Ominous thought for Steve, but I had to consider him an unknown still. Kimball? Clearly out of the game. The other guy? Also an unknown, but unlikely to be an issue. If Neils kept talking, I'd keep asking. In the meantime, I had to cobble together some sort of plan that didn't involve a bullet in my chest and this maniac on the loose.

"So you make and sell pixie dust," I pressed. "For fighters?"

"The creator of the drug only releases small amounts of it at a time," he murmured. "It's basic supply and demand."

"And that's you?"

His teeth sparkled when he smiled. "That is me."

"He's unhinged," Ellie murmured, so low I could barely make it out. "He's speaking in the third person. We have to get out of here."

I squeezed her hand again.

"It's hard to get a hold of," Neils continued, "and the effects are powerful, so it sells for thousands of dollars per hit. Most people will do anything for more of it." He frowned, then brightened. "I thought of calling this the Hungry Games, you know, instead of Survival Club."

"This?"

He gestured around us with a wave. "The fight. The cabin. The Hungry Games. Because these people get so hungry for another hit. Sounds less . . . ridiculous."

"People like Steve come to fight . . ."

"And their reward is a hoard of the stuff. So much pixie dust that, with the right skill," Neils shrugged again, as if to say *what can I do*? "one could make a hundred thousand dollars when they sold it. With the 70% kickback to me, I believe I could be a very rich man."

"Is that what you want?" I asked. "Money?"

"Power."

"It's the same, isn't it?"

Neils laughed, but it rang dark and empty. Something I'd expect from a hollowed-out soul. He stepped off his dirt clod and took a step toward us. I sent him a warning glare, and he paused. I attempted to decipher whether or not I had the time to grab the gun and wrestle it from him. He must have seen the calculation in my gaze because he lifted the gun. I stared down the barrel for a full second before I lifted my hands.

"You don't have to do this," I said. Panic filled me like smoke. *Ellie*, I thought. What terrible curse gave her to me minutes before I would lose her?

"Yes." A stark expression crossed his face. "I do."

A shot rang out.

* * *

Shrapnel in the muscle felt like hot acid. A busted shoulder felt like crushing despair. I expected a gunshot to the chest to feel like fire.

Instead, there was silence.

I opened my eyes. No bright white light waited. No pain ricocheted through my body. For a full five seconds, I felt nothing but Ellie as she trembled in my arms.

"Dev?" she whispered.

A moment passed before I realized that I hadn't died, nor had I been shot. In the breath between the barrel staring down my eyes and the sound of a shot, I'd whirled around and covered Ellie with my body.

"Are you okay?" I asked.

"Yes."

Movement drew my eyes overhead. Steve stood at the top of the hill above us, a pistol in his hand. Blood drenched his right pectoral muscle. He breathed heavily. Sweat glistened on his face and dripped down his cheeks. His skin had a grayish tinge.

I glanced back. Neils lay on the ground, a hole torn halfway through his face.

"Don't look," I said to Ellie.

She gripped my shirt, her arms wrapped around my waist, and buried her face into my neck. I splayed my hands across her back to keep her close, then canted her so she couldn't see the destructive mess that she'd once considered a friend.

Above us, Steve's arm lowered. The gun dropped to the leaves and slipped out of his reach when it slid closer to me. He dropped to his knees with a grunt. His gaze lowered to mine. I'd seen that look before. The slow bleeding of life. The sucking, gasping breaths of the dying.

"Why?" I asked.

"You were both . . . kind."

I paused. "I'm sorry, Steve. I'm sorry this happened to you."

He dropped to his side with a groan. "I never wanted this. Never . . . asked for it. Now, it will be gone."

Ellie buried her face in my head with a little cry. I tightened my hold on her and pressed a kiss into her hair. Steve had just saved our lives. Maybe he didn't deserve accolades, because he'd played a part in this nightmare, but in the end, he'd done the right thing.

"Thank you," I said.

His glassy eyes softened, then closed. Slowly, the desperate gasps ebbed. Ellie pulled herself so close she'd merged into me. I kissed the top of her head again, still shocked to have her fitted against me without death between us, and let out a slow breath.

"It's over," I whispered as I ran my fingers through her hair. The gesture was meant to soothe me. "It's over."

My mind raced with what to do next. First priority: locate the radio. Call for help. Find coordinates and give them. Get to the truck? No, stay here? See what the responder said, then do that. Wait for help to arrive. Hernandez, he'd come. Probably with another ranger. Maybe? The thoughts streamed through my mind one at a time until they nearly consumed me.

Ellie's sniffle brought me back. Tears dropped onto my neck until she pulled away and tilted her head back. Her lower lip trembled.

"We almost died."

I reached up and brushed the hair out of her face with my hands. "I'm sorry. I'm sorry about—"

She shook her head. "No. Don't."

My heart cracked right down the middle when tears welled back up in her eyes. When was the last time I'd seen her cry? Years. Years ago. So many that I'd forgotten how beautiful the emotions made her.

"Ellie, I love you."

She went completely still. Her heart leapt into her eyes, both frightened and hopeful and I knew at that moment that my world would never be the same.

"You do?" she whispered.

"I've always loved you. From the moment I saw you hiding behind the counter in the Frolicking Moose to this one. The years in North Carolina were torture without you. I thought you hated me. That we'd never speak again. Then after I almost died so many times on deployment, I swore I wouldn't let another moment pass without telling you how I felt."

She swallowed, the graceful column of her neck smooth and elegant. I trailed my fingertips to the hollow at the base of her neck, where I'd wanted to kiss her all my life. Feel the pulse of her heart against my lips. The thought robbed my breath until I gave into it. She tilted her head to the side to let me press my lips there and sighed.

"You're mine, Ellie." I kissed the side of her neck, her jaw, then braced her face in my hands. "You always have been."

"What does that mean?" she asked, wide-eyed vulnerable.

"It means that I won't live without you. That you won't leave my world, my sight, until you have to. That I'm going to spend the rest of my vacation convincing you to give up everything and follow me across the country. It means that if you tell me I can, I will kiss the breath out of you again and again and again. I will kiss you the way I've always wanted to kiss you." My trembling hand touched her cheek. "Ellie, it means I give you everything."

Her lips caught mine again. She held my face in both her hands. I locked my arms around her as the bottom fell out from my world. She pulled me close until space didn't exist. Her legs locked around my waist. I clawed her closer until I couldn't breathe, her lips slanting over mine in a kiss that had been tucked away for years.

Everything I once knew about Ellie totally unraveled. I lost myself in this new side of her. She pulled away with a gasp, and half a sob. Her forehead pressed to mine.

"I don't want to leave you again. I don't want you to leave me. I accept that we can't live every waking moment together, but we can always have each other. Because Mama was wrong. She was wrong." She pressed her lips to mine, then pulled away. "I love you. I love you. I love you."

I locked her in my arms with the feeling that I couldn't

breathe. Relief left me weak, and the past three years of questions, fear, and dreams evaporated into mist. Everything had come together.

And Ellie was mine.

Chapter Twenty-Three

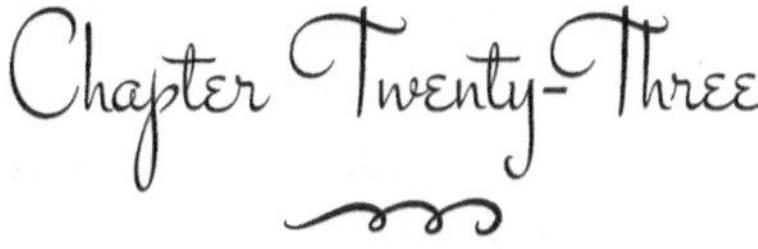

ELLIE

"Here."

Hernandez draped a blanket around my shoulders and gazed at me with concern. I had a sip from a thermos filled with coffee that he'd conjured from the depths of his vehicle, and my ravenous stomach did a little jolt. Despite the warmth of the fading afternoon, the straight black coffee drove comfort all the way to my bones.

"Thanks."

Devin bumped my arm, a hand held out. With a little smile, I passed the thermos over to him. He had a sip, then a long, long draught. I watched his throat move as he swallowed, unable to tear my eyes off of him.

"Slow down, stallion," I murmured with an adoring smile.

He laughed and passed it back. "That," Devin declared, "is the best coffee I've ever had."

"That new girl, Dahlia, knows what she's doing. Funny, too." Hernandez motioned to me with a nod. "Have some more. We're going to ask a lot of questions soon. You'll need some caffeine. I have some protein bars, too. Let me grab them for you."

Despite missing meals and days of dreaming of what I'd eat

first, I couldn't fathom eating right now. A general queasiness lived in my body. Devin had shielded me from the grisly parts of what we left behind, for which I was grateful. But my mind quickly substituted all the things I didn't see. The boxes I had tucked away for so long kept flopping down, defeated. I stopped fighting them and let the shocked feelings flow with a powerful sense of relief.

Devin loves me, spiraled the thought. It buoyed me up amid all this horror. *He has loved me this whole time.*

Aside from the general shock of his confession, I couldn't help but feel a giddy relief. A disbelieving awareness that we'd danced around the same feelings for years. If one of us had just gotten up the gumption to *say* something, maybe all of this could have been avoided.

Except, that may not have been the right path either.

After all I'd learned about myself without him, and the path that life set both of us on, I couldn't imagine any other circumstances that would have served us better. Now, we knew our path.

And we were on it together. Totally. Entirely. Completely. No questions asked, no dreams held back.

"Ellie?"

Blinking out of my thoughts, I glanced up to see Hernandez staring at me expectantly. Too late, I realized they had been talking to me and I'd missed it.

"Sorry."

Devin's arm lay heavy on my shoulders. "Give us a sec?" he asked Hernandez. He nodded and stepped back, calling for someone else with a quick whistle. Devin curled me closer into him. I leaned into his side.

"I don't want to talk about it with him," I whispered. Tears filled my eyes again. "I just want to go home."

"Me too."

Panic seized me when I realized that *home* meant away from Devin, and I couldn't fathom the thought of being away from him. Not now. Not after all that—

"You won't leave me?" I asked without attempting to hide my panic. "You'll stay? Come to—"

"I'm not leaving." He put a hand under my chin and tilted my head back. The tips of his fingers caressed a gentle line down my cheekbone and my throat, then he gripped my neck in his hand. "After we're done with this, we'll go to Mav and Bethany's. You get first dibs on a super-hot shower. I'll be in the other room, trying not to picture you in that shower and all the things I want to do to you."

A roguish gleam in his eyes sent heat through me, sending away the darkness of the past few days.

"While we're getting cleaned up," he continued, "Mav will fix us a massive meal. I'll call my parents, they can come over. I'll tell them everything so you don't have to, and we just get it done. Then, you and I will go into your old bedroom and fall asleep for the next three days together. You will be in my arms the entire time. Got it? There are no other alternatives."

Relief swam through me. "Got it," I whispered and sagged against him in relief.

"We have to talk to them first," he said, "but we can do it together. Okay? I've got your back."

Macabre week aside, my lips twitched. *My* Devin was definitely back. In fact, he'd never really left.

"Sounds like a dream."

He pressed a kiss into my temple. "It's going to be all right, Ellie. Everything will be all right."

Chapter Twenty-Four

DEVIN

Ten Days Later

Mom's old camo banner with *Good Luck Devin* scrawled across the front flapped across the entrance of the Frolicking Moose. An extra "^ *and Ellie*" had been added underneath the obnoxious red-white-and-blue lettering in white paint that still dripped.

The smell of charbroiled meat and barbeque sauce filled the air, along with the happy shrieks of my niece and nephews as they galloped around the parking lot. My big sister, Kendra, pretended to be annoyed with them when they asked, "Is grandpa *really* cooking cow brains?" She gave a heartfelt eye roll, ruffled their hair, and said, "Yes, and they're good for you."

Warm sunshine fell on my face as I surveyed the mingling crowd. Half of Pineville filled the place now with warm chatter. At my side, Ellie said, "Everyone is showing up. I didn't think there would be so many people."

Her glossy black hair shone in the sunlight and spilled down her back. The ends curled on her shoulder, covered with an emerald green shirt that so perfectly matched her eyes, I couldn't stop looking at her.

"They're showing up for you," I murmured into her temple, then planted another kiss on her. She hooked an arm around my back and pulled me into her. As if we could *get* any closer.

Ellie's gaze hovered over Lizbeth, who lingered not far away, her pregnant belly visible through her shirt. Bethany stood next to her with a bottle of water in hand, while her son galloped in and out of the coffee shop with my youngest niece. Sauce smeared their faces and shirts. Small American flags waved in their hands. Next to Bethany stood Maverick, his prosthetic leg gleaming, while Mark said something in his usual animated way.

Behind it all worked the new full-time barista and Frolicking Moose tenant—a girl named Dahlia. With tireless energy, she pumped out macchiatos like she was born to it. Her cheeks had high color, and her dark eyes were bright with amusement. Hernandez nearly choked on his coffee when Dahlia tossed a lid on his to-go cup and slid it all the way down the counter, into his awaiting hand, like a bartender. When she said something I couldn't hear, Dagny laughed until she doubled over.

The Frolicking Moose would be just fine without Ellie.

"I'm going to miss this," Ellie whispered.

Her voice caught a little bit. Ever since *the disaster*, as she called it, her emotions had been more unbound than I'd ever seen. Like she'd finally accessed them again after not giving in for years.

My fingers squeezed hers. "You don't have to—"

"Don't say it." She sent me a chilling glare. "Don't even finish it."

Unbothered by her tough display, I just laughed. "I won't. But you need to know it. You're giving up a lot to be with me."

"It's worth it."

She softened, because Ellie was never really that tough in the first place. Inside the shop waited two bags stuffed totally full, two carry-ons, and a box full of treasures she'd dug up from their old house and always carried with her. Once the barbeque ended, Maverick and Bethany would drive us to the airport in

Jackson City and Ellie would fly home to North Carolina with me.

"I belong with you, Dev," she murmured. "Even if there's sadness in letting go here, I want to be with you there more. Adventure *finally* awaits."

"Yes," I whispered, and my heart wrung itself out like an old rag. "You do belong with me." I glanced at my watch with a little hiccup in my stomach. "We need to leave in ten minutes. Are you ready?"

"Yes." She smiled up at me. "I'm finally ready for you, Devin Blaine."

As if she sensed our conversation, Mom cut across the black-top, her hair gently wafting around her shoulders as she approached. A radiant smile filled her eyes from the moment she learned that Ellie and I had finally been fully open with each other.

"Seen it for years," she'd said breezily. "I knew you'd come around. You're stubborn, like your father."

Now, she held out her arms and Ellie stepped readily into them. They embraced for a long time. Once Ellie pulled away, she returned to my side. Mom's eyes filled with tears as she looked at me.

"You are sure you're ready for this?"

"Finally," I said. "Yes."

She laughed, but it was teary. Her gaze traveled between us, then landed back on me. "You're one lucky man, Devin Blaine."

Ellie grinned when I squeezed her hand. "Trust me, Mom. I know."

Mom embraced me, her arms tight around my waist. Then she stepped away, wiped the tears off her cheeks, and made space for Dad to step up. He spit out some gruff advice, told me he loved me, then dissolved into tears when Ellie hugged him goodbye. I hid an affectionate eye roll.

Of *course* only losing Ellie pushed him to the brink of emotion.

One at a time, people began to fade away. I hugged, joked with, and cajoled more people than I thought possible. The anxiety of being home had burned away one piece at a time, particularly after a few video calls with my psychologist after the disaster. A long, in-person appointment with her awaited tomorrow. Ellie would attend with me. Together, we'd create an action plan to tackle the PTSD—both from this weekend and the deployment. Something we'd both need.

A long road awaited, but this time it wasn't a lonely one.

Daniel stepped up to Ellie with a grunt. She stared at her boss from the Outfitters for a moment before she did the unthinkable and hugged him. He stiffened like a board, then wrapped his arms around her.

"Best damn guide I've ever had," he muttered into her shoulder, then stepped away. "You keep it up, Ellie. Those mountains need you when you get back."

She smiled wide. "I'll be back, Daniel. Give me three years. Then I'll return and run the store while you retire. Got it?"

He grinned. "Got it." Then he turned to me with a threatening finger. "You're the only twenty-one-year-old I can tolerate. Don't lose your position by doing something stupid, all right? You wouldn't face just Maverick if you break her heart again. You'll face all of Pineville."

Ellie laughed when I pulled her into my side again.

"Roger, sir."

Daniel's lips twitched with a smile, then he nodded, shook my hand, backed away, and disappeared into the gathering. As the crowd thinned out, only Bethany, Maverick, my parents, and a few others remained behind. Bethany walked up, eyes sparkling and happy.

"You're taking my girl, Dev," she said. Then she winked. "It's about time."

Behind her, a booming laugh rippled out of Maverick. He stepped up behind her, put a hand on her shoulder, and said,

"Let's get the two of you to the airport. It's time for your next great adventure."

I pulled Ellie into my side and kept her there.

Where she's always been mine.

Forever.

Smoke and Fire

A SNEAK PEEK INTO THE 7TH BOOK.

The growing plume of smoke on the horizon behind Pineville did not give me any warm fuzzies. A wildfire in the mountains was not how I wanted to start the week, and certainly didn't lend much hope for an easy, low-key time in the mountains.

To that end, the romance book sprawled open on the counter behind me also did not give me warm fuzzies. Far worse.

It gave me butterflies.

"Fantastic," I muttered darkly.

The last thing I needed right now was a romance novel. One that I actually liked. It only made my bad mood even worse. The water heater in my RV failed this morning, which certainly didn't help my wrathful disposition. Not to mention a plastic taste in the water, which meant a filter had probably gone out. Yesterday, thanks to a deranged Lizbeth on a book bender, I'd forgotten to stock up on milk, so I had no breakfast at home. My alarm had gone off twenty minutes late, which meant I barely managed to change out of my PJ's before stumbling into work.

The whole smeared-mascara-messy-bun appearance would have to cut it today.

I shoved another romance book onto the shelf on the far wall of the Frolicking Moose Coffee Shop and reached for the final one. Lizbeth had pulled off ten different books as other romantic suggestions for you to get started in the genre, Dahlia. Because we aren't cave people here. We recognize romance as a powerful force in this world, so get reading already.

I eyed the last book warily. She'd been so serious when she said that. I'd cracked a smile that had slowly deflated, like a dying balloon, when I realized she'd been serious.

Dead. Serious.

She actually believed in romance. That romance made wonderful things happened—instead of terrible things. Instead of pain and loss and mourning and . . . separation. An uncomfortable feeling grew inside me, like my stomach was lined with itchy wool. I shoved the encroaching thoughts away when the smoke plume drew my gaze again.

Speaking of actual powerful forces . . .

Should I call that fire in, or something?

Lizbeth's chatter filled my brain again when I shoved the last romance book back onto the shelf and prayed she wouldn't actually ask me for a full, written review of the novel she'd all but shoved into my chest yesterday.

There will be a report tomorrow. She'd pointed a finger at me, as stern as I'd ever seen her before. Don't think you can fake your way through this book. I know it inside and out, and the rest of the series, too.

Instead, I turned my back to the smoke plume and faced the book that waited for me on the counter.

I frowned at it.

"What," I muttered, "am I going to do with you?"

Historical is the way to go if you have any love of untouchable men from the past, Lizbeth had said with all the efficiency of a librarian while she searched through her back to find this particular book. I can talk about Jamie Fraser all day, but until you read his brogue, it's nothing. Plus, you can't go wrong with Regency. I mean all that sexual tension wrapped up in subdued societal expectations of physical touch between men and women? I swoon just thinking about it.

She'd shuddered then, and that's when I had realized just how in-over-my-head I'd become. When the ten historical romance novels she'd suggested went unread for two weeks, she finally figured out I hated history—on any level, I loved to forget history—then she'd immediately squealed with joy.

My hope to extricate from her romantic obsession immediately disappeared.

Then you must read Jess! It's fate.

She'd nodded firmly once, as if that cemented it, then shoved five books at me.

No one knows who she is, but she. is. brilliant. She doesn't write with a last name, only has a Twitter profile but nothing else, never runs ads, never appears on social media, and tops the romance charts every. stinking. month. She has twenty novels in one series and I've made it through the first eight for the tenth time in the last four days. Start at the beginning with Life is a Freaking Dream.

Leery again of just how much I liked Life is a Freaking Dream after only 100 pages, I meandered back to the counter and stared at the splayed cover.

In all fairness, at least Life is a Freaking Dream didn't have giant, heaving bosoms and a man with a chest so chiseled it looked like a painted sculpture. The subtle, text-based front had stylistic scrollwork with a mixture of contemporary and Victorian that drew my attention. To be honest, the cover reminded me of my favorite cousin, Tabitha. And I liked Tabitha, and I did like Lizbeth when she wasn't on a maniacal book bender, so gave this book a chance.

Now I didn't want to put it down.

"Sorry," I whispered to the book. "I'm sorry. I love you, I just don't want to love you because you're not real and I don't want hope. Hope sucks. And the reality never matches up to the book and romance leads down dark paths and . . ." I shrank smaller, poking it with my index finger and a gentle, "Sorry."

The book folded back together, probably in protest of my rejection, and sat there with a silent little huff of annoyance.

My gaze slid back to the horizon through the front windows of the Frolicking Moose Coffee Shop.

Now that ugly column was a reality I could focus on.

My brow grew heavy. I'd been in and out of the mountains around Pineville every summer since I was six, but I'd never seen a plume of smoke that thick, that dark, and that close. The hairs on the back of my neck stood up.

Fire.

I shuddered.

In the thick mountains that wrapped around Pineville like long, evergreen arms, fires were portent to disaster. The bigger the smoke plume, the greater the pit in my stomach. Pineville had just become my home. I'd finally parked my travel trailer in a place with actual electricity and water hookups.

I was not leaving.

So I pointed to the smoke with a firm growl. It deserved a good scolding.

"You stay over there." Then I jabbed a thumb to the espresso machine, near where I stood behind the coffee shop bar. "I'll stay here. We're square. Got it? Capeesh? Understood? I may live in an RV, but I don't need to be uprooted again so soon, okay? I'm here to stay . . . all winter!"

The plume shifted ever-so-slightly in the wind.

"That's what I thought," I muttered, and turned my back to it and the book. The book stared at me while I bustled around, ignoring its existence. Surely not thinking about Amalia and Rodrigo, or whether Rodrigo would return home from the war and understand the real depths of Amalia's love for him.

"By heavens, Rodrigo!" I cried, unable to help myself. "She bloody loves you, man. Get over your own pride!"

And I snatched the book off the counter to dive back into it.

Lost in the swirls of unrealistic romance, but I story I couldn't peel myself away from my if even my boss Bethany popped in, I forgot about the shop. No one wondered in for a coffee, and I didn't move from my position.

Until, twenty minutes later, a green bus-like truck pulled up outside, parking near the edge of the lot. The words ROCKY HOTSHOTS had been painted across the top in black letters.

With a sigh, I shoved a napkin into the pages and set the book aside. Rodrigo and his fiery kisses would have to wait.

Outside, grungy men spilled out of the strangely-colored bus in matching yellow jackets, green pants, and haggard expressions. They huddled together in a meeting while the bus hissed and turned off. I watched them from behind the counter and played my favorite game.

Match the drink with the drinker.

"Definitely a cappuccino for that guy," I murmured, eyeing a tall, lanky figure with a scraggly beard that looked as if it'd been set to flame on one side. "Straight coffee for the other. Black, no creamer, one sugar for Mr. Short-and-Scrumptious."

The concoctions amused me until the HotShots climbed back into the bus and left. Bemused, I forced myself away from the book to do the maintenance log on the fridge and a few checks. Dagny would be in to take the next shift, and I would not be caught derelict on duties while reading a romance novel.

Less than two minutes later, I'd grabbed the book and fallen face-first back into Amalia and Rodrigo.

The crack of the door brought me out of my reverie. My gaze darted to the clock—it had been thirty minutes!—as the door jangled open. With a squeak, I whirled around to face the front of the shop and shoved the book off to the side.

"Welcome to—"

The words died on my lips.

A pair of stormy eyes peered at me from an angular face.

One of the HotShots.

A rough beard streaked with brown and hints of blonde drew my gaze to a strong neck and shoulders. The smell of smoke entered the room with him. None of that startled me. Not even the obnoxiously yellow shirt, muted by layers of grime and filth, or the dark green camp pants. A wildland firefighter, clearly. No doubt called here to that nasty plume of smoke that had—albeit slightly—widened in the past hour so that I'd been drooling over Rodrigo again.

The expression of panic in the Hotshots eyes, despite a casual, put-together mein, arrested me almost completely.

That wasn't normal.

"—the Frolicking Moose," I finished.

What could possibly have a man like him look terrified like that? He shifted forward and I noticed a computer under his left arm for the first time. When he spoke, it seemed to rumble in his chest.

"Internet."

I tilted my head to the said. Wait . . . what? What was that? A caveman request? It wasn't even a question. Peeved now that I'd been pulled from Rodrigo for this—even if he was smoky hot—I countered.

"Coffee shop."

He frowned. His gaze dropped to the countertop, as if seeking something, then landed on the book. The muscles around his lips tightened.

I bristled.

Great. He was going to judge me to be a simpering woman that read romance novels at work. That would put me into a label and a category without knowing me at all or the truth behind my life and who I was. The judgment already built up in his gaze, like a gathering storm. Oh, that's exactly what I saw in his a-little-too-attractive face right now. Condemnation.

Judgment.

For the most part, I liked almost everyone I met. It's why a coffee shop in a small mountain town near the end of summer ended up being an ideal job. Something about this tough guy, however, set my teeth on edge. Definitely wasn't that masculine appeal.

Nope. Not that.

He scowled. "I need to use the internet."

"Okay."

Utter silence followed, and I felt his annoyance deepen in the weighty pause.

"If you are asking," I drawled to his obnoxious quiet, "if we have internet, the answer is yes. Hot and cold running water too, if you like that kind of modern upgrade, but the outhouse is out back if you need it. Password is on the board."

If possible, his frown deepened.

Tough crowd.

Time to get this guy out of here, so I slapped on my brightest smile. The kind that almost crackled with the underlayer of tension within it. He seemed to notice as well because his gaze darkened.

"What can I get you to drink?" I asked, just to get rid of him.

"Coffee. Straight."

I choked back a laugh. My Match the Drinker game had been absolutely spot on—like always.

He turned to head toward a table. "And protein."

I opened my mouth to clarify that, but decided not to. No reason to force him to outdo his quote of words for the day. I bet he operated his life with less than twenty words per day.

Instead, I grabbed a cheese-and-sausage bagel, a mug off of our wall collection with a picture of a scowling cat on it—oddly appropros—and slung coffee into it. By the time I worked my way to his table with requested nourishment, he had his laptop open and had sunk deeper into his foul mood.

I set it down, eager to sneak away without a word, but then he grabbed my wrist. The burn of his skin went all the way to my bones.

And I knew that everything had just changed.

If you can't wait to get more of the sizzle between Dahlia and Bastian, visit www.katiecrossromance.com to grab your copy or stay tuned with updates.

Ellie and Devin first met me about thirteen or fourteen years ago.

I can't remember the details. The only thing I do remember is a deep yearning for a relationship as deep as they had. Their friendship and depth of relationship were actually inspired by an NSYNC fan fiction story that I followed on an Angelfire website back when I was twelve or thirteen.

(And boy, if that doesn't date me, I don't know what does!)

I wrote Ellie's original story on Google Drive while working night shifts at a pediatric hospital. My dating life was tough on a good day, and I longed to connect with someone that just *got* me. The story poured out in surprising speed.

So a few years ago, I revisited those Google documents. One thought led to another, and the initial concepts for *The Coffee Shop Series* began. Even though Ellie ended up being book six, she was the original inspiration for all these stories. She was going to be book one, was nudged to book three, then finally to book six.

This was her rightful place.

It's rare that I finish a novel with the feeling of *this is exactly how I wanted this to puzzle together*, but it's how I wrapped WILD

CHILD up. I'm so proud of the two of them, and gratified to bring her to light after so many years.

Acknowledgments

First and foremost, a huge and heartfelt thank you to Christy and JaiHo, the original readers of Ellie's first iterations (which are so painfully boring I'm not sure how you made it through!)

Thank you for supporting my work when I didn't even know I was an author. I was just a kid in a grown-up world trying to find her way.

To my team and all your quick responsiveness to really tight deadlines—thank you for bleeding on my work, pointing out my strengths and faults, and making me a better team leader and author.

To my readers, I hope that Ellie and Devin live up to everything you wanted them to be. I know they did for me.

To my family, you are my life, my drive, my inspiration. I adore every single one of you and appreciate your loving support for this wild child right here.

Also by Katie Cross

The Health and Happiness Society

Bon Bons to Yoga Pants (Lexie)

I Am Girl Power (Megan)

You'll Never Know (Rachelle)

Hear Me Roar (Bitsy)

What Was Lost (Mira)

The Health and Happiness Society Collection

Finding Anna

Coffee Shop Series

Coffee Shop Girl

Lovesick

Runaway

Fighter

Shy Girl

Wild Child

Smoke and Fire

Clean Sweep

Protect Me

About the Author

Katie Cross is ALL ABOUT writing epic love stories and wild places. Creating new books is her jam.

When she's not hiking or chasing her two littles through the Montana mountains, you can find her curled up reading a book or arguing with her husband over the best kind of sushi.

Visit her at www.katiecrossbooks.com for free short stories, extra savings on all her books (and some you can't buy on the retailers), and so much more.

www.ingramcontent.com/pod-product-compliance
Lightning Source LLC
Chambersburg PA
CBHW061541210726
48287CB00006B/2038